THE FIXER

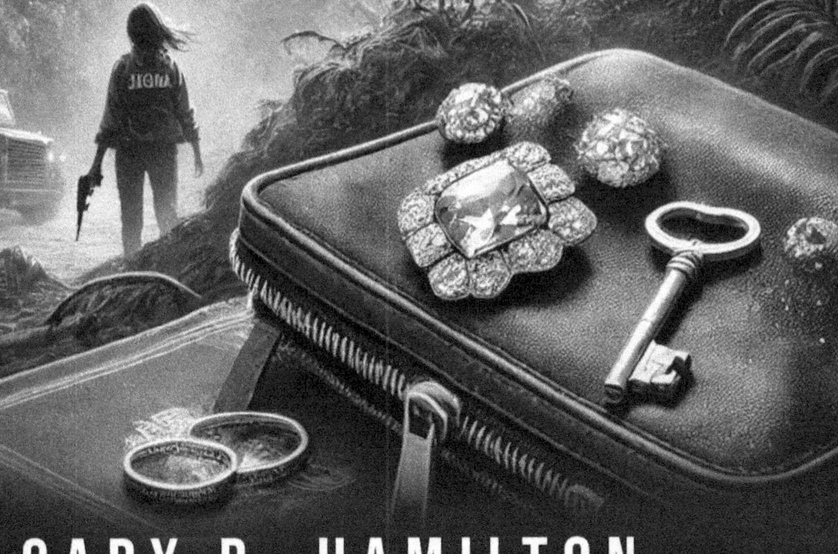

GARY R. HAMILTON

THE FIXER

GARY R. HAMILTON

Copyright © 2025 by Gary R Hamilton

CITIOFBOOKS, INC.
3736 Eubank NE Suite A1
Albuquerque, NM 87111-3579
www.citiofbooks.com
Hotline: 1 (877) 389-2759
Fax: 1 (505) 930-7244

Ordering Information:

Quantity sales. Special discounts are available on quantity purchases by corporations, associations, and others. For details, contact the publisher at the address above.

Printed in the United States of America.

ISBN-13:   Softcover   979-8-89391-502-0
                eBook   979-8-89391-503-7
                Hardback   979-8-89391-504-4

Library of Congress Control Number: 2025900566

This is a revised version, and therefore new and improved.

Table of Contents

CHAPTER 1 – Mr. Mbozi!

One year ago

Jean Michel Mbozi thumps the mahogany table with such force that the empty glasses jump and those with water wobble, prompting the owners to reach out and steady them. The soldier at the panelled wood door shuffles his feet and then relaxes as he removes his hand from his side arm, resuming his At Attention posture.

"I will not be spoken to in this way!"

"Mr. Mbozi …"

"You promised me a fair, negotiated settlement if I brought my people to the table …"

"Mr. Mbozi …"

"… and this is how you treat me?"

"Mr. Mbozi …"

"We are a sovereign country. We are not cow dung under your shoes that you simply scrape off and dispose of like …"

"Will you shut up! God damn it, man!"

There is stunned silence in the room. Mr. Mbozi looks across the table with his mouth open, stalled in mid-sentence, his eyes wide open. The only audible sound is the hum of the fan, labouring in its task of futility.

Mr. Johnson mops his brow, takes a deep breath, and scratches behind his ear with his little finger. He does not like losing his temper, or for that matter showing any sign of loss of control. "This is as good as it will get." He says slowly.

"But last year we were getting seventy-five cents on the

dollar." Mr. Mbozi objects.

"Mr. Mbozi. With all due respect, look around you."

Slowly, Mr. Mbozi and his party follow Mr. Johnson's arm as he gestures around the low ceilinged, single room structure in which they are meeting. To their right, sunlight is streaming through the east-facing window, its inexorable path to the dusty concrete floor partially interrupted by the edge of the mahogany table. A green lizard lazily sits motionless on the window ledge. Suddenly, its tongue flicks out and catches a fly, and for a few moments there is detectable movement of its lower jaw and throat, before it becomes motionless again. Behind Mr. Johnson, a gibbon flickers between the slits in the louvered window as it brachiates through the trees in the distance. To their left, the floor standing fan slowly circulates the warm air blowing in through the open west-facing window. Mr. Johnson picks up his handkerchief, leaving a layer of moisture on the table, and again mops his brow. He surveys the Mbozi party.

The attaché, sitting to Mr. Mbozi's right, has intelligent looking, bright, round eyes that match his young round face, and bright white teeth. His navy-blue suit looks like it was tailored on Savile Row.

The security officer standing behind Mr. Mbozi is overweight and has a very unsteady gaze. A bead of perspiration ebbs its way down his cheek before he uses a thumb to flick it away. His dark suit is crumpled, and his shirt collar looks like it is a size too small.

The woman on Mr. Mbozi's left is a mystery to Mr. Johnson. He has to force himself to avoid staring into her alluring, light brown eyes. Her very low, black afro enhances her long, high cheek-boned face. Despite the uncomfortably warm conditions in the room, not a bead of perspiration can be seen on her face. She seems to be impatient for proceedings to end, glancing at her watch on a regular basis, and not really taking any interest in the discussions. He does not recognise her as Mr. Mbozi's wife from the Intelligence pictures he has seen, nor does his information shed any light on her identity, nor was she formally introduced when the meeting began. Mr. Johnson feels some unease, but he is not sure why.

"Fifteen cents." Mr. Johnson says quietly, refocusing his attention on Mr. Mbozi.

Mr. Mbozi shifts in his chair, "This is …"

Mr. Johnson holds up a very thin hand, its whiteness contrasts starkly against the dark complexions of Mr. Mbozi's party across the table.

"Fifteen." He says more firmly.

"Twenty?" Mr. Mbozi asks feebly.

Mr. Johnson's shake of his head is almost indiscernible. Mr. Mbozi drops his head and after a moment's pause, nods. Mr. Johnson opens his briefcase and slides a neat stack of papers across the table and places a silver Parker pen on top. Mr. Mbozi reluctantly glances at the papers, and then looks at his attaché, who promptly picks up the papers and starts reading, quickly flicking through them.

"Wait! This says fourteen cents. I thought we just agreed to fifteen?" The attaché says, his deep voice bouncing off the bare, whitewashed walls, resonating in the small room.

"Does it? Didn't I mention my one percent fee? I'm sorry."

"What? This is outrageous!" The attaché barks. He starts to push the papers across the table. Mr. Mbozi softly but firmly grabs his attaché's arm.

"Mr. President. I must insist that we walk away from …" The attaché starts.

"No." Mr. Mbozi rebuffs. "At this stage we have no choice."

In a hushed tone, the attaché leans closer to Mr. Mbozi, 'Monsieur le Président. Avec tout le respect … (*Mr. President, with all due respect …*)'

"In English please." Mr. Johnson says, but Mr. Mbozi holds up his free hand, turns to his attaché, and nods for him to continue.

"… I am sure the French would show us more respect than these greedy dogs."

"The French have been clear about what they want in return, and that price is too high to pay."

"English, please." Mr. Johnson interjects.

The attaché ignores Mr. Johnson, "Surely someone in Europe will listen to reason. We are being raped by these people. They have no class, no tradition, no pedigree."

"English?" Mr. Johnson asks, showing his frustration.

Mr. Mbozi holds up his hand again. He turns back to his attaché, "You may be right my friend." Mr. Mbozi starts to release his hand from his attaché's arm, when the mystery woman reaches over and softly puts her hand on the stack of papers.

"Qu'est-ce? Vous préférez être souillée par des hommes en chapeau haut de forme et de perruques bouclées? (*You prefer to be defiled by men in top hats and curly wigs?*) Their head gear distracts you from the pain that you feel? Who were the imperialists who enslaved us for centuries? Suddenly we can trust them?" Although she matches the hushed tones of Mr. Mbozi and the attaché, the venom in her words make the attaché subconsciously shrink in his chair. "We do this now to set the stage for a new beginning. We will learn who are our friends, and who are our enemies." She looks Mr. Mbozi in the eye, and then suddenly smiles, the very small diamond embedded in her nose twinkles. "Jean Michel, you have a choice, but you must make it soon. In thirty seconds, maybe a minute, the guard is going to become ill. It should then take me about twenty seconds to kill this white fool and the guard, just before our snipers open fire on the guards around this camp."

"How?" An incredulous Jean Michel whispers.

"The Americans are overconfident. Sign the paper Jean

Michel or let me kill them. If you sign, this is a bed in which we must lay, but only for a time."

Mr. Mbozi looks from the 'diamond' woman to his attaché, who curtly nods his head and positions the top sheet of paper in front of Mr. Mbozi. Mr. Mbozi quickly signs the paper, and with no further notice or ceremony rises from the table.

"Mr. Johnson, I can't say this was a pleasure, but I was probably naive to think that it would have been." He turns and strides towards the door, his party hurriedly follows. The soldier unsteadily steps aside.

The metal reinforced wooden door is flung open by the attaché and a wall of hot air crashes into the room. Mr. Johnson, standing behind them, instantly turns a brighter shade of pink. He watches as the Mbozi party climb into their Toyota Land Cruisers and disappear into the heavy foliage. The soldier pushes past Mr. Johnson and stumbles out the door. Mr. Johnson briefly glances at the soldier retching in the bushes beside the concrete bunker before closing the door as he re-entered the room. Back at the table, he retrieves a bulky satellite phone from his briefcase.

"We're all set. Start putting things in motion." He walks back to the door, loosens his tie and smiles. "Can someone get me something cold to drink?" He shouts as he opens the door and steps back out into the jungle heat.

CHAPTER 2 – Uncle, Uncle!
Six months ago

Pye! The sound of the slap hangs in the air before being carried away on the wind.

"How yuh so fool fool? Eh?"

"Ow! Yuh never have to knock me so hard."

"To blerdnaught! How much time me must talk to yuh? How de blerdnaught you figet de battery?"

"Me no know."

Pye!

"Ow!"

"Nephew! De backup system work off de battery. How it mus' work widout it?"

"Me sorry, Uncle."

"Blerdnaught!"

In the fading light of dusk, Nephew looks down from their position, at the top of the radio tower, at their distant pickup truck parked in the clearing amongst the trees and overgrowth below. His knees buckle for a moment, and he remembers that he is not supposed to look down, but a curious ambivalence overcomes him as he closes his eyes and imagines himself falling, flying, falling, flying, falling. The wind roars in his ears, and when he opens his eyes, he is momentarily confused. He sees a cloudless blue sky! He can feel the warmth of the sun on his face!

Pye! Nephew shakes his head. It is now dusk, the wind has a cold edge to it, and it has started to drizzle.

"Nephew! Stop daydream! Is work we a do!"

"Me sorry, Uncle."

Nephew cautiously inches away from his uncle so that he is just out of arm's length. He pulls up the collar of his blue overalls to protect his neck from the wind and rain, and reverses his white Radio 98.5 FM emblemed baseball cap. As he pulls the cap tighter over his head, he ruefully runs his fingers over the side of his face where he has been slapped. He can feel each finger impression of his uncle's hand stinging on his cheek.

"Nephew! Nephew!"

Nephew looks up to see his uncle gesticulating at him. The wind makes it hard for him to hear what Uncle is saying. He holds out his arms with his palms up, and Uncle points at his own waist, and then at Nephew's waist. Nephew looks down and then remembers that he is carrying the tool belt. Without looking up, he inches closer to Uncle and unbuckles the belt, flips it off and holds it out. The weight of the belt surprises him, and in order to maintain his balance he has to take his free hand off the stanchion, but his non-regulation Nike Air track shoes don't have the necessary grip on the damp metal bar. If Nephew had been a gymnast, he would have been proud of the headfirst flip that he inadvertently performs, but since he isn't, and he is one hundred feet off the ground, he screams in terror as he plunges towards the overgrowth below. The ten feet of slack in his rope harness suddenly halts his descent with an audible thud. It takes a moment for the shock to wear off, and the air to return to Nephew's lungs.

"Whoa! Whoa! Save me, Uncle! Save me!" Nephew screams, as he hangs head down, his feet thrashing around as he tries to right himself.

"Hold on bwoy! Stop panicking." Uncle reaches for his flashlight that is fastened to his overalls, and shines it at Nephew, in the hope that it will calm him down. Uncle then starts to make his way down the tower, and he notes that Nephew's kicking has abated. "De rope will hold you. If yuh did wear de boots yuh supposed to wear yuh wouldn't slip."

A furious gust of wind blows Nephew violently into the tower, and the shock of the impact causes him to start thrashing around even more violently than previously. By this time, Uncle has almost reached Nephew, and one of Nephew's flailing kicks lands on Uncle's knee, momentarily causing Uncle to lose all feeling in that leg. The incapacitated leg buckles, and the pain and surprise slows Uncle's reactions making him a split second slow and a tad too late to grasp the nearest bar as he falls. Remembering his training, Uncle relaxes to lessen the effect of the fall and the recoil of the harness rope, but another kick from Nephew lands on Uncle's jaw, knocking Uncle unconscious, rendering him helpless to remove the rope that has been entangled around his neck, and within two minutes Uncle is dead. Asphyxiated.

"Uncle! Uncle! Lawd, me a go dead!" Nephew screams as he peers down at the limp body of his uncle, ten feet below him. Another gust tugs Nephew's cap from his head, releasing his short reddish-brown locks. His arms flounder about in vain, trying to catch the cap before it starts its wayward descent towards the ground below. In desperation, Nephew instinctively pulls out his penknife from his pocket and frantically cuts away the rope that is holding him. His miscalculation does not fully register until a split second before his head hits a rock at the base of the tower and breaks his neck.

CHAPTER 3 – Wrong Way Lenny
Still 6 months ago

"With regret, Radio 98.5 FM announces that Barry TT – '*So nice dem name 'im twice*', will not be hosting the planned outside broadcast due to the pending arrival of Hurricane Lenny. Regular programming will be replaced by a special Hurricane Watch, hosted by Harriet Hughes throughout the day, and Peter Jones throughout the night. Radio 98.5 FM is the station that will keep you fully informed of all 'Wrong Way Lenny's' movements as it approaches Jamaica, so don't touch that dial. The new broadcast tower on top of Blue Mountain will enable us to reach more people throughout Jamaica with breaking news about this weather system. Stay tuned for news, sport and music from Radio 98.5 FM. Right now, we switch to Harriet Hughes for the latest on Hurricane Lenny."

"Thanks Chris. Hurricane Lenny has already caused some damage as it caught meteorologists unawares. This is the first hurricane in over one hundred years that is following this west to east trajectory through the Caribbean, starting in the Gulf. This Category Four hurricane did some early damage over the Blue Mountains area last night with strong winds blowing down power lines and trees …"

* * *

"Ugh! Aargh!"

"Mister, are you sure you going to be ok?" The pilot looks across at the slim, ruddy complexioned man with the clean-shaven head. A scar that runs from the top of his head down to his left ear still makes the pilot uncomfortable a day after he had first seen it back in the Congo rain forest. During their stopover in the Andes to refuel, he almost stirred up the courage to ask, but a steely look in the eye of his passenger had convinced him not to ask about the circumstances. Even in the low glow from the cockpit instrumentation, the ominous scar is noticeable and sends a small shiver down his spine.

"Just fly the bloody plane and get us to our destination." The slim man says in a clipped Afrikaans accent.

The plane takes another sudden dip as it hits another air pocket.

"Ugh! Aragh!" The South African drops his head between his legs and buries it into a barf bag. After a few moments he raises his head. "Why the hell is it so rough?" He asks weakly. "The flight across the Antarctic Ocean wasn't like this."

"It's that damn hurricane. I think they call it 'Wrong Way Lenny'. We are flying in its wake."

The South African looks at his watch, "We've been flying for over three hours now and we would normally see shoreline lights by now. Where the hell are we?"

The chubby pilot taps a few dials on the instrumentation panel and looks around. The South African looks around also. The darkness around them is thick.

"I think …"

"You think? You have got to be joking mate!"

"We are heading north, but we had to alter course to the west because of the hurricane. It was blocking our path, so I took a more westerly course for a while."

"And?"

"And I am trying to get my bearings now. I believe we are somewhere between Jamaica and Puerto Rico."

"You believe!"

"Hey, my Mama never grow no fool!" The pilot glares at the South African. "By my rough calculations we must be somewhere in the vicinity of Jamaica, but since I don't see any lights, we must be between those islands, otherwise I would have expected to see lights." If the light was better in the cockpit the pilot's red complexion would have given away how angry he is at being challenged by his passenger. After all, he has twenty years of experience, and if it wasn't for his weight problem, he would probably still be flying jets for the US Air Force.

"Don't you need to check in with local air traffic control when flying over islands?"

"Hey. Come on now." The chubby pilot snorts. "It's not like we are your jolly American Airlines scheduled flight." He shakes his head and snorts again.

"Save the lip. I don't know how this shit works." Comes the gruff response.

"Well, I assume we are incognito for a reason."

"Are we? Who told you that? What do you know?" The scar-headed Africaans turns in his seat to face the chubby pilot. The pilot notices that his passenger starts to reach inside his windbreaker jacket.

"Did I say I knew anything? I am just making stupid assumptions. I mean I am an inquisitive guy and our route from central Africa to Florida isn't exactly conventional. So, I figure we don't want to be seen, and you don't want to be searched. Am I right?"

"Maybe you think too much."

The chubby pilot glances over at his passenger and feels a chill. Even in the low light of the cockpit, he can make out the cold, steely glare of his passenger. The scar seems to glare at him too. The pilot snorts again. "As I said, I make stupid assumptions all the time. It's because of my active imagination. My mother tells me that ..."

"Hey, what is that ahead of us?" The South African is staring through the windscreen.

The pilot refocuses his attention ahead.

What is that?

Instinctively he leans forward, as does the South African as they both peer out the windscreen to determine what they are seeing.

"Oh my God!" The pilot flings himself back in his seat and pulls back violently on the yoke, simultaneously increasing the throttle. "Come on! Come on!" He shouts. Beads of sweat appear immediately, and his shirt collar is visibly wet in seconds.

The South African is thrown back in his seat. The barf bag slips from his hand and crashes into the back wall of the cockpit, splashing vomit across the door, "What the fuck is it?! What is it?!" He screams.

"It's a mountain, gawddarn it!"

The engines scream as the plane tries to ascend at the rate the pilot demands of it, complaining as it climbs every foot. Both men wait. The foliage on the mountainside suddenly becomes very clear and distinctive in the flying lights from the plane as it gets closer and closer to the mountain. If they were religious men, they would have started praying at this point. The seconds pass interminably, until finally the mountain is no longer visible through the windscreen, and all that can be seen is the blackness of the angry night sky. After a few seconds the pilot pushes the yoke forward, reduces the throttle, levels the plane and starts laughing, his snort gets louder with each breath.

"Why the hell are you laughing?!?" The South African demands.

"Cause gawddarn it," the pilot wipes his forehead with the sleeve of his short-sleeved shirt, "we just cheated death my friend." He punches the yoke. "Looks like we are over Jamaica, but there are no lights. I guess the hurricane knocked them all out." He continues to snort.

"What about other tall structures or hills?" The South African asks nervously.

"No chance! We just cleared the south face of the Blue Mountains. Nothing higher than this mountain on the island."

The South African adjusts his position in his seat, pulls his handkerchief from his back pocket and mops his brow. The cockpit smells raw from the vomit that is dripping down the back wall and door, and he thinks about opening the cockpit door, because the smell is beginning to make him more nauseous than the rough ride.

"Now what the fuck is that?"

"What?" Asks the pilot absentmindedly, as he is busy checking his instrumentation.

"That!" The South African declares, pointing emphatically ahead. A beam of light seems to be hovering in mid-air and swaying from side to side. "Is it a UFO?"

"Of course not! You believe in those things?"

"I believe in what I can see. And I see a light hovering in mid-air!"

The pilot begins mumbling.

"What was that?! What the fuck did you say?!" The South African barks.

"Huh?" The pilot turns to the South African with a distant look in his eyes.

"I asked you what the fuck did you say? Do you know what that is?" The South African is now pointing emphatically.

"I was going through all the possibilities, and I can't figure it out. It looks like a dangling streetlight, but we are much too high up for that. I'll climb above it to be safe." The pilot pulls lightly back on the yoke and sees the light descend below the dashboard. They both relax and sit back in their seats, only to be violently thrown forward as the radio tower rips off the wing of the aircraft. The pilot fights gallantly to bring the plane under control, but this time the plane summarily ignores his efforts and within seconds after the collision, the plane crashes into the Blue Mountains.

CHAPTER 4 – Janet, Are You OK?
In the present

Janet drifts across the room. She holds her gown like an imaginary partner and waltzes around the room, her polished toes easily gripping the plush carpet of her hotel suite. Janet giggles and squeals. Her cheeks hurt. Even her long, dark, curly hair bounces with joy. She closes her eyes, losing herself in the sound of the music coming from the band on the pool-side terrace below. A familiar chord is struck, and Janet can see her father holding her, whirling her around and around in their living room at home, during one of their regular impromptu dance sessions. Or were they lessons? Janet was never sure. Her father enjoyed introducing her to the music he loved from his extensive vinyl collection, and she loved learning the subtleties of the two-step and three-step waltzes from him.

I guess they can be both. She thinks.

Janet sings the chorus of the Manhattan's 'Kiss and Say Goodbye' on the top of her voice, in harmony with the fairly good lead vocalist from the band. She hugs her gown closer and pretends to be swooned by her debonair partner. Janet giggles, throwing her head back and increasing her pace across the floor, deftly switching from a two-step to a three-step.

"Let's not rush anything, darling." Janet whispers to her imaginary partner. "We have all night." She swishes her hair from side to side and giggles.

"Ow!" Janet crashes to the floor, and rolls across the soft carpet, her momentum is stopped by the glass sliding door leading out to the patio. It takes a few minutes for Janet to extract herself from the tangled mesh of her gown and the heavy gold, red and brown patterned drapes that had just a few seconds ago hung elegantly from the ceiling. Janet sits up and looks around at the drapes now lying in a heap at her feet, and the glass, oval, coffee table that is standing with its hind legs in the air.

"Oh no! What have I done now?"

She struggles to her knees and shuffles across the carpet to look more closely at the table, and with a sigh of relief, confirms that the expensive looking table is undamaged. Steading herself, Janet carefully eases the coffee table down onto all four of its sturdy wooden legs. Out of the corner of her eye, Janet notices a red streak across the off-white carpet, leading from the pile of curtains towards the coffee table. In horror, she looks down and notices a gash on her shin, where blood is slowly seeping and running down her leg.

"Oh no!" Janet exclaims and runs to the bathroom. She soaks a towel in cold water and presses it against her shin, which also helps to ease the throbbing.

How am I going to explain the blood on the carpet? Mom is going to kill me! Janet looks around the bathroom for anything that she thinks might help. *If only we had some Arm & Hammer. I'm sure that would work.* Janet thinks.

"Hold on!" With a pronounced limp, Janet makes her way to the mini bar. "A ha!" She says triumphantly as she extracts a bottle of tonic water. "This should do it!" She opens the bottle and pours it liberally over the blood trail, and hurries to the bathroom for another towel. For the next fifteen minutes, Janet sits in her underwear and patiently pats the carpet dry.

Only a forensic team could tell that blood has spilt on this carpet. Janet thinks as she admires her handiwork.

The telephone rings, startling Janet. She stretches over to the bedside table from her sitting position and picks up the phone.

"Hello?"

"Janet? Are you ok?"

"Oh, hi Dad. Yes. Why do you ask?"

"You've been gone for almost an hour. Your mother and I had started to worry."

"It's been that long?"

"Is something the matter? Do you want me to come up?"

"No. No Dad. I'm ok. I'll be down shortly."

"Ok. Did you get the stain out?'

Janet gasps. *How did he know?*

"Janet?"

"I … I"

"Girl, what is the matter with you? I'm coming up there."

"No! Don't! I … I just had to use the toilet."

"Was it something you ate? Didn't you have the same meal as I did?"

"Yes. No. I mean, it's not that. It's, it's that time of the month."

There is silence on the line for a few seconds. "Oh." Janet's father clears his throat. "Sorry." He clears his throat again. "Did you get out the wine stain?"

"Wine stain?"

"Yes, the red wine stain from your gown."

"… from my gown?' Janet mutters. "Oh! That stain! I forgot!"

"You forgot? That was why you went upstairs in the first place. Are you sure you're ok?"

Janet giggles. "Yes, Dad. I'm ok." She pauses. "What did Mom say again?"

"Turn it inside out and run cold water …"

"Yes! Yes, I remember now. You're the best, Dad. Be down

in a jiff." Janet hangs up the phone, picks up her gown and hurries to the bathroom, without a limp.

CHAPTER 5 – Bomb!

"No, not now! Not now!" Kenneth Johnson tries not to slow his pace as he fumbles around, searching for his phone in the pocket of his windbreaker. He glances at his watch while removing his receipt-bloated-wallet from his pocket. He has even less time than expected, as his connecting flight is less than an hour from now. As he enters the Immigration Hall, he freezes in dismay and stares at the horde of people in the hall.

I'll never get through this in time to catch my flight!

Kenneth's attention is brought back to the present by the incessant ringing of his phone. He retrieves his phone, "Hello?"

Kenneth finds himself amid a sea of people as a throng of passengers descend on the Immigration Hall. Someone knocks Kenneth's wallet from his grasp, scattering his wallet, passport, credit cards, immigration and customs forms across the tiled floor.

"Hello! Hello! Hold on! Hold on! I have to pick up my things. Give me a second."

A woman with wide hips and large buttocks, dressed in high heels and carrying a very large bag, bustles by Kenneth.

Kenneth shouts. "Stop!"

Too late! The heel of her right shoe lands on a credit card, causing the woman to slip violently. In an effort to regain her balance, the woman throws her arms out in front of her, resulting in the bag that she was carrying being thrown high into the air.

* * *

Dezray Veronica Charles is the last passenger to get off the flight. With much difficulty, the Caribbean Airlines attendant helps her with her bag. The flight had left Montego Bay late because Dezray, who liked to be called DVC, had insisted, very forcefully, that her bag had to be properly secured and protected from damage. Initially, the first-class flight attendants had wanted her to place it in the overhead compartment, but DVC informed them that if her very expensive vase broke,

"Dem would 'ave hell fi pay. Yuh nuh know seh me is DJ Little Shrimp's woman!"

After the Captain joined the heated discussion, it was agreed that the bag would be placed in one of the front compartments, with blankets placed around it to cushion it from any turbulence.

Now she is making her way towards the Immigration Hall, quietly cursing herself for her overindulgence. If she was honest with herself, she would admit that she got carried away by the dream of seeing herself on the cover of Home and Garden magazine, in front of their new home in Boca Raton that Little Shrimp bought with the proceeds from his latest tour. When she saw the vase, she knew that she would look fantastic standing beside it by the enormous mahogany front door, with the new white Lexus strategically parked to the side, its custom gold grill catching the eye of the reader, and sure to impress. She knew exactly where the camera man needed to set up to get the right shot. She must remember to ask the gardener to plant some roses nearby to add colour.

"Cho! Dis bag so damn heavy! How dem nuh have no trolley fi me carry mi sing ting dem? A wha' kinda airport dis? Cho!" As DVC makes the long trek towards the Immigration Hall, she slows, "Whoa, my corn a bun me! Cho!"

DVC sighs in relief when she sees the signs for the Immigration Hall, only for her hopes to be dashed when she sees the waves of people approaching an already crowded hall. "Rahtid! Me nah 'tan up in dem yah shoes fi hours a wait pon nuh line!"

She quickens her step and lengthens her stride. Despite the weight of the bag, she is determined to get to the shortest line before the sea of people who have just arrived in Miami. DVC sees a man off to her right stooping down on the tiled floor. She wonders for a moment what he is doing, but then refocuses on her goal at hand, getting to the front of a line as a quickly as possible. She redoubles her efforts and lengthens her stride even further. She hears a shout, but DVC doesn't make out the words over the noise in the Immigration Hall, when suddenly, her right heel slips out from under her. In her attempt to regain her balance, DVC throws her arms forward and loses her grip of the bag. In horror, DVC watches her bag flying high into the air towards the white ceiling with its recessed florescent lights.

"No! Mi bag! Ketch mi bag!" She screams as she falls to the floor.

* * *

Norman loves Star Trek. Jean-Luc Picard is his favourite captain, although he thinks Spock is the coolest ever. Last summer he had tried to stretch his ears so that they looked like a Vulcan's. He couldn't understand why his mother over-reacted the way she did when she walked into his bedroom and caught him trying to hang himself from his ears. He had worked out that his body weight was just enough to make his ears stretch appropriately, but his mom would not listen to his theory or look at his calculations.

Mothers!

Norman could not believe his luck when he walked into the bookstore in Heathrow airport and saw the Star Trek Chronicles on the shelve, a series of six books in one package, including some great artwork. Thankfully, he had enough of his spending money left to cover most of the price, and he begged his dad for the rest of the money.

It is awesome!

He is now reading the book as they walk towards the Immigration Hall. It had been a long flight, and even with the book, Norman had trouble finding things to keep himself entertained throughout the entire flight. He had slept for about half the flight, watched a movie, and then read for the remainder of the time. He had asked his mom if they were there yet once, and the expression on her face convinced him that he shouldn't wake her to ask her that question again for the rest of the flight. They had been delayed on the tarmac after landing, something about there being congestion on the ground, but Norman had taken the opportunity to get fully engrossed in his Star Trek bible. Norman had put on his headphones and turned up the sound on his iPad just loud enough that he could hear his mother's voice but not hear what she was saying. He wanted to concentrate on every fact and detail in the book, and he was finding it hard to do that with all the hubbub from the passengers, and his mom and dad talking. The light got a lot better for reading as they got closer to the Immigration Hall, with its very high ceiling, white tiles, walls and ceiling, and the innumerable lights in the ceiling. Normally, Norman would have stopped to count the number of light bulbs, but he was getting to a really interesting part of the story.

Captain Kirk's Starship Enterprise was under attack from the Romulans. Disaster was imminent because the Romulans had deployed a new device called a Refraction Bomb that could be used at even warp speeds. Norman was trying to understand the technical explanation of how the bomb worked, and admiring the artist's impression of the bomb, when he saw something rise above the rim of his book, flying towards the ceiling. He glanced at it, and back at the artwork of the Refraction Bomb.

Wow! That looks just like the bomb. He thought.

Norman excitedly tugged at his mother's dress and shouted,

"Hey Mom! Look, a Refraction Bomb!"

* * *

Squatting, Kenneth could feel the wave of silence coming towards him before he could hear it. He can see the confused expressions on the faces of many passengers as they slowed down. Hushed questions are being asked.

"Bomb? Bomb? Did you hear someone say bomb?"

Kenneth's attention is drawn to the bag, as it reaches the peak of its flight. Its rapid descent reminds Kenneth of a roller coaster, and even though Kenneth braced himself for the landing, he is unprepared for the sound, which seems to be amplified by the unusually hushed atmosphere in the hall.

Everything stops.

The large buttocks woman screams, and then pandemonium breaks out in the Immigration Hall.

"Bomb! Bomb!" are the screams from the panicked passengers, as they run towards the exits ignoring the armed personnel. Those who are too slow are knocked aside or knocked over. A loud siren blares, and a loud-speakered voice instructs people to remain calm and follow the guidance of the officers.

After the chaos, Kenneth uncurls his muscular six-foot-two-inch frame from the fetal position he had adopted to protect himself from the stampeding people and looks around the hall. Astonishingly, the Immigration Hall is now empty, except for the wide hipped woman who is sobbing a few feet away from him. There are passports and papers strewn across the hall, and for a moment Kenneth feels a wave of panic. He frantically looks around and sighs when he sees his passport and wallet neatly wedged against a column, almost as though someone had placed them there out of harm's way. There is no sign of his credit cards, but that is OK. As long as he can get home, that is the most important thing. He can always get replacement cards. Pain racks his body as Kenneth gets up and gingerly makes his way over to the column to pick up his passport and wallet. As he bends down, he senses a presence. Kenneth slowly repositions his body so that he can see who is standing behind him. The first thing he sees is the barrel of a gun. With some effort, Kenneth adjusts his focus to the fresh face behind the gun.

Rhatid! Is wha dis? Kenneth thinks.

He runs his index finger and thumb over his stubble length moustache and goatee beard, as he ponders the situation.

"Sir! Can you stay where you are and not move!"

"I'm just picking up my passport and wallet. Is that ok?"

"Sir! Please don't move!"

"Can I stand up?"

"Sir! Don't move!"

"Look! I can't stay in this position much longer. Either I sit down or stand up. Which would you prefer?"

Kenneth can see the confusion in the young man's eyes. The officer glances from Kenneth to the woman who is still on the floor, with the trampled bag she was carrying now some distance away. Despite the momentary confusion, Kenneth notices that the young man's eyes are steady and focused, and his hands did not shake as he keeps the gun trained on Kenneth, but his stance is not what it should be. His weight is too over-balanced over his left leg. For a moment Kenneth thinks about taking advantage of this weakness, and then he remembers where he is, and decides against it.

"Look kid ..." Kenneth glances at the 'U.S. Customs Service 1789' emblem on the shoulder of the young man's uniform, with its scales of justice and a key, and quickly corrects himself, "... sir. I don't want any trouble. I'm going to raise both my hands over my head, slowly turn around and then stand up."

Kenneth starts his manoeuvre, being sure to maintain eye contact with the officer. The young man shifts his position, stepping slightly backwards as he watches Kenneth. As Kenneth completes his manoeuvre, he can hear running booted feet approaching from behind the column. In a blur, Kenneth is handcuffed and bustled through the Immigration Hall. Kenneth is dumped in a small room with only a wooden table and a metal chair in one corner of the room. His muscles complain. An overweight man with grey thinning hair limps into the room within seconds of Kenneth's arrival.

"You're in big trouble mister." He announces triumphantly.

"Oh?" Kenneth says. "For what?"

The overweight man pulls up his trousers waist and glares at Kenneth, "Terrorism!"

CHAPTER 6 – Mike Tyson

Kenneth eases himself into the comfy leather chair, while his wife, Jenny, strategically places some additional cushions around Kenneth to support his sore body.

"You sure you up to this?" John Jefferson IV asks. His friends call him Jay. He prefers that to Junior, mainly because it distinguishes him from the other 'Johns' in his family; his father, grandfather and great grandfather, which may seem ironic if you saw them all in the same room. They were all as dark as midnight, no more than five feet five in height, with the physique like the Hulk. If not for the age differences between the men, one could be forgiven for concluding that they were quadruplets. The likeness is striking. "Man, you look like you just got whooped by George Foreman."

"Nah man." The rough-neck Marshall chimes in before Kenneth can respond. "It look more like Muhammad Ali."

"What you talking about?" Eric slowly strolls up to Kenneth. Everyone looks on with interest. Eric bends down and stares at Kenneth's face, his brow knit. He swivels on bended knee to the small group of friends that are gathered on the grilled patio to welcome Kenneth home, with a grave expression etched on his round Chinese face. "It was definitely Mike Tyson." Eric declares.

Laughter erupts. Kenneth looks on in despair. His closest friends, Jay, Eric, Lisa and Marshall are all crying from laughter! Kenneth's gaze drifts over to Jenny.

"Jenny! How can you be laughing too?" Kenneth asks with a pained expression on his face.

"I'm sorry darling, but it is funny." Jenny says, wiping her eyes with a napkin.

Jenny had met Kenneth in university during Carnival, when she had been a Carnival Queen, and he had been one of the float builders. Their relationship had a rocky start, because she is a 'red Jamaican', from one of Jamaica's old money families of the colonial days. 'Red Jamaicans' are often descendants of the plantation owners, families that came from Europe in the 16th and 17th century, while Kenneth is a 'brown man', of mulatto descent. Mulattos are often the descendants of slave masters and plantation owners, and their slaves. Many plantation owners came to the New World in search of building their wealth, but it was arduous work and inhospitable conditions, so they left their families behind, and many had new families in the New World with their chosen slaves. Jenny's parents did not approve of her dating a brown man.

"Alright, alright. The joke done now!" Kenneth says forcefully, which makes them laugh even more.

Eric Sean Lee holds up a hand to get everyone's attention. Eric is a Mathematics professor at the University of the West Indies. Something of a child prodigy, Eric entered university at age fourteen. His mother was from Hong Kong, and when she recognised his talent, she taught him at home in the evenings and weekends. By twenty, Eric had doctorates in both pure and applied mathematics and then spent the next decade traveling around the world working with the brightest minds on some of the most advanced technological challenges of our age. Eric has never been able to talk about most of what he has worked on because he was always restricted by a non-disclosure agreement. However, one evening Kenneth and Eric were kicking back, *'beating some juice'* in his study listening to some 1960's soul music. They must have been on their second, or maybe it was their third, flask of Wray and Nephew when Eric whispered to Kenneth that he wanted to share with him a project he had worked on for NASA, on the Space Shuttle's flight characteristics. Eric figured Kenneth would appreciate the artistry and genius of the solution because of his military background. He explained that one of the extraordinarily difficult problems NASA had to solve in the early days was the variability in the flight characteristics of the Shuttle when it transitioned from spacecraft to hypersonic in thin air, to hypersonic in thicker air, to supersonic, to transonic. There are no practical ways for a human pilot to know when to use which control in which way at a particular time. The maths and programming needed to have computers take over the use of the control thrusters, the body flap, and the tail or elevons for specific manoeuvres during different phases of flight instead of the pilots was a significant technological problem to solve. Eric's eyes were on fire as he described the machinations he went through to figure out the maths, and then, Bang! He slammed his hand down on the table. It hit him. This was a variation of the Navier-Stokes fluid dynamics equation, if, and only if, they were able to measure the air density within a reasonable error deviation. The maths was a thing of pure beauty. Kenneth nodded his head and smiled, giving Eric a high five.

These types of projects paid very well, but Eric hit the jackpot when he was recruited to become a Quant on Wall Street, writing mathematical models that forecast financial market behaviour. As the ripe old age of thirty approached, he met his blonde-haired, blue-eyed love, Lisa, a pediatrician. Eric, got married, and started a family and the lure of traveling vanished. When the University of the West Indies offered a professorship, with a seven-figure salary, house and car, Eric jumped at the opportunity to settle down with his young family.

"So let me get this straight." says Eric, who holds up his hand and composes himself. The laughter subsides. "After they couldn't make the terrorist charge stick, they decided to give you a cavity search, just for good measure?"

Kenneth frowns and shifts uncomfortably in the chair, "Yeah."

Eric's fat cheeked face twitches, as he tries to maintain a

serious expression. "That's ..." he snorts, as he tries to hold back a giggle, "that's just ..." he starts chuckling, "that's just not right." Eric is laughing now, along with everyone else on the patio.

Kenneth shakes his head and sheepishly buries it in his hands. It is not long before he feels hot breaths and wet tongues on the back of his hands. He looks up to see Caesar and Sheeba. The two nine-month-old German Shepherds whimper, their tails slowly and hesitantly wagging from side to side. Caesar bows his head and whimpers again, slowly edging forward to Kenneth. Sheeba leans forward, stretching her neck and sniffs Kenneth suspiciously.

"It's ok guys. It is me." Both dogs wag their tails enthusiastically when they hear their master's voice. Kenneth hugs them. "At least someone still loves me."

"Aww!" comes the chorus from the group.

After another minute or so, Eric, ever the logician, asks, "So who called you?" Running a hand through his short, spiky hair.

Kenneth looks up from the puppies at Eric, "You know, I don't know." Kenneth turns to Jenny, "Can you get my phone? I think it is upstairs, probably still in my travel bag." When Jenny returns, Kenneth checks his phone. "I don't recognize the number."

"Well since that call managed to earn you a cavity search, I would call and find out who the rhatid caused all this grief." Jay offers, which starts another bout of laughter.

Kenneth shakes his head and tries to ignore them as he dials the number, "Hello. This is ..."

"I know who it is Mr. Johnson. Thanks for calling back."

"Who is this?" Kenneth asks, using his free hand to tell everyone to be quiet.

"My name is Donald Martin. You don't know me."

"Ok." Kenneth hesitates for a moment, "So how can I help

you Mr. Martin?"

"I need your help. My daughter Janet is missing."

CHAPTER 7 – The Martins

Donald and Catherine Martin sit down beside each other in the five-seater leather sofa. Mr. Martin's low curly hair is completely grey, as is his very full moustache. His long face and limbs give him the appearance of being very tall, although he is less than six feet tall. Mrs. Martin is almost the same height as her husband, but appears much taller, probably because of her bolt straight back. Her thick jet-black hair combed into one, completes the persona of an old-style headmistress or matron. After serving them a drink, Jenny sits beside the Martins, while Kenneth sits opposite them in his leather chair that has been moved from the patio into the living room.

Despite the late hour, Eric is still there, and as is customary for him, he is sitting on the marble floor with his back resting against the wall, his legs stretched out in front of him and his track shoes resting beside him, with his left big toe sticking out through his bobby socks. Lisa has left to take their son, Andy, home to bed, and the only other person still in attendance from the evening lyme is Marshall, who is standing in the open archway that leads to the dining room. Kenneth first met Marshall in high school.

* * *

Kenneth watched the scene from across the classroom. A group of boys from one of the classes in his year was playing box-football during their lunchtime break. The box had been kicked out of the window of the classroom, and they shouted to a new transfer student who was walking by to throw the box back into the room.

The new transfer student, with his short uncombed afro, ignored the shouts and walked by. The box-football playing group took this as a sign of disrespect and hurried out the door to confront the new transfer.

"Aye bwoy! What do yuh? Yuh nuh hear we a call yuh?"

"Yuh a disrespek wi? Eh bwoy?"

The group surrounded the new transfer, blocking his path and stopping him from turning away. Kenneth watched as the boy slowly takes off his watch and slides it into his pocket. The boy looked at the group of six boys that surrounded him, scanning them up and down, and shuffling his feet. The six boys had larger statures than the new transfer, and Kenneth feared the worse. So, Kenneth slid from his grey metal chair and walked slowly but purposefully across the classroom. The boys noticed the shuffling feet of the new transfer.

"Aye bwoy. Yuh nervous?"

"Yuh fraid?"

"Yuh a go piss yuhself?"

The boys started laughing and menacingly tightened the circle around the new transfer. Then Kenneth recognised and associated boxing patterns to the new transfer's shuffling. Suddenly, before the six boys could launch their attack, the new transfer dropped his hips, threw a lead hook to the solar plexus of the biggest boy in the group and then the new transfer dropped him to his knees with an uppercut to his jaw. The new transfer then shuffled over to the next biggest boy and stunned him with a jab and cross combination to the head. The boy fell flat on his face and didn't move. The other four boys looked on with their mouths wide open in shock. Before they could decide what to do Kenneth jumped into the centre of the group.

"Guys. The new kid meant no disrespect." Kenneth said calmly, holding up his arms. "Let's stop while we are ahead on this one, shall we?"

The four boys looked at each other and after a few tense moments shrugged their shoulders in unison. Kenneth grabbed the new transfer's arm and dragged him away from the group, guiding him towards the canteen. As they entered the canteen, the new transfer stopped and looked at Kenneth.

"Me nah look no friend." The new transfer said as he ran his long dark fingers through his short uncombed afro.

Kenneth matched the intensity of his screw face, "No problem."

The new transfer glared into Kenneth's green eyes, before giving him a simple nod and strolling away to join the patty line. No one really understood their relationship dynamic back then. No one really understood it now, but no one questioned their loyalty to each other.

* * *

Kenneth grimaces as he slowly leans forward in his chair, "Mr. and Mrs. Martin, I thought it best if we talked face to face, instead of over the phone. Why did you call me?"

Mr. Martin sighs. Mrs. Martin takes Mr. Martin's hand and softly pats it.

"I, we were hoping ..."

He stops and takes a deep breath. He looks at his wife. Mrs. Martin returns his look and squeezes his hand. Mrs. Martin turns to Kenneth.

"This is extremely difficult for us. Our daughter Janet has not been seen for the last three days." Her voice is steady, firm, almost stern.

"Have you spoken to the police?" Kenneth asks.

Mr. Martin gently clears his throat, "We ..." He hesitates, looks at his wife and then continues, "we believe they may be involved."

"Oh?" Kenneth says.

"What evidence do you have of that?" Eric asks.

"Well …" Mr. Martin starts.

"Hold on." Kenneth holds up an arm. He leans further forward in his chair. "We are getting ahead of ourselves. First tell us what happened."

Mr. Martin explains how the family had taken a short break at a hotel with some friends. It was something they did occasionally, like many other Jamaicans. A beach is no more than a thirty-minute drive from most parts of the Corporate Area, or the suburbs of Kingston and Saint Andrew, while the closest of the famous tourist resort areas is no more than a ninety-minute drive away. A long weekend is always a favourite time to chill out at a nice hotel. Mr. Martin related his last conversation with Janet. She never came back down to the poolside after leaving them to clean a wine stain from her dress.

"It's my fault." Mrs. Martin blurts out, catching everyone by surprise. "I should never have insisted that she go and remove the wine stain. If she had stayed with us, she would still be here with us." Her voice trembles and she struggles with the words. Mr. Martin hugs her, his long arm extending around her shoulder.

"Catherine, you don't know that, so please stop tormenting yourself."

"Mrs. Martin. All we can do now is focus on the positives." Kenneth offers.

"So, you said Janet is eighteen?" Eric asks.

"Yes."

"And you're sure she hasn't gone off with some young man?"

Mr. Martin soft eyes show a glint of anger, and Mrs. Martin stiffens and glares at Eric.

"Young man! That would not be proper!" Mrs. Martin says

sharply.

"I'm sorry, Ma'am. I didn't mean to …"

"Yes, you did!" Mrs. Martin cuts off Eric. She pauses and takes a deep breath, "But it's ok. Although we are old, we are not naive. We know the temptations out there for young people today. We had Janet when we were almost beyond my childbearing days", she smiles at Eric, "but we were young once too." She looks lovingly at Mr. Martin.

"Look, we want to be completely honest with you, Janet is young at heart. Very much so." Mr. Martin says

"You mean she is retarded?" Marshall asks.

"No, no. She is a straight 'A' student, but …" Mr. Martin looks at his wife, searching her face, "I'm struggling to find the words that best describes her. Some would say she is naive. She sees the best in everything and everyone. She rarely sees the bad side. She loves life and its beauty to the fullest."

"So, she wore …" Marshall stops, "I'm sorry. She wears rose pink glasses."

Mr. Martin responds quickly, without acknowledging the slip by Marshall, "I guess that is one way of saying it. We have protected her, because we strongly believe that her disposition is a gift, not a hinderance. As children, this is how we all saw the world …"

"Yes, but we all have to grow up." Marshall interrupts.

"Indeed, but then we hate instead of love, and as a result there is more grief instead of laughter."

"That's the reality of life." Marshall chirps.

"Yes, unfortunately, but I tell you the truth," Mr. Martin's voice rises in volume, "unless you change and become like a little child, you will never enter the kingdom of heaven."

Marshall involuntarily takes a step back and rubs his stubble beard. No one speaks.

Mr. Martin continues, breaking the awkward silence. "It's a message we have come to understand because of Janet. That is why we have protected her. We have tried to allow her to grow up in her own time. She always brings laughter to a room, lifts hearts, helping people to see light in the gloom. She ..." Mr. Martin's voice trails away.

"This brings us full circle, why are you here?' asks Kenneth.

Mr. Martin looks at Kenneth. His eyes well up and he says softly, "We have nowhere else to go."

The sound of a chirping cricket drifts into the room with the cool and gentle breeze through the open glass louvers on either side of the bay windows that front the living room. "Why do you say the police are involved?" Eric asks, as he wipes his eyes.

Mr. and Mrs. Martin look at each other. "To be honest, we don't know that to be true." Mr. Martin offers, "but the investigation just doesn't feel right."

"What do you mean?"

"An officer promptly came by the hotel and took our statement. He was a nice young man. He radioed the station while he was with us, and said someone would be over very soon to look at the room and look for any clues. We waited for the rest of the evening, and no one came by. We called the station the following day, and they said the officer had taken ill and would not be back at work the rest of the week. We asked what was happening with the investigation and they said it would have to wait until the officer was back at work. We asked if his report had been submitted and acted upon, and we were told that the information could not be shared with us. We called the Commissioner's Office, and they said they could not interfere in a local investigation at such an early stage. We can't wait until next week to find out if something is being done to find Janet."

"Why do you think I can help?" Kenneth asks.

Mr. and Mrs. Martin exchange brief looks.

"We," they look down at their laps in unison, "we have heard about your past." Mr. Martin offers, his voice noticeably lower in volume.

"Our Pastor suggested that we call you." Mrs. Martin adds quickly. They don't look up at Kenneth. "He said you have the ability to fix things."

* * *

"You know I wouldn't normally ask, but I won't be able to do anything for a few days until I am a hundred percent. I'm only asking her to use her connections to make some inquiries. Nothing more."

Mr. and Mrs. Martin and Eric have left, leaving only Marshall. Marshall rubs his chin for a while, and then nods, "Ok. I'll ask her. Kathy will do anything to make an impression with you and Jenny."

"I hope she doesn't think that she has to impress us?" Kenneth counters.

"Come on, Kenneth. Really?" Marshall says with a pained expression on his face.

"What?" Kenneth looks at Jenny for support.

"You can be exacting." Jenny says patting Kenneth on the shoulder. Turning to Marshall, she smiles, "Marshall, you know that any friend of yours, is a friend of ours."

Marshall gets up and kisses Jenny on the cheek. "You have a big heart. That's why we all love you." He heads for the front door. "We'll be in touch." He shouts as he closes the door.

CHAPTER 8 – No Q

The back door opens and slams shut immediately.

"Tun off de damn light." Comes the rasping voice from outside.

Kathy reaches up and switches off the roof light. The back door opens and quickly closes.

"You ok?" Kathy asks as she starts to turn around.

"Is wha yuh a do? Look in front and don't tun round!" The raspy voice barks. Kathy snaps back to face the front of the car. They are parked under a large mango tree on a side avenue, facing East Street in downtown Kingston. Kathy has deliberately chosen this spot because it is shaded from any of the streetlights by the overhanging branches of the mango tree.

A minibus honks its horn on East Street as it slows to pick up passengers at the bus stop just south of the avenue.

"What's wrong?" Kathy asks.

"Is who dis? Yuh supposed to come alone." The voice says from the back seat.

Kathy looks across at the driver of the car, "Jeff is my associate. We work together at the Gleaner. His name is …"

"Hear me, woman! Me need money. Now!"

"You'll get your normal fee for helping me when …"

"No! Dat cyaan work!"

"Why? What's going on?" Kathy is distracted by a commotion in front of the car.

Fifty yards away, a multi-coloured mongrel dog runs across

the road and scampers towards East Street. A stone crashes into the zinc fence after flying over the dog's head and a bare-chested man in shorts runs out of a nearby gate swearing. A woman runs out after him, her large breasts are barely being held in check by the thin vest she is wearing.

"Mine yuh kill de dawg!" She screams.

"De bomboclawt dawg fi dead! How him come fi nyam off mi dinner? Is what you was doing?" The man picks up another stone and throws it down the street into the darkness in frustration. The scrawny mongrel dog emerges from the darkness into the beam of a yellow halogen streetlight, now trotting. Suddenly, the stone thuds into the dog, causing the dog to yelp and then scamper off in a panic towards East Street. Then, there is a squeal of tires and a loud bang. Kathy, Jeff, the informant and the underwear clad couple watch as the mongrel bounces across the road. An angry minibus driver swears and shakes his fist at the prostrate mongrel, before revving his engine and powering away in a cloud of diesel smoke. The bare-chested man looks at the dog in the distance, nods his head, turns and marches back through the gate. The large breasted woman looks from the prostrate dog to the man and back to the dog, before running after the man gesticulating.

"Is wha yuh do to de dawg? Is wha yuh do?" She shouts. A door slams, and her voice is no longer discernible.

"Dem a come fi me. Me have to run." The raspy voice says between gasps.

"What? Who? Why?" Kathy asks, still distracted by the dog laying in the middle of East Street.

"Woman! Yuh nuh hear what me a seh? Me need money now!"

"What? I don't understand." Kathy says, now fully engaged in the matter at hand. "Tell me what happened!"

"Money woman!" The raspy voice demands.

Kathy spins around in her seat and glares at the wiry thin man in the back seat. "Tell me what is going on!" She barks.

"Me nuh have time fi dis." The man opens the door. Kathy reaches over the seat and grabs him on the shoulder as he tries to get out of the car. He screams as Kathy holds his shoulder and falls back in the car. Kathy pulls away from him in shock. Her hand is moist, and initially she thinks it must be from perspiration, but her fingers start to stick together as the seconds pass. Kathy hurriedly opens the glove compartment and takes out a slim flashlight and shines it on her olive complexioned hand.

It was covered in blood!

Kathy and Jeff spin around and look at the wiry man. They gasp as the beam of the flashlight illuminates him as he lies on the back seat groaning. The left shoulder of his shirt is crimson with blood!

"What happened to you?" Kathy screams.

"Shut up woman! And tun off de light!"

Kathy turns off the flashlight. "What happened?" She asks in a hushed shout.

"Dem shot me! What it look like?" The informant says through clenched teeth.

"What! Why? I don't understand."

"I did send mi bredren fi ask some questions bout dis girl yuh a look fah. Me never see him for two days, so me go look for him. Dem shot up him house and kill him and everyone in him house." He is now sitting upright in the back seat. He grunts between each sentence as he straightens himself.

"Where?" Jeff asks.

"Jungle."

"Then that nuh normal?" Jeff quips.

"Is wha yuh a seh?"

"Yuh bredren probably mix up in some business that went bad."

"Any business him was into, was Don business, and me know bout it. Dis was different."

"Why do you say that?" Kathy asks.

"Dem leave a message. '*No Q or UNX.*'"

"What does that mean?" Kathy asks.

"No questions. Or you next."

"What!?!" Kathy exclaims.

"How you know the message was related to his killing?" Jeff asks skeptically.

"Dem write it pon de wall where dem dump de body dem."

"So?" Jeff says.

"In blood."

"Oh my!" Jeff exclaims.

Kathy gasps and covers her mouth. "How did you get shot?" Kathy breathes.

"When I ran out of the house dem was waiting for me. I managed to beat de fence, but dem a look fi me now."

Kathy hesitates, "Before I give you the money, I need to know what your friend found out."

"Woman, yuh nuh hear wha me seh?"

"Yes, but the only way to solve this is to understand it. What did your friend find out?"

"Me nuh know. Him dead before me chat to him."

"You sure?"

"Woman!"

"Ok." Kathy nods at Jeff. He reaches under the seat and hands Kathy a brown manila envelope. She reaches into the envelope, and with the aid of the flashlight counts out some bills. "Here is ten thousand." She says as she leans over the back of the seat and gives it to the informant.

"Dis is all? How far yuh tink me a go get wid dis?" He spits back.

"Ok." Kathy reaches into the envelope. "Here is another ten thousand."

The informant grabs the money and disappears out the door into the darkness. Jeff gets out of the car and closes the back door. When Jeff gets back in the car Kathy notices that Jeff is shaking.

"Do you want to step down from this one?" Kathy asks.

Jeff is silent. His head is bowed.

"Jeff? Did you hear me?"

"What? You said something?"

"Are you ok? Do you want to step down from this one? I can fly solo on this."

"No, no. I can do this." Jeff says emphatically.

"You don't need to prove anything to me, Jeff." Kathy says softly.

"I know, but I need to do this."

"Are you sure?"

Jeff hesitates and then nods his head, "Yes. I am sure." He clenches his fist and does a fist pump.

He is really growing up fast. His grandmother must be so proud of him. Kathy thinks.

Kathy nods at Jeff, who starts the car, and they drive away in silence.

CHAPTER 9 – Yes Grandma

Kathy walks into the lecture hall. She always walks with purpose, with her head down, to the lectern in these sessions. She is wearing a stylish purple jacket with a white silk camisole blouse, over a slim cut black jeans pants. She feels good today.

Today was going to be a good day.

When Kathy reaches the lectern, she looks up and scans the amphitheatre styled hall. She is surprised to see that the hall is full.

Whoa! This has never happened before.

"Good morning, ladies and gentlemen." Kathy waits, looking around the hall. "Come on, you can do better than that. Good morning, ladies and gentlemen."

"Good morning, Ma'am." The sound rolls down the amphitheatre.

"I am so pleased to see so many of you here. The turnout suggests that the title of this year's open lecture has piqued a lot of interest. Unless you are all in the wrong lecture hall."

This generates a lot of laughter and a rumble of discussion.

Kathy picks up a sheet of paper off the lectern and reads from it. "We are here to discuss our national motto – Out of many one people. What are the inherent implications of our motto on our implicit right to reparations?" Kathy looks around the lecture hall. "Are you all in the right place?"

There are a lot of nodding heads, smiling faces, and a hum in the hall.

Kathy flashes a broad smile, "Great. Let's get going. The islands of the Caribbean have a shared history of being 'discovered' by explorers from Europe. Jamaica in 1492, Antigua and Barbuda in 1493, Trinidad and Tobago in 1498, St Lucia in 1499, and Barbados in 1536, to name a few."

A young lady in a white polo shirt and jeans enthusiastically puts up her hand. Kathy points at her.

"Ma'am, St Lucia was discovered in 1502 by Christopher Columbus. You said 1499."

"What's your name?" Kathy walks slowly from behind the lectern, looking at the student who made the comment.

"Vicky Jones."

"Thank you for bringing that up, Vicky. You are correct, the information we previously had indicated that Christopher Columbus discovered St Lucia in 1502. But recent evidence suggests that Columbus' navigator, Juan de la Cosa, had set foot on the island three years earlier, in 1499. Juan kept his own notes, separate from those of Columbus. He makes references in them of a journey he and a small crew made north of Trinidad. They could see an island to the east and thought about diverting there but decided to hold their northerly course and landed on an island. His description of the twin peaks on his approach suggest he was describing the Pitons mountains. His notes are still being verified but the community is pretty much convinced that he set foot on St Lucia in 1499."

This revelation sparks a lot of discussion in the hall. Another hand shoots up. Kathy points at the young man.

"How do we know if any of the discovery dates are accurate?"

Kathy chuckles, "Well, we do the best we can to verify and validate the information we have about our history." She pauses and strolls slowly around the platform. "The reality is that history is written by the victors not the vanquished. In our capacity as an independent university that represents the interests of the West

Indies, we have the privilege and responsibility to do right by our constituency. The University of the West Indies is very proud of the advancements and contributions we have made in medicine, law, hospitality management and human sciences in the region." Kathy looks around the hall, "As much as I would love to expound on UWI's achievements, that is not the purpose of this lecture, but please, keep the questions and discussion points coming." Kathy walks back to the lectern and looks at her notes. "What our little deviation highlights is the minefield we are dealing with when we revisit the complex and multi-layered history of our people. Malcolm X coined the following term when he was asked about what he was thankful for during a Thanksgiving holiday in the US. He said, 'We didn't land on Plymouth Rock, Plymouth Rock landed on us!', referring to the black American descendants of African slaves who were captured, shipped and enslaved in the Americas by the millions, having no choice in the matter." There is a chuckle throughout the hall. "So, it was with us. This was not an immigration choice but a brutally, enforced mass migration of cheap labour to enrich the nations in Europe. Our ethnic diversity was also not a choice. Initially we had white, the plantation and slave owners, and black, the slaves. Then over time we had the mulattos, or 'brownings' as they are called today, which were the offspring of the slave owners and slave mothers. There was no bleaching back then." This brings a roar of laughter in the hall. "Then, we saw the introduction of Chinese and Indian indentured labourers with the abolition of the slave trade in the 19th century. And we should not ignore the voluntary migration that took place across islands in search of opportunities for work or wealth by white workers. All of this sets the background and foundation for our cultural and societal mix that we have today. The lecture title is focused on the Jamaican national motto, 'Out of Many One people', but for completeness I should mention the mottos of the other islands I have so far mentioned. Trinidad and Tobago, 'Together we Aspire - Together we Achieve'; Barbados - 'Pride and Industry'; Antigua and Barbuda - 'Each endeavouring, all achieving'; St Lucia – 'The land, the people, the light'. The common theme is to inspire a people to come together to achieve because our history has been all about dividing us."

Kathy captivates the audience for longer than the prescribed hour for the lecture. As it approaches the two-hour mark, Kathy holds up her arms.

"Gentle people, this has been a wonderful time together, but I must draw it to a close. I'd like to draw your attention to one interesting fact that should convince you, if you are not already convinced, that reparations are just. The Abolition Act was passed by the British parliament in 1808. Full emancipation of slaves occurred with the reading of the Emancipation Declaration on the first of August 1838. One of the reasons it thirty years to transition from abolition law to emancipation is because of the debate about how to compensate the slave owners for the loss of their property. For the sake of time, I'm oversimplifying the issues, but I think you get the point. The British government took out a loan in 1833 and paid twenty million pounds, the equivalent of about 300 million pounds today, to the slave owners. The government only finished paying off that loan in 2015. 2015! What did the slaves get? Absolutely nothing!"

A young man in the back of the hall, on one of the top tiers, slowly puts up his hand. It is noticeable that no one is sitting near him. Kathy points at him, "Yes sir."

"So dis preparation ting. Dem a guh do NBA testing to decide who get de money?"

Kathy knits her brow and scratches her head, looking at the young man with a red, green and gold knit tam on his head, and a knotty goatie beard. His eyes were slightly glazed, and red. Kathy suddenly nods and claps her hands together, "Ah, I get it now. You are asking how reparations will be paid out to the current generation, and whether it will be done via DNA testing. Is that correct?"

The hall erupts in a roar of laughter. Kathy is smiling until she notices the young man shrink in his seat, bowing his head.

She quickly raises her hands over her head.

"Keep it down, keep it down. What's your name?" Kathy calls out.

"Jeff, Ma'am."

"Jeff what?"

"Jeff McDonald, Ma'am."

Kathy reaches out to the lectern to steady herself. "You're Jeff McDonald?"

"Yes, Ma'am".

After a pause Kathy says, "Well Jeff. That is a really good and considered question." Jeff's posture becomes a little straighter. "It is one of the most difficult questions that is being debated. How should reparations be paid more than 200 years after slavery has been abolished, and almost 200 years after the full emancipation of said slaves?"

A lot of hands shoot up across the hall. Kathy chuckles.

"I'm glad to see that there are so many ideas. I'll just leave you with this. The GDP of the English-speaking Caribbean is about 85 billion US dollars. Our debt to GDP ratio is in the range of 70%, about 60 billion. So, what about cancelling that debt?"

All the hands drop as numerous mini huddles form across the hall in deep discussion.

Kathy continues, "Some argue that the amount is disproportionate, but consider this. The dot com bubble crash caused a 5 trillion-dollar loss in stock market value, and the subprime mortgage crisis wiped 13 trillion dollars off the real estate market in the US only. These losses were covered and supported to enable the stock market to stabilise, companies to reinstate their value and the mortgage market to recover. We are asking for about 1% of the dot com crash to be invested in our region to allow us to get on our feet and build our countries. Is that too much to ask?"

The hubbub in the hall grows in volume.

Kathy steps back from the lectern, "I think that may be a great topic for another lecture. Thank you very much for your time and attention."

The audience rises as one in thunderous applause. The moderator climbs on stage and walks up to the lectern.

"We want to thank Dr Kathy Akers for her riveting lecture as our guest speaker for our annual Professor lecture series on issues of social significance within the Caribbean. Please thank Dr Akers."

The applause gets even louder. Kathy smiles, gives a curt bow with her hands clasped in front of her chest, waves and walks off stage.

While standing outside the lecture hall with the moderator and a few professors, Kathy sees Jeff leaving the hall by one of the exits at the back of the hall. She excuses herself and hurries over to catch up with him.

"Jeff!"

Jeff stops, startled by the call.

As Kathy approaches him, the strong smell of marijuana hits her. "I wanted to commend you for your question, but I'm concerned. Aren't you Miss Dorothy's grandson?"

"You know my grandmother?" Jeff's eyes are wide open.

"Yes. I got into trouble in my teens, and she mentored me through it. She clipped me behind the ears a few times when I would see her down at KPH."

"KPH? The Kingston Public Hospital?"

Kathy looks down at the ground before looking Jeff in the eye. "I got knocked up, then had complications and lost the baby." An uncomfortable silence sits with them until Kathy speaks, "Miss Dorothy is so proud of you."

Jeff steps back and looks away.

"She mentioned that she was worried about you."

Jeff steps back further.

"She asked me to …"

"Hear me. I and I nuh need nuh nannying."

"I and I? What are you doing? You a rasta now?"

"Glory be to the father and to the maker of creation. As it was in the beginning, is now, and ever shall be, World without end; Jah Rastafari, Eternal God Selassie I, the lion of Judah."

"Jeff, come on. Talk to me."

"I don't know you. Who is you?" Jeff spits.

Kathy retrieves her phone from her jeans pocket and dials, "Hello. Miss Dorothy? Yes, it's Kathy. I have someone who wants to talk to you." Kathy offers Jeff the phone. Jeff stares defiantly at the phone for a few moments, then his shoulders sag and he slowly takes the phone.

"Hello Grandma … Yes Grandma … Yes Grandma … Yes Grandma. But, but … yes Grandma." Jeff takes a deep breath. "Yes, Grandma." Jeff hands the phone back to Kathy. Kathy puts the phone to her ear.

"Yes Miss Dorothy. Of course. I will do anything for you. Goodbye." Kathy hangs up. She glares at Jeff. "I expect to see you in my office on Monday morning." Kathy softens her gaze and smiles, handing him a business card. "Don't worry, I'll be gentle."

CHAPTER 10 – She Dead!
Back in the present

"Can she travel now?"

"Maybe a day or two. The swelling around her eye is almost gone."

"And the cut on forehead?"

"The doctor said the stitches can come out today."

"You fool."

"You said that already."

"I told you to question her, not beat her brains out."

"I get that now."

"You have cost us many days."

"I know." After a few seconds of pregnant silence, "Do you want me to send her up with one of my people?"

"Mr. Albert, are you stupid as well as foolish?"

"What?"

"A police officer accompanying a missing girl through the airport. How many red flags do you want to raise at the same time?" After a short pause, "No. I will come and get her personally. Make sure she is ready." The phone line goes dead.

"One day me a go kill dat bastard."

∗ ∗ ∗

Kenneth opens the front door and watches as Eric walks from his car, deep in animated discussion with Jay. Kenneth's driveway is horseshoe shaped, with gates on either end of the horseshoe. The driveway curls around a well-manicured lawn, with a small rose garden in the middle of it. As they approached the front door, Marshall's car pulls up, and he and Kathy jump out and hurry towards to the front door.

Kenneth leads them all through the door, through the marble floored foyer into the room to the left, the living room. This is one of Kenneth's favourite rooms in the house because it always makes him feel energized. The room is always bathed in bright sunlight that streams in through the large bay windows on either side of the front wall. The brightness of the room always seems inconsistent with how cool the room always feels, aided by a cool breeze that regularly blows through the perennially open side windows. The honey white walls are tastefully complemented by a generous number of potted plants that exhibit colourful flowers, buds and lush green leaves. Kenneth picks up a remote to turn down the music that can not only be heard but can also felt throughout the house.

Jenny appears at the archway entrance to the living room. "Hi everyone. You just missed lunch. Do you want something to eat or drink?"

"I'll have a Red Stripe." Eric replies.

"Wray and Nephew with milk." mutters Marshall.

"Appleton and coke." said Jay.

"Wait, Jay? I didn't see you come in. I thought you were supposed to be in England." Jenny says surprised.

"Yeah. They postponed me. I leave tomorrow."

"Ok." Jenny says and then looks at Kathy.

"I'll have something soft." says Kathy.

"Would tropical juice be ok?" asks Jenny.

"Yes. That is fine."

"Kenneth?"

"Some coconut water, dear. Thanks."

"And no one wants anything to eat? I have ackee and saltfish with festival." Everyone declines and Jenny disappears down the hallway to the kitchen.

"Ok gentle people. Where are we?" Kenneth looks around the room.

Kathy takes a deep breath, "We may have stumbled into something big here."

Jenny walks in with the tray of drinks, and places them on the individual side tables, and then relaxes in an easy chair beside Kenneth.

Kathy takes a sip of the drink, "Very nice. What is it?"

"Tropical juice, with mango and Ting." Jenny points toward Kenneth with her lips. "I can't take the credit. Kenneth made it. He has been bored around the house, so he has been experimenting with different drink flavours and dish recipes. He's come up with some interesting and tasty drinks and food.'

"Nice. Very unique flavour."

Marshall leans over and takes a sip. "Nice boss. Add a little whites and it would be perfect."

"I agree, but I have had to lay off the alcohol so that I can recover quickly." Kenneth turns to Kathy. "You going to keep us in suspense all afternoon."

Kathy relates her experience the night before with her informant, Walker, who had been bleeding in her backseat. Everyone is visibly disturbed.

"Did you call the police?" Jenny asks.

"Jeff is talking to them now." Kathy's cellular phone rings. She glances at the phone and doesn't recognise the number but decides to answer it anyway. "Hello, Kathy Akers here."

Kathy hears a rasping voice screaming in her phone, "She dead! She dead!"

CHAPTER 11 – It's The Police!

"What? Who's dead? Who is this?" Kathy stands up and hurries towards the living room door and steps into the foyer.

"Is what kinda trouble yuh get me mixed up inna?"

"Walker? Is that you? Who is dead?" Marshall hurries to Kathy's side.

"Bomboclawt! Mi baby mother! Dem couldn't find me, so dem go to her house and kill her!" Walker screams.

"How do you know it was related?" Kathy breathlessly asks.

"Dem find the letters 'UNX' on the wall. Painted in her blood."

"Oh my God!"

"Is wha' yuh get me into?" Walker cries into the phone.

"I don't know. I am so sorry." Kathy can't help herself and the tears start to roll down her face.

"Me need more money."

"How much do you need?"

"A hundred bills."

"Ok. That's a lot but I need to talk to my manager to get that sort of money. I'll see what I can do. Meet me at seven o'clock." The phone goes dead. Kathy collapses into Marshall's arms.

* * *

Kathy and Jeff stoop behind the wall of the church across the intersection, and watch Walker turn off East Street and head away from them towards the car. Before Walker can reach the car, headlights illuminate the small lane. A large rat, almost the size of a small cat, scurries away from a pile of garbage and disappears down the water drain at the side of the road. Walker freezes and quickly raises his arms above his head. His left arm is visibly lower than his right, and there is a small blood stain near the shoulder of his white shirt. Walker is bracketed by lights from two jeeps, one before him and one behind him. Kathy can make out the silhouette of a man climbing out of the vehicle facing Walker and saunters towards him. The silhouette stands arms akimbo a few feet in front of Walker. Kathy cannot hear what is being said, but she can see the man aggressively pointing at Walker, who seems to be cowering under the imaginary weight of the forceful appendage. The man walks up to Walker slaps him across the face. Walker stumbles backwards from the force of the blow, and then there are two light flashes. It takes a moment for the loud explosions to reach Kathy and Jeff. Walker drops to his knees and then topples over, flat on his face.

"Oh my God!" Kathy gasps.

"They just murdered Walker!" Jeff exclaims.

Suddenly, there is a barrage of gunfire from four men standing in front of Jeff's car which was parked about fifty yards further down the lane from Walker's lifeless body. Jeff's car rocks from side to side, and the windows explode as the bullets bombard it. Jeff and Kathy duck below the wall and look at each other in shock. Out of a sense of caution, Kathy and Jeff had decided an hour earlier to vacate the car and hide behind the wall of a church about one hundred yards away, across the 4-way intersection of East and Charles streets.

"Kathy, we have to go! When they realise we are not in the car they will come looking for us." Jeff blurts out, his black eyes are as large as saucers.

As suddenly as it started, the gunfire stops. Kathy and Jeff keep as low as they can and scamper across the dusty yard of the church on East Street from where they had observed the terrifying incident. They jump over the westside chain-linked fence and run around the corner of the building and enter Johns Lane, before they hear the startled shouts behind them.

"We need to get back to the Gleaner!" Jeff shouts, his barrel chest, crew cut and booming voice reminding Kathy of a sergeant major, as they sprint across the car park of the adjacent building, heading north along Johns Lane.

They are about a quarter mile from the newspaper building. They hear the engines starting behind them and the screeching of types. Kathy and Jeff dig deep and sprint faster up the slight incline towards the Gleaner Company building on North Street, Kathy's long athletic strides helping her pull away from the short-legged Jeff. At the top of Johns Lane, they turn right on to and across North Street without looking to see if any traffic is coming, when they hear what sounds like the first vehicle entering East Street from the lane, apparently driving north, the wrong way up the southbound, one-way East Street. It takes Kathy and Jeff seconds to run the block from Johns Lane to reach and cross East Street. Only one hundred yards to go!

"Open the gate! Open the gate!" Jeff bellows as they run towards the building. Kathy always wondered how such a large voice could emanate from such a small man. A guard pushes his head out the guardhouse, recognises Kathy and Jeff and quickly jumps to action. The large gate starts swinging open within seconds. Jeff and Kathy dive through the twenty-foot gate, and without prompting, the guard shuts the gate behind them. Jeff and Kathy scurry into the guardhouse and sit with their backs against the wall as the first vehicle skids to a halt outside the gate.

"We a look fi some gunman dat just come dis way. Yuh see anyting?" A voice shouts at the guard.

"No, me no see nuting. Is what dem do?" The guard answers.

"We just have a shoot-out wid dem down de road. We kill

one of dem, but we tink two of dem get weh."

"If me see anyting me will call yuh. Who me must ask for?"

"Just call Special Squad. Dem will patch you tru." The engines gun violently, and the vehicles speed off east, along North Street.

"Oh my God, Jeff. It's the police!" Kathy whispers. "The police just murdered Walker!"

* * *

Jay jumps out of his chair, "Let's not jump to any quick conclusions. This murder is horrific, but unfortunately, there are far too many of these in Jamaica every day. We have no idea what this guy Walker has been involved in. This could be related to any other underhanded activity he has been involved in. This is not concomitant."

Jay looks around the eight-seater dining table at Kenneth, Eric and Marshall. Jenny had invited the group over for brunch before Kenneth takes Jay to the airport, and they are seated at the dining table after a hearty meal of mackerel rundown and green bananas. Kathy is in an animated discussion on her phone, pacing from one side of the room to the other. The pastel yellow drapes flutter in the breeze. Marshall kills a mosquito that had landed on his forearm.

"Jay is right. We have to tread very carefully here. Inspector Albert's Special Squad is a very decorated unit. Maybe this is a case of a few bad apples." Kenneth says.

Jenny walks into the room, "I say we stay out of this. What has this got to do with us? Why should we get involved? The risks seem far too high."

"That is true, but innocent people are being hurt. The Martin girl is still missing, and now these two young men are dead." Kenneth objects.

"Two?" Marshall says.

"The informant and his friend." Kenneth responds. "Oh, wait. Oh my. I just remembered that the friend's entire family was killed."

"And the informant's girlfriend." Jay offers grimly.

"And that is why I think we let the authorities handle it. The body count seems to be rising quickly." Jenny appeals as she walks around the table. "We are not the police."

"Yes, but …" Kenneth objects.

Jenny stops and pulls a chair out from the table and sits down, interrupting Kenneth. "We are dealing with cold blooded murderers with badges."

"Well, we don't have any evidence of that." Jay interrupts.

Jenny glares at him. Jay quickly examines his navel, as Kathy sits down beside him.

"We must not get involved." Jenny insists.

Kathy's phone rings again. She looks at the display with some apprehension, and then relaxes when she recognizes the number, "It's my manager." She answers the phone, "Hello Craig."

"I've been trying to get hold of you. Your phone has been busy."

"Yes. I was speaking to …"

"Jeff is dead."

"What?!?" Kathy whispers into the phone.

"He didn't come into the office this morning. We tried to call him, but he didn't answer. So, I sent someone around to his apartment. He was found shot to death in his bedroom."

"No! This can't be happening!"

"There is more. The gunmen wrote the letters 'K UNX' on

the wall in blood."

"What?!? Oh my God! No!"

"Do you know what this is about? I know you and Jeff were working together on an assignment for the last few days."

"Yes, we were. But I can't talk about it yet."

"Well, you'll have to talk about it soon. The police want to talk to you. Inspector Albert called …"

"What? What did you tell him?"

"I told him I would try and track you down because you hadn't been in this morning."

"Ok. Don't tell him anything. Craig, I'll get back to you. I have to go."

"Kathy? You don't want me to tell Inspector Albert anything? The police?!? What's going on?"

"I don't know what is going on. I need some time to figure this out and clear my head. Bye." Kathy hangs up. "Jesus Christ! Shit!" Jenny flinches. "Sorry. Excuse my French."

"What's going on?" Jenny asks.

Kathy relates her conversation with Craig. The group sits in quiet reflection. Kathy rests her head on the table, cushioned by her forearm, and starts crying. Jenny walks over, pulls up a chair and consoles her. Marshall puts his arm around Kathy and kisses her neck. The only sound in the room is Kathy's sobbing.

CHAPTER 12 – That's Our Proof

Kenneth looks across the table at Jenny. Slowly, everyone's gaze settles on Jenny. Jenny looks around the table at each face.

"Ok, ok. We are now involved. That's obvious. So, what's next?" Jenny finally blurts out.

"Kathy has to go." Kenneth says quietly.

Kathy looks up, raising her head from Marshall's shoulder, "What?"

"You have to leave now."

"What? You're kicking me out of your house?"

"No, no, the second message was for you. They are coming for you."

"What?"

Marshall sits up in his chair, "Kenneth, have you been drinking? What are you talking about?"

Eric chimes in, looking at Marshall and Kathy, "Of course, how did I miss it? The K is for Kathy." He said softly.

Kathy involuntarily shivers. Marshall hugs her more closely.

"I think you have to go now, and you can't risk going home." Kenneth says.

"Go? Go where?" Kathy asks.

"I think you should go straight to the airport. I'm taking Jay to the airport, and you should come. Buy a ticket to Miami."

"Miami?!? And stay where?"

"You can stay at our house there. I think you should go with her Marshall. It won't take them long to make the link between the two of you."

"I can't do that. Do you know what you are asking?" Kathy blurts out.

"Hey man, you are asking a lot." Marshall points out.

"Look. Whoever these people are, they don't play around. If," Kenneth looks across at Jay, "if, as it appears, that the police are involved, who do we trust and who do we seek help from?" Kenneth asks.

Kathy begins to protest, when her phone rings again, which causes her to jump. Kathy lets it ring a few times as she composes herself. She looks at the display and frowns because she doesn't recognize the number.

"Hello."

"Ms. Akers?"

"Yes. Who is this?"

"This is Inspector Albert, from Special Squad."

Kathy covers her mouth with her hand and drops the phone on the table.

What's the matter? Malcolm mouths and he reaches for the phone.

"It's the police. Inspector Albert." She whispers frantically.

Kenneth hurries across the room and comes back with paper and pen. He scribbles on the paper - *You have to talk to him!*

Kathy shakes her head. Tears rolling down her cheeks. She keeps her hand over her mouth. She is hyperventilating.

Kenneth circles the words on the page and underlines them vigorously. Kathy shakes her head. Marshall hugs her tightly. Kenneth scribbles on the paper -

He will know that you know.

Kenneth glares at Kathy. He scribbles again -

You must!

Kathy shakes her head vigorously. Kenneth picks up the phone and hangs it up.

"Listen!" Kenneth says firmly.

"Hey!" Marshall objects. "Take it easy."

Kenneth takes a deep breath. "Look. Inspector Albert is going to call back shortly. We don't know if he is involved in this."

"Yes, we do." Kathy rebuts.

"How can you know that?"

"This is an unlisted number."

"And that makes him guilty of murder?" Jay quips. Jenny spins around and glares at Jay, who quickly finds his navel interesting again.

"Kathy. Kathy dear." Jenny says soothingly, redirecting her attention on Kathy. Kathy is sobbing in Marshall's chest. "Kathy, we need to use this opportunity to find out if Inspector Albert is involved in this." She says quietly. "Can you do this?"

"Tell him you dropped your phone, and it disconnected the line." Kenneth blurts out. Jenny looks at him sternly. Kenneth looks at Marshall, pleading with him with his eyes. Marshall strokes Kathy's hair and then pulls her away from him.

"Kathy, listen. Kenneth is right. You have to do this." Marshall says.

"I can't." Kathy sobs.

"You can. You're strong, and I know you can do this." Marshall says soothingly. "And you have to." He says with some emphasis.

Kathy's phone rings again. Kathy's red and puffy eyes grow wide. Marshall picks up the phone and holds it out to her. "Come on Kathy. You can do this." He says quietly, but firmly. He pulls out his handkerchief and softly wipes her eyes. He smiles, "I know you can do this. For Jeff."

Kathy takes the phone and the handkerchief. She takes some deep breaths and answers the phone.

"Hello?"

"Ms. Akers?"

"Yes. Is this Inspector Albert?"

"Yes."

"I'm sorry. My phone dropped and disconnected your last call."

"That's ok."

"How did you get this number?"

"I am the police."

"This is an unlisted number. I know that it isn't possible for you to get this number."

"Your office gave it to me. Can't remember who it was, but the person was very helpful."

"Oh … ok. How can I help you?"

"We want to speak to you about some murders that took place last night and today. Can I send a car for you?"

"Some murders?"

"Yes. Very unfortunate. Anyway, if you tell me where you are I can send an unmarked car to bring you down to the station."

"There's no need. I can just drive down to see you."

"No, I don't want to put you to so much trouble. Let me send a car. I am sure you will be distressed by the pictures and our discussions. It may be hard for you to drive back afterwards."

"Ok. I'll be at the office in about an hour. You can send a car to pick me up from there."

"I have a car near your home right now, if you are near there it would be easier for us to pick you up there."

"No, I am not near home at the moment. Much better to meet me at the office."

"Ok. Tell me what you are wearing, so my team can identify you. I don't really want them going into an office with guns. It may be alarming for the other employees."

"Sure. I'm wearing a red jacket over a black pants suit."

"Ok. Good. You should see my officers waiting outside when you arrive at the office. They will show themselves when they see you. Thanks for your time."

Kathy hangs up. The tears are gone, and her eyes are steely cold as she looks around the room at the alarmed and inquiring expressions on everyone's face. "Busha George is involved." Kathy says with finality.

"How do you know?" Jenny is the first to get the question out.

"He said he got my number from my office. There is a company policy to never give out our unlisted numbers, to protect our journalists. He was also insisting that I be picked up by one of his unmarked cars, instead of allowing me to drive down to the station."

"Humph! That's why you lied about what you are wearing?" Jenny nods her head; an admiring smile breaks out across her face.

"Yes. And everything just feels wrong about this. And he said there is a car near my house! How does he know where I live?" Kathy is wearing a blue mid-calf length shift, with a yellow jacket.

Jay haltingly puts up his hand, "I'm sorry. But that is the basis of your conclusion? Busha circumvents your systems to get your phone number and address and that makes him a murderer?"

"You tell me Jay. What would be the reason for an honest cop to steal my number and address and lie about it instead of just waiting for the channels to work?" Kathy shots back.

Jay bears his palms in front of his chest, "I'll grant you that. But murder? That is a huge jump from simply hacking some data to get a phone number and address. Don't you think?" Jay looks around the table.

"Well, this just feels wrong. Something is all wrong about this." Kathy turns to Marshall, "Are you ready?"

"Ready?"

"Yes. To go to the airport. I think we should take Kenneth's advice."

"Are you sure?"

"Absolutely. I think we better make tracks before Busha George gets suspicious."

Jenny walks out of the room and returns with some keys, 'These are the keys for the house.'

"I have to swing by my house and pick up my passport." Marshall says. "Do you have yours?"

"Yes. Always walk with it. A journalist is always supposed to be prepared for the unexpected." Kathy smiles wryly. She turns to Kenneth, "So what's the plan?"

Kenneth suddenly looks very tired. He stretches, rubs his head, and with elbows on the table he rests his head in his hands. "Go to Miami and get to our house as soon as possible. Don't worry about clothes. You can go shopping after you settle. I would suggest getting a new phone when you get there and throwing away the one you have right now. Call us when you get there. The rest of us will try and find out what is going on and meet you there in a few days."

"What's the address?" Kathy asks.

"Let me write it down for you." Jenny reaches across the table for a sheet of paper and pen in front of Kenneth.

"Oh my God!" Kathy exclaims.

"What?"

"I have to call Miss Dorothy!" Kathy breaks down and buries her head in Marshall's shoulder.

"Miss Dorothy?" Jenny asks.

Marshall responds quietly, "Jeff's grandmother. She helped Kathy when she got into trouble as a teenager. Miss Dorothy asked Kathy to mentor Jeff a few years ago when he got mixed up with some bad company." Marshall hugs a sobbing Kathy.

"I don't even know if she knows." Kathy sobs. Kathy slowly picks up her phone and dials. "Hello. Miss Dorothy? This is Kathy."

"So nice to hear your voice, Kathy. How yuh do mi dear?"

"Oh, I've had better days Miss Dorothy."

"Hush. Nuh mind mi dear. Life. What can I tell you that you don't know already?"

"Well, I have some very bad news to tell you."

"What is it? Tell me."

"It's about Jeff. He was killed this morning."

"Oh my Lord! Oh no!" Miss Dorothy breaks down in tears. Kathy cries with her.

"I'm really sorry, Miss Dorothy. I feel responsible. I'm so sorry."

Miss Dorothy blows her nose. "What? How are you responsible?"

"Jeff and I were working on a story, and we seemed to have crossed paths with some very bad people. I think those people killed him. I should have never got Jeff involved."

"Oh Kathy. Don't do that to yourself. I'm heartbroken that Jeff is dead, but I don't want to lose you too. You saved Jeff and he loved working at the Gleaner, and he loved working with you. If the Lord called him home, then I grieve but I know he loved the Lord, so I will see him again. All I ask of you that you find these people and you make them pay! Yuh hear me?"

"Yes, Miss Dorothy." Kathy sniffles.

"You go and do what yuh have to do and come back and mourn with me when yuh done. Yuh hear?"

"Yes, Miss Dorothy." Kathy says with more conviction.

"I want justice for my Jeff."

"Yes, Miss Dorothy."

"Hold on, someone knocking at the gate. Let me see is who. Oh, is the police. I assume they have come to tell me about Jeff."

'Miss Dorothy! Don't tell them that you spoke to me. Act like you are hearing the news for the first time."

"What? Why?"

"It's important. I'm trying to get to the bottom of his death. There are some people in the shadows who are involved, and I need to hide from these people, and protect you."

"Don't worry about me."

"These are powerful people, Miss Dorothy. Please do as I ask."

"Ok Kathy. I'll try my best. You take care of yourself now."

"Yes, Miss Dorothy." Kathy hangs up the phone.

Everyone around the table watches Kathy, waiting. "What did Miss Dorothy say?" Marshall eventually asks.

"The police just stopped by to tell her about Jeff." Kathy dries her eyes. "And she said we should catch the bastards who did this!" She says with defiance. "Let's get going." She gets up with purpose from the table.

"Guys, are we really sure about this?" Jay asks.

"I see what you guys are saying, but the evidence is very flimsy." Eric concurs.

"Hey." Jenny exclaims. "Isn't that Busha George on the

TV?" She hurries over to the TV and picks up the remote. She points the remote at the wall mounted flat screen TV and turns up the volume.

"… lunchtime breaking news - Jeremiah Walker was shot and killed by police in the vicinity of Spanish Town Road earlier today. Reports are that he pulled a gun and opened fire on a police patrol as it drove past. He was pursued on foot into Tivoli Gardens where a gun battle ensued. A search of the area revealed Walker's body with gunshot wounds to his head and torso. Inspector George Albert said that Walker was a notorious gunman who the Special Squad had been tracking for some time. Walker is reputed to have been involved in the shooting deaths of three young men in Arnette Gardens last week, and the brutal murder of a Gleaner journalist, Jeff McDonald last night. Inspector Albert congratulated his team on their effective work, reporting that their closure rate of gun related crimes stands at an impressive 85%, significantly higher than the 30-40% reported by the rest of the police force. Inspector Albert said that his team's methods may be a little unconventional, but the statistics show that they deliver results."

The pictures of Busha George and Walker are replaced by a clean-shaven young man on screen, dressed in a blue suit and tie. He smiles briefly as he reads the next news item about increased foreign currency reserves.

Jenny mutes the TV. "I guess that's our proof. They must have moved the body to Tivoli Gardens after they shot him on East Street." She looks at Eric and Jay, who simply nod, and they all head for the front door.

Kenneth takes Jenny's hand as they walk towards the car, "I can fix this." He whispers in her ear.

"I know. I know you can." Jenny kisses him on the cheek.

They drive to the airport in silence. Kenneth pulls into a space in front of the Departures terminal. Marshall and Kathy jump out of the back of the car and hurry towards the terminal without saying a word. Kenneth walks to the rear of his BMW

540i to help Jay take his luggage out of the trunk.

"Hey Jay. You be careful. We don't know who these people are and how far their reach is."

Jay stops with a startled look on his face, "You think they would try and reach me in England while I am there?"

"Don't know. Just telling you to watch your six."

Jay salutes, "Yes sir, Commander."

Kenneth smiles and hugs Jay. "We have been through our fair share of troubles together."

"Yes. That much is true."

CHAPTER 13 - Geronimo
Ten years ago

Seal Team 7 Bravo arrived at the rendezvous coordinates at 0400 as planned. Despite the unusual hour, a casual observer could be forgiven for thinking that the group of casually dressed, head-gear clad men were normal. It would take a keen eye to notice their athletic physiques, slightly oversized knapsacks and military issue khaki boots below their khaki slacks. After entering the two-storey, sand coloured house, the group quickly and silently disperses throughout the house, searching all of the sparsely furnished rooms.

"No one here, Commander."

"Roger that." Kenneth says. "Ok. Secure the location. Our British friends have no doubt encountered some resistance enroute. Make sure we can cover them if they come in hot."

"Roger that sir." Chief Petty Officer (CPO) Hernandez gives the orders to the 8-man squad, "Double time, I need two topside; one covering the approach and the other covering our location's six. I need four on the perimeter on the compass." The men quickly get to work on the tasks at hand.

At about 0500, a call comes over the comms.

"In coming. Coming in hot. Could be our British friends."

"Roger that. They are supposed to give us a signal, so we know it is them." Kenneth says looking out one of the four windows facing their approach. "It should be a red flare, shot to the east, against the sun rise. Flares are always going off in this area so no one will think anything of it."

A red flare goes up, its light trail streaks across the semi-dark sky towards the east.

"Ok. It's them. Sparce cover fire as needed. Comms silence." CPO Hernandez says.

Two dust covered Toyota pickups are speeding towards the house Seal Team 7 Bravo is occupying, deftly swerving between hand carts, cows, bales of hay and piles of garbage. Thankfully, at this hour there are no people in the streets. Two of 7-Bravo team run to the 6-foot, wooden gate and open it just in time for the vehicles to drive through. They close the gate behind the vehicles. A group, that looks eerily similar to the 7-Bravo team, alight the vehicles. They follow the 7-Bravo team members inside the house.

"Commando Officer Jefferson, you're late." Kenneth says as the team enter the house. He has a stern look on his face.

"Commando Officer Jefferson at your service, Commander Johnson." John Jefferson Jr. bows differentially towards Kenneth and stares at him.

Kenneth holds his stare. The tension in the room is palpable as the two units congregate and face off in the entrance hall of the small house, watching their leaders stare each other down. Suddenly, a smile breaks out across Kenneth's face.

"I thought you Brits were always on time." Kenneth quips.

"Maybe it's my Jamaican heritage." John responds.

"Jamaican?"

"Yes. My father is from Jamaica, but I was born in England."

Kenneth laughs, "So was I. Well, I was born the US, but my parents are Jamaican."

The two men man-hug briefly and share a good laugh, relaxing their teams.

Kenneth points to his team, "Meet Navy Seal Team 7 Bravo. Chief Petty Officer (CPO) Hernandez, Petty Officer Third Class (PO3) Collins, and Smith, Dennis, Henderson, Simons and

Tenison."

"Tenison? Are you related to Alfred Tennyson, the Poet Laureate?" John asks.

Tenison laughs, "No. I get asked this all the time. My name has one 'n' and an 'i' instead of y."

"Ok." John points to his team. "Meet Royal Marines, 40 Commando Unit, Delta squadron. Sergeant Jones, Corporal Martin, and Arthur, Gunther, George, Bernard and Laurent."

Sergeant Jones steps forward and theatrically points at John, "And this is Commando Officer John Jefferson the fourth."

Seal Team 7 Bravo look quizzically at John.

John looks angrily at Sergeant Jones and then shakes his head, "It's a family thing. I carry the name of my great grandfather, grandfather and father. My friends call me Jay."

"Now that formalities are concluded, let's get down to the task at hand." Kenneth walks over to the table in the adjoining room through a double door frame. Maps have been laid out on the table. The men from both squads follow Kenneth into the room. "What have you been told so far?" Kenneth asks.

"First and foremost, that we are not here, and no one is supposed to know that we are here." Jay says.

"Yes, although when the hostages are gone, I think they'll figure out that we were here. They're just not supposed to know who. I'm guessing a joint mission allows for plausible deniability."

Everyone around the table nods in unison. No one takes their eyes off Kenneth.

"Our mission is to rescue the hostages. Our exfil is from a LZ fifty clicks south, just across the border. Blackhawks from USS Abraham Lincoln will pick us up there. Central Ops Command is on USS Abe Lincoln with the call handle Geronimo. We will lay low today. Zero hour is 0200 tomorrow night. Satellite imagery shows that there are trucks on site that we can commandeer to transport the hostages. Your two pickups will run fore and aft." Kenneth looks at Jay, who nods. "There are twenty-five hostages. Our intel says they are being held in this building to the north of the compound. We will split up into three groups. We'll hit the compound from east, south and west, sweeping and cleaning to the north building. I need a pair to then prep a truck for us." Kenneth looks around the group.

Laurent and Tenison put up their hands.

Kenneth nods, "Good. The trucks are parked two buildings over to the west. I need a pair to send out comms to clear our path to the border and then disable their comms." Kenneth looks around the group again.

CPO Hernandez and Gunther put up their hands.

Kenneth nods, "Their call signs are in this pouch." Kenneth slides a black pouch across the table towards CPO Hernandez. "You and Gunther study them throughout the day. They have two machine gun towers. East and west. Our snipers need to take those out before we can approach."

Dennis and Corporal Martin give a thumbs up.

"When we get to the building, we need to use optics or thermals to confirm the position of the hostiles and their proximity to the hostages. We'll decide on how we take the hostiles when we know their positions. There are two entry points. Here and here." Kenneth points at the map. We'll split entry."

"How do we go in?" Jay asks.

Kenneth glances at CPO Hernandez before looking at Jay, "Dez and I have been discussing that. Depending on the location of the hostiles we can use flash bangs and go in loud and fast. If locations are not suitable, we pick and sneak, knives only until we are all inside."

Jeff examines the map and nods. "I don't like having to make the decision on the fly, but I think you are right."

"Ok. We have twenty-one hours to zero hour. Get some

rest guys." Kenneth looks around the room and nods. The group disperses quietly.

* * *

At 0200, all the teams are in position. Jay, leading the Echo Team, is at the east entrance. CPO Hernandez, leading the Whiskey Team, is at the west gate. Kenneth, leading the Sierra Team, is positioned at the south entrance.

"Geronimo. This is Deacon. We are at position Foxtrot." Kenneth says into the satellite radio.

"Roger that Deacon. Are we a go?"

"Hold Geronimo." Kenneth says into the radio. Kenneth switches to the local comms, "Jay? Are you set?"

"Roger, Kenneth. Set." Jay responds.

"Dez?"

"Roger, Commander. Set." CPO Hernandez responds.

Kenneth switches to the radio, "Geronimo. We are a go."

"Roger that Deacon. You are a go. Oversight is in place."

"Echo and Whiskey. We are go. Dennis and Martin. Go!"

Corporal Martin in the Echo Team, and Dennis in the Whiskey Team, both fire two shots at their assigned machine gun towers in unison. The two guards in the east and west towers drop where they stand, the bullets hitting their mark just below the base of the skulls of their targets. Kenneth observes with night goggles and immediately signals his team to move. Kenneth leads his team through the cut wire fence and they silently crab walk their way in the darkness past each building. Central Ops Command's Oversight observes as the three teams move from building to building, stopping briefly at each, long enough to assess any threat. At one building Oversight notices multiple sources of bright, concentrated heat light up the screen on the opposite side of a building that Sierra team has just approached.

"Deacon. Hostiles on the north side of your building. Looks like smokers."

"Roger that, Oversight." Kenneth whispers. He stops the team. "Hendy?"

Henderson shuffles past Kenneth and slowly sticks a black, thin, optical wire cable around the edge of the building to peer around the corner. The image of four men in shorts smoking in a huddle shows up on a palm-sized screen on his forearm. Henderson holds up four fingers and points in the direction of the men. Kenneth points at Henderson and PO3 Collins and then points at the ground. He then motions for Smith and Laurent to follow him. Kenneth sets off in the opposite direction from their original direction of travel and the threesome work their way around the building until they are on the opposite side of the building from Henderson and Collins.

"Hendy. Tell me." Kenneth says.

"Four hostiles. Facing away from building. Shoulder arms. No clean approach." Henderson responds.

"Any other threat?"

"Negative."

"Roger that. Ok. We have to avoid a fire fight. So, night googles. Double tap. Centre mass and head shots. Lights, hostiles and then building. On my mark." Kenneth whispers. Kenneth pulls on his goggles, as do Smith and Laurent. "Three, two, one, mark."

In a crouching stance, Kenneth quickly goes around the corner of the building. He fires at the single lightbulb on the wall above the door, suddenly engulfing the area in darkness. Kenneth's group runs towards the door. There are eight spits and the sound of four sacks crumpling to the sandy ground as Kenneth runs through the door of the building. The building only has two rooms, a long room with two rows of six cots and another room that looks like a shower and latrine. A body starts to rise from one of the cots. Kenneth shoots him through the head. The body falls back in the bed, but a loud clatter rings across the wooden floor as a metal object falls out of the bed. Multiple bodies begin to rise. Kenneth, Smith and Laurent clinically shoot each body centre mass and in the head. Kenneth surveys the room and walks to the door.

"Hendy, bring those bodies inside." Kenneth looks at Smith and Laurent. They run outside to help Henderson and Collins with the bodies.

Five minutes later, all the bodies are accounted for, each positioned in a bed with the team making an effort to cover any obvious wounds and blood from detection by a casual observer. After a quick inspection the team leave the building and continue towards the hostage building. Sierra Team meets the Echo and Whiskey Teams in a dark clearing facing the hostage building.

Kenneth looks at Tenison and Laurent. "The truck depot is to the west. Go prep one for us." Kenneth says. The pair take off to the west. He swivels to Hernandez and Corporal Martin. "The radio room is beside the truck depot. We need a clear path to the border." The pair are about to leave when Oversight calls.

"Deacon. We have bogeys inbound."

"How much time do we have?"

"I'd say about ten minutes."

"Roger that." Kenneth looks at Hernandez and Martin. "Anything you can do to redirect the bogeys and buy us time will be helpful."

The pair nod and disappear in the darkness. Kenneth looks at Jay.

"What do we know?"

"We count six hostiles. One by each of the two entrances and four at various distances around the hostages."

"And the entrances?"

"Single bolted on the inside. Double hinge."

Kenneth rubs his chin. "With bogeys inbound we don't have much time for delays or finesse."

"Flashbangs and charges?" Jay suggests.

Kenneth nods, "A firefight is the fastest way."

The group splits, with Kenneth leading the Seals and Jay leading the Royal Marines.

"Optics." Kenneth whispers when his team gets to the entrance.

Corporate Collins hurries to the door and slips the optics wire under the door. The image appears on the screen on his forearm. Collins holds up one finger. Kenneth nods at Simons. Simons eases forward. He deftly shapes and deploys the C4 charges on the positions of the hinges and the dead bolt using the screen. He plugs in the detonators, unwinds a role of wire and fastens it to a small box with a switch and button on it. Collins flicks the switch, and a small red light comes on. Collins nods at Kenneth. Dennis positions himself by the window beside the door and pulls two hockey puck looking objects from his vest. The rest of the team pulls back from the door, out of the blast radius of the C4.

"Jay. We are ready." Kenneth says over the comms.

"Hold." Jay says, as he watches Bernard set the plastic explosive charges. The team withdraws. Jay looks at George, who is crouched with two hockey puck looking objects by the window near the door. "Ready." Jay says over the comms.

"On my mark." Kenneth says. "Three, two, one, mark."

Collins and Bernard push the buttons on their small boxes, and Dennis and George throw their hockey pucks through the windows at the same time.

Bang! Bang! Pop! Pop!

The teams rush through the doors as the doors are falling

to the ground. Kenneth, with night goggles on, enters first. The hostile who was near the door is on the floor, groping for his gun. Kenneth kills him with a headshot. Collins, Smith, Simons and Henderson rush past Kenneth. Jay's team come in through the door on the other side of the building at the same time. The headshot from Jay drops the hostile on his knees near his entrance door. Eight more muffled shots from the team extinguishes any resistance. The only sound in the room is wailing and whimpering from the hostages.

Kenneth assesses the situation, "Are there any civilian casualties?"

The team hurries around the hostages who are assembled in the centre of the room.

"Stay down please, ma'am."

"Please stay seated, sir."

"Do you need medical attention, sir?"

"We'll be giving you an update shortly, ma'am."

"Please stay calm, sir. We should be leaving soon."

"Quiet please. You are safe now."

Kenneth listens patiently to the advice being given by his team before he speaks into the radio, "Geronimo. How much time before the bogeys arrive?"

"Six minutes."

"Roger that, Geronimo."

"Commander, no causalities. Just a few cuts and bruises." Kenneth hears over the comms.

Jay walks up to Kenneth, "We going to try and run for it?"

"No. We won't even finish loading the truck in six minutes." Kenneth says thoughtfully.

"So, what's the play?" PO3 Collins asks as he approaches Kenneth.

Kenneth looks around the room as the team calms the hostages. "Funnel and Choke." He mutters.

"What was that?" Jay asks.

'Funnel and Choke." Kenneth repeats with more conviction.

"Do we have enough manpower?" Collins asks.

"It will have to do."

"What is funnel and choke?" Jay asks.

Kenneth picks up a small table and steadies it. He rolls out the map of the compound on the table and pulls out a pen flashlight from his vest. "Geronimo, how many vehicles are inbound? And what types?"

"Two troop transports and a pickup with a mounted gun. Looks like a 50 cal." Geronimo responds.

"Roger that Geronimo." Kenneth looks at Jay and Collins. "We're going to have to work fast." He points to the map, "This road here looks good enough."

Collins peers at the map, "Yeah, it will do for three vehicles."

"Do for what?" Jay asks.

"Dennis and Martin. I need you in the machine gun towers. Sniper duty. Stat!" Kenneth calls.

"Roger." Dennis and Martin respond and run out.

"Tenison and Laurent. We need a truck at the hostage building now!" Kenneth says over the comms.

"You mean the transport?" Tenison responds.

'No. Another one for a Funnel and Choke for the inbound bogeys."

"Funnel and Choke? Do we have enough manpower?" Tenison asks.

"We need to make it work."

"Roger that. Be there shortly."

"Pick up Collins outside the building. He will show you where to go."

"Jay, did you find a barracks enroute?"

"Yes, sleeps twelve. It was quiet so we left it be." Jay says.

"This is going to get really noisy, so we need to cover it now."

"Roger that. I'll take George and cover it." Jay turns to leave.

"Jay."

Jay stops and looks at Kenneth.

"You know the assignment?"

"Yes. Anyone who leaves dies."

Kenneth nods and Jay leaves with George. Kenneth calls over Sergeant Jones and pulls him to the side. "Try to keep everyone calm. They will hear a lot of explosions and gun fire. This is by design, and if we do our jobs, we will be back for you very soon. I'll leave Arthur with you." Jones nods. "Everyone except Jones and Arthur on me." Kenneth calls and runs through the door.

Kenneth leads Smith, Simons, Henderson and Bernard through the dusty streets at a dead run until they reach the lane where the truck is parked. Kenneth peers around the corner of the building at their chosen road. The road is a single-lane, 30-yard, dirt road with wood and brick single-storey buildings lining it on both sides. The best attribute of the road is that it was in complete darkness.

"Geronimo. What is the ETA of the bogeys?"

"Two minutes."

Kenneth huddles with the group. "Deploy to the roofs along the length of the road. Open fire on my call." The team disperses.

Two minutes later, the headlights of the pickup truck

appears along the road, followed by the lights of the two trucks.

Kenneth whispers into the comms, "Dennis. Take out the pickup driver and gunner on my mark. Martin, stop any rabbits at the rear."

The pickup and trucks slowly roll down the road. Kenneth scans his waiting team, who are peering over the edge of the buildings lining the road. Just before the pickup gets to the end of the road, Kenneth says, "Tenison! Now!"

The commandeered truck is driven out in front of the pickup. The pickup slides to a stop a few feet from the truck, causing the trucks to also brake suddenly.

"Dennis! Now!" Kenneth calls.

The pickup driver's head snaps back and the machine gun operator falls off the back of the pickup.

"Truck drivers! Now!"

The windscreens of the two trucks shatter from the gunfire from the team on the roofs, and the two drivers slump over their steering wheels.

"Watch for any hostiles coming out of the trucks." Kenneth calls over the comms.

There is silence. Kenneth waits. The team waits. There is no movement.

"Flashbangs and grenades at the ready." Kenneth whispers into the comms. Kenneth raises his arm.

"Hold! Hold Commander!" Martin shouts into the comms.

"Hold team!" Kenneth calls. "What is it, Martin?"

"Something is not right. Hold."

After a few seconds of silence, Kenneth calls, "Martin?!?"

Martin peers through his sniper scope, "Women."

"What?"

"Women, sir! There are women in the back of the trucks!"

"Women soldiers?"

"No sir. They …" Martin pauses.

"They what?" Kenneth asks impatiently.

"They are dressed like they are going on a date, sir."

"What?" Kenneth asks. Kenneth thinks for a moment, "Ah, I get it. Stand down team."

"What?"

"What is it, sir?"

The comms channel is full of questions.

"Conjugal visits guys." Kenneth says chuckling.

"Ah."

"Really?!?"

"Say what?"

"Looks like our hostiles were planning a party." Kenneth offers. "Any movement, Jay?"

"No. Everything quiet here at the barracks." Jay says.

"Ok, Jay. Come on back. Jones, start preparing the hostages for transport."

"Roger that, sir. Not soon enough. I've had enough of this place." Sergeant Jones says over the comms.

"Saddle up boys. We are going home." Kenneth says over the comms.

"Geronimo. We're packing our bags and checking out." Kenneth says into the radio.

"Roger that Deacon. Safe journey home."

CHAPTER 14 – Not Haha Funny
In the present

"Mr. Johnson, do you have any news for us?"

"No, I'm sorry Mrs. Martin. We have been hitting walls everywhere we turn." Kenneth says into the phone.

"It's been almost a week now."

"Yes, I know. We're trying."

There is silence on the line. "Tell me the truth Mr. Johnson."

"Yes?"

"What are the chances of finding Janet alive after all this time?" The whisper is so faint Kenneth has to strain to hear the words. Kenneth starts to speak but hesitates.

"It's ok Mr. Johnson. Just tell me the truth."

"The odds are not good."

"Thank you for your honesty."

"You're welcome, Ma'am. Is there anything you have not told us that may help? Anything at all? Even if it seems to be unrelated."

"Well, Janet was in Miami a few weeks ago."

"When was this?"

"Ahh … Donald, when was Janet in Miami?" Kenneth can hear a muffled conversation before Mrs. Martin comes back on the line, "It was three months ago."

"Anything unusual happen?"

"No, in fact something really funny happened. She was given free tickets to anywhere in the US."

"And that is not unusual? That doesn't sound funny."

"I guess it wasn't haha funny. It was more 'that's nice funny'." Mrs. Martin says after a pause. "She said she got the tickets because she gave up her seat on an overbooked flight. She came home a day late as a result. They even put her up in a hotel for the night." Mrs. Martin voice trails away towards the end of the sentence.

"Why are you remembering this now? It didn't come up during our meeting."

"Well, something else funny happened two days ago. Someone broke into the house."

"And that's funny?"

"No. Not haha funny. 'Strange funny', in that the only thing they stole was Janet's passport."

* * *

Jenny looks up from her crossword puzzle.

"Devon House? What are we doing here? You taking the scenic route? Or you got lost?" Jenny chuckles at her joke and looks across at Kenneth. Her smile freezes. She notices that he is glancing in the rearview mirror very often with a very worried look on his face. "Kenneth, this is not funny. What's the matter?" She starts to turn around to look behind.

"Don't do that! You may alert them." Kenneth says hurriedly.

"Alert who?"

"Don't know who they are. I noticed them when we were downtown. I decided to take a few circuitous routes to see what would happen, and unfortunately, they have continued to follow us." Kenneth and Jenny had spent most of the day doing business downtown at the Scotia Centre, Bank of Nova Scotia's head office at the corner of Port Royal and Duke Streets. They are now driving north along Hope Road, its four lanes busy with early evening rush hour traffic in both directions. The traffic has not yet reached its peak, so Kenneth is able to monitor the progress of the tailing black Toyota Cressida without too much effort, which also means that they can follow him without too much effort. Kenneth slows down and changes lanes into the slower moving left lane. He notices that the black Toyota also slows down and slips in behind a white pickup van about three cars behind them.

Kenneth peers into the driver's side wing mirror, waiting for the right moment. Out of the corner of the wing mirror he sees a trail of thick smoke.

This could be my opportunity! Kenneth thinks.

He glances over his right shoulder to see a 40-seater Isuzu bus overtaking the two lanes of north bound traffic, in the wrong lane. The bus is so full that no light can pass through it, and it is leaning to the left from the weight of the people standing on the entrance step of the bus. The bus swerves violently back into the northbound right lane a few yards behind Kenneth, narrowly missing another bus going in the opposite direction. Drivers vigorously blow their horns in protest.

"Hold on." Kenneth says, glancing over at Jenny to make sure she has on her seatbelt. Jenny puts down the crossword puzzle book and holds on to the armrests of the seat. Kenneth guns the BMW and swings into the right lane in front of the bus. The tyres of the bus scream in protest as the driver hits the brakes. Kenneth braces himself in anticipation of the impact, but the acceleration of the BMW and deceleration of the bus work in concert, like the feint and parry of dueling swordsmen. Kenneth checks his rearview mirror and sees the Toyota Cressida try to change lanes, but it is blocked by the bus and the traffic it has just overtaken.

This is my chance! Think!

Jenny leans forward and points to Kenneth's right. Kenneth follows Jenny's finger and then looks over at her.

"Got it!" Kenneth shouts.

Ahead of them, the traffic lights at the intersection with Ardenne Road are just changing to red for the traffic entering Hope Road. The oncoming southbound traffic is beginning to roll into the intersection in anticipation of their green light. Kenneth presses his horn continuously, turns on his hazard lights and pulls into the lane of the oncoming traffic. Horns are blaring. Car drivers are swearing. Bystanders are staring and pointing in bewilderment and shock. Kenneth maneuvers the BMW onto Ardenne Road as the traffic light turns green, releasing the Hope Road south bound traffic. Kenneth races along Ardenne Road into Trafalgar Park. Jenny looks behind.

"The intersection is completely blocked by the south bound traffic. Nothing from the north bound lanes can get into Ardenne Road!" Jenny shouts.

Kenneth races through the Trafalgar Park community, covering the one-mile distance to Trafalgar Road, the other major road that borders Trafalgar Park, in just over a minute. The BMW enters Trafalgar Road in a power slide, narrowly missing a Honda Civic being driven by an old woman with a full head of grey hair and wire rimmed glasses perched on her long nose. Her mouth and eyes open wider and wider as the cars come closer together, and she throws her hands up in the air as they narrowly miss each other. Kenneth would have waved an apology, but he is too busy trying to recover the car from the slide and then accelerates through the Knutsford Boulevard and Trafalgar Road intersection, just before the traffic lights turn red. Kenneth checks his mirrors.

"Do you see them?" Kenneth asks.

"No. I think you lost them."

"I'm not taking any chances. Is there any reason why you need to return to the house?"

Jenny thinks for a moment, "No, I don't think so."

"I'm going to swing by and pick up the kids from karate

and head to the airport. Call Eric and ask him to stop by the house to get our passports. We're not sticking around to find out what those people want."

CHAPTER 15 – Kissmeneck!

Kathy runs up to them as they exit the glass double-door exit of the Miami International Airport Immigration Hall and hugs them. The children first, then Jenny and finally Kenneth. Kenneth notices that her eyes are very moist.

"I am so glad that you are all safe. I have been fretting since we got your call this afternoon."

"What are you doing here?" Kenneth asks.

"I am so glad to see you too Kathy. It was so thoughtful of you to come and pick us up." Kathy says trying to mimic Kenneth's voice, causing the children to break out in laughter.

"I'm sorry. I was just surprised to see you and Marshall." Kenneth nods at Marshall.

Kathy steps back, "So wait? If it was Marshall alone you wouldn't be surprised."

"That's different." Kenneth objects.

"How?"

"Please!" Jenny interjects. "Let's get to the house and then we can talk about this." She grabs Kenneth and pulls him in the direction of the exit. "You've got to cut her some slack." Jenny whispers harshly at Kenneth.

"What?" Kenneth objects.

"You know what I am saying." Jenny whispers gruffly.

"But …"

"Kenneth!"

"Ok. Ok."

The kids, Ken Jr - 12, Jackie - 11 and Jason - 9, run past them on the way to the car park.

"Hey kids! Slow down!" Kenneth shouts after them. Jenny and Kathy start jogging after the kids. Before Kenneth can break into a run, Marshall grabs him.

"Hey Kenneth!" Marshall pulls him close, as though he is giving him a man-hug, "Isn't that Janet? The girl we are looking for."

"Where?"

"Just coming through the glass doors."

"Kissmeneck!" Kenneth exclaims under his breath. Kenneth and Marshall huddle together, like long lost friends renewing a lifelong bond, adjusting their position so they can both watch the progress of a young woman and a man in horn rim spectacles, with a scar on his clean-shaven head. Janet is wearing a pair of jeans and blouse, both of which look a size too large for her athletic frame, and she seems to have a slight limp. Marshall starts to move towards them, but Kenneth grabs his arm and nods towards two clean-shaven Suits following closely behind.

"Packing?" Marshall asks. Kenneth nods. "You know them?"

"No, but they look like government, possibly federal." Kenneth responds.

"How can you tell that?"

Kenneth stares into Marshall's brown eyes briefly before diverting his attention back to the group, who have gone through the outer doors and walked about twenty yards away from the exit and stopped. Kenneth and Marshall stand near the exit, mingling with a group of laughing woman who exited with three trolleys stacked high with suitcases.

Kenneth takes his vibrating phone out of his pocket. "Yes Jenny?" He listens for a moment. "Send Ken for the keys. We are still back at the terminal, right by the exit. Tell him to look for Marshall. I may not be there." Kenneth hangs up.

"What?" Marshall asks.

"Follow my lead. We may or may not get an opportunity." Kenneth says quietly. He watches the group with Janet closely. The two Suits are standing on the edge of the sidewalk, looking in the direction of the oncoming traffic, while Janet is standing a pace behind them beside the bespectacled man, his left hand gripping Janet's right arm. Kenneth leans over to Marshall.

"Flag down a taxi. Stop the taxi over there," he points diagonally past the spot where Janet is standing, but across on the central median, "and keep the back door open." Marshall walks away.

One of the Suits holds up his arm, and Kenneth turns to see a black Escalade fifty yards away put on its indicator. Kenneth checks on Marshall and sees him waving a taxi over to him. The taxi is having trouble making it over to where Marshall is standing because of a white stretch Hummer limousine that is trying to maneuver away from the curb.

Come on! Hurry up! Kenneth thinks. He looks over his shoulder.

The Escalade is now twenty yards away. The Suits separate. The closest Suit to Kenneth takes Janet's arm. She tries to pull away, but he roughly pulls her towards him, almost causing her to fall over, and takes a stride closer to Kenneth. The bespectacled man steps back, and the other Suit takes a step further away from Kenneth.

Check! Kenneth thinks.

Kenneth looks over at Marshall. The taxi has finally pulled over and Marshall is opening the back door and leaning inside. Kenneth starts to walk slowly towards Janet's group.

The Escalade pulls up. The Suit furthest from Kenneth opens the back door for the bespectacled man and then opens the front door for himself. The Suit with Janet pulls her behind the car, and they walk towards the other side of the vehicle. Kenneth quickens his step. He is within five yards of Janet when the Suit opens the back door.

Checkmate!

"Taxi!" Kenneth shouts and holds up his arm and brakes into a jog. He bounces into Janet, throwing her into the rear quarter of the vehicle, and she starts to fall to the ground.

"Sorry!" Kenneth shouts.

The Suit stoops to help Janet get up. Kenneth quickly brings his knee up and slams it into the Suit's temple. The impact causes the Suit's knees to buckle, and he crumples to the ground.

Kenneth hardly brakes stride. He grabs Janet and whispers in her ear, "Your mother sent me."

They quickly jog towards the taxi, dodging rental pickup vans and hotel buses. They slip past the happy women who are now taking their suitcases off the trolleys and stacking them on the sidewalk. As he sees Kenneth and Janet approaching, Marshall turns and walks away from the taxi, in the direction of the parking building. Kenneth and Janet are climbing into the back of the taxi when Kenneth hears the shouts behind him.

"Where is she?"

"Where did she go?"

"You fools!"

"Drive." Kenneth says firmly.

"Where?" Asks the taxi driver.

"Orlando."

"What?"

Kenneth glares at the taxi driver, "Drive as though you are going to Orlando. I'll tell you where we are going when we get out of here." Janet tries to look back, but Kenneth pulls her head down. He turns to the driver. "Don't attract any attention when you pull away."

The taxi pulls away from the curb and merges into the traffic. Kenneth slowly raises his head above the seat and looks back to see the Suits and the bespectacled man running around looking for Janet. Kenneth slides down in the seat and smiles.

CHAPTER 16 – When Are You Coming Home?

"Is that really you baby?"

"Yes Mom, it's me." Janet is crying, laughing and trying to talk to her mother and father at the same time. She is sitting on a light grey coloured beanbag beside the telephone in Janet and Kenneth's Palm Beach home. The sunken living room has two similarly coloured four-seater modular sofas positioned around two sides of a large handmade square Indian rug that Jenny picked during their vacation in India last year. The rug is orientated as a diamond, with the open end facing an entertainment system adorned wall, and the other end of the rug encircled by the sofas. The telephone is set on a small cedar table positioned at the far end of one the sofas.

"How are you, Janet?" Mr. Martin asks. "Did they hurt you … in any way?" The concern in his voice comes across the phone line loud and clear.

"No Dad. Not in the way you are thinking?"

"So, what did they want? Why did they take you?" Mr. Martin presses.

"That's what I intend to talk to Mr. Johnson about. He said it is better if I don't tell you too much."

"When are you coming home?" Mrs. Martin asks.

"I guess I'll be on the next flight home." Janet says, looking inquiringly over at Kenneth, who is in deep discussion with Jenny, Marshall and Kathy. The group is gathered around the end of the other sofa, across the room. Kenneth looks over to Janet and motions for her to give him the phone as he walks over to her.

"Mr. and Mrs. Martin, this is Kenneth."

"Hello Mr. Johnson. Thank you so much for getting back our Janet." Mrs. Martin responds effusively.

"You're very welcome. It's ironic that we found her when we weren't looking."

"We have been praying incessantly and feverishly ..." Mr. Martin says. A phone rings in the background and there is a pause on the line.

"... And the Lord has answered our prayers." Mrs. Martin chimes in.

"Excuse me Mr. Johnson, while I answer my cell phone." Mr. Martin interjects.

"So, when are we going to see Janet?" Mrs. Martin asks.

"We have been talking about that ..." Kenneth starts to say.

"Hello. Hello."

Kenneth pauses, confused by the intrusion.

"Sorry, Mr. Johnson?"

"Yes?" says Kenneth, still a little confused by the disjointed nature of the conversation.

"It's Donald Martin again. That was the police. An Inspector Albert. Good news! He said he has some news for us about the case, so he said he is coming over in the next thirty minutes to speak with us."

"Hold on. Busha George just called you?" Kenneth asks in surprise.

"Yes. He said ..."

"Leave the house now!" Kenneth says urgently.

"What?"

"Leave the house now. No, hold on, let me think for a moment."

"Mr. Johnson, this is ..." Mr. Martin says.

"Please! Can I have some silence for a moment, I need to think."

"Mr. Johnson, you are very rude, and I would ask that ..."

Kenneth beckons to Jenny, hands the phone to her and walks away, pacing the full length of the living room behind the sofas.

Jenny puts the phone to her ear.

"... to be on the next flight. Do you hear me?" Mr. Martin is saying.

"Hello." Janet says in the handset.

"Hello?" A confused Mr. Martin responds.

"I'm sorry Mr. Martin. Kenneth gave me the phone while he thinks through the problem." Janet says.

"What problem? We have our Janet back. We are not interested in any other problems." Mr. Martin voice is beginning to rise in volume.

"To be honest, I don't know. But I do know that Kenneth is not usually wrong when it comes to these things." Jenny says while watching Kenneth pacing.

"Young lady, we greatly appreciate all your help, but I think we would very much like to put an end to this matter now."

"I'm sorry, I ..." Jenny is saying when Kenneth walks over and gestures for her to give him the phone.

"Mr. and Mrs. Martin, I am going to ask you to follow my instructions to the letter. This is very important, and you don't have much time."

* * *

"Hey Dad, you want to play FIFA?" Ken Jr. shouts from upstairs.

Kenneth walks out of his study to the bottom of the spiral staircase and looks up. He sees Ken Jr. looking down at him from the balcony outside his bedroom. "What did you say?"

"Do you want to play FIFA?"

"Sure. Come on down."

Jason runs out of Ken's bedroom. The boys are sharing bedrooms to make space for everyone, "I want to play? Can I play?"

"You don't have FIFA for three players, dummy." Ken Jr scolds.

'But I want to play. Daddy, can I play?"

"Sure, you can." Kenneth smiles up at Jason, who can just see over the balcony.

"Aw, come on Dad. It's too easy to beat Jason. I wanted a challenge." Ken Jr complains.

Jackie saunters out of her room, "Hey Kenny, how about I play you? Would that be challenging enough for you?"

"Aw come on. Girls don't play football." Kenny says exasperated.

"What? Yes, they do." Jackie shoots back.

"No, they don't." Kenny says emphatically.

"But I want to play!" Jason shouts.

"Hey guys." Kenneth says.

"Yes, they do."

"No, they don't."

"Daddy! I want to play!"

Jenny walks out of the living room and joins Kenneth at the foot of the stairs. "Hey! Hey! What's going on here?" Jenny shouts.

The kids all start shouting at the same time.

"Mom! I want to …"

"Stop! Stop!" Jenny holds up her arms.

"Mom!"

"Stop!"

The kids fall silent.

Jenny takes a deep breath, "First of all, Kenny, apologise to Jackie."

"Why?"

"You know that girls play football. You were being mean-spirited."

"But …"

Jenny holds up a hand to Ken Jr. and shakes her head, "No, sir."

Ken Jr. holds down his head. There is silence as everyone waits. Ken Jr. looks at Jackie, "I'm sorry."

"Well, I don't think that …" Jackie starts.

"Jackie! No! Show grace." Jenny says, holding up a hand towards Jackie, shaking her index finger.

Jackie stops, looking at her mother. She looks at Ken Jr, "I accept your apology." She mutters.

"What was that?" Jenny says. "Can you hear me?"

"Yes, Mom." Jackie says.

"Well, I expect to be able to hear you."

"I accept your apology." Jackie says to Ken Jr. "Did you hear me now?" Jackie glares at Jenny.

"Careful young lady." Jenny warns.

"Yes, Mom." Jackie eventually says after a brief stare-down with her mother.

"Now that that is settled. Why don't you play a game where

all four of you can play? You all enjoy playing tennis. Why don't you play virtual tennis doubles?"

"We have virtual tennis?" Ken Jr asks excitedly.

"Yes, we bought it the last time we were here." Kenneth interjects.

"Yaaayy!" The kids start running down the stairs.

"I'm playing Djokovic!" Kenny shouts.

"I'm playing Federer!" Jason shouts.

Kenneth kisses Jenny on the cheek. "You are awesome."

"Thanks." Jenny slaps Kenneth on the bottom and walks towards the study.

"Where are you going?" Kenneth asks.

"I'm going to watch a movie while you guys play your games. There's a new Kevin Hart comedy on Netflix that I have been meaning to watch. Have fun."

CHAPTER 17 – It's Not Obvious

A few hours later, the phone rings in Kenneth's study. Kenneth hurries from the living room where he had been trying to relax with Jenny after a great session of virtual tennis doubles with the kids. They are watching one of Jenny's favourite romcom movies, Sleepless in Seattle.

"No, no. Listen to me." Jenny can hear Kenneth saying agitatedly into the phone. "You have fly out of MoBay, not Kingston, and into Orlando. I've reserved a car there for you to pick up. You'll have to drive down from Orlando."

"Do you really think all of that is necessary?" Eric asks over the phone.

Kenneth takes a deep breath, "To be honest, I don't know. I don't know who these guys are, but they seem to be well connected. We just need to take some extra precautions. Bring your gear. We'll probably have to do some modeling."

Eric sighs into the phone, "Ok. We'll see you in the morning."

* * *

The car is still moving when the back door flies open. Eric has to hurriedly slam on the brakes to avoid Mrs. Martin hurting herself as she tries to leap from the car when she sees Janet standing with the group by the white double sash front door to Jenny and Kenneth's five-bedroom Palm Beach home. When the car screeches to a halt, Mrs. Martin sprints towards the house. Kenneth and Jenny step aside and allow Janet to walk towards her mother and fall into her arms. Mr. Martin is only two steps behind. The threesome merge into one. Sobbing emanates from the collective mass of bodies as they stand hugging in the brick driveway.

Kenneth and Jenny greet Eric, Lisa and little Andy, and after waiting a few moments they decide to quietly go inside, leaving the front door ajar for the Martins.

* * *

"This is all about a bag?" Mrs. Martin asks in surprise.

"I guess so." Janet responds, shrugging her shoulders.

"The bag, where is it now?" Kenneth asks.

"Probably at the hotel where I stayed overnight."

"Haven't I told you not to accept bags, or any articles from strangers when you are flying. They even ask you at the desk when you check in." Mrs. Martin scolds.

"I know. But he looked so harmless. I didn't see any harm in carrying it for him." Janet's voice trails off, and everyone falls silent in the living room.

"What could be in that bag that is so valuable?" Kathy wonders, breaking the silence.

"None of this would have happened if I hadn't forgotten the bag." Janet chastises herself.

"You don't know that baby." Mrs. Martin consoles her. The Martins are sitting on one of the modular sofas, while Kenneth, Jenny, Kathy and Lisa are sitting in the other sofa. Eric and Marshall are sitting on the rug, positioned at either end of the sofa with their backs against the sofa base.

"It's probably not what is in the bag, but what the bag leads to." Eric says absentmindedly.

"Huh?" Everyone looks at Eric. It takes a few seconds for Eric to realise that everyone is staring at him.

"What?" Eric says, looking around the room.

"What did you just say?" Kenneth asks him.

"What? I don't know. What did I say?" Eric asks turning to face Lisa over his right shoulder.

"Something about the bag leading to something." Lisa offers.

"Oh. That. Isn't it obvious?" Eric says, looking around the room. Everyone stares back at him with blank expressions, slowly becoming frustrated, waiting for Eric to explain.

"What?" Eric asks.

"I hate when he does this." Jenny says exasperated. "No! It's not obvious. Isn't that obvious!"

"Sorry. It just appears to be logical in light of the evidence." Eric begins. He stops and stares out the window closest to him. Everyone waits. Kenneth is going to say something, but Lisa holds up her hand and puts her index finger to her lips. They wait. Eventually, Eric turns his attention from the window to Janet, "If you had remembered the bag, you would be dead now."

"Oh my Lord!" Mrs. Martin exclaims, grabbing Janet and hugging her tightly.

"Damn!" Marshall exclaims, shaking his head.

"I'm sorry to alarm you Mrs. Martin. But it is …" Eric pauses and looks across at Jenny, "it is incontrovertible." He slips off his track shoes and lowers his head. "Listen. Let's walk through this." Eric runs his hand through his short, spiky hair. "If this bag contained something valuable or illegal, it would have been smuggled, not taken in hand luggage. The contents are inconspicuous in the hands of a teenager, but very prominent if carried by a certain type of person."

"Prominent?" Kenneth asks.

"Well, maybe not prominent. Let's say it may attract the wrong type of attention for these people."

Everyone nods.

Eric continues, "It was being carried into Jamaica, and we are aware of at least three people who have been murdered to protect this item."

"Protect?"

"Ok. I'll give you that." Eric says, rubbing his chin. "Maybe not protect, but as inquiries about Janet triggered violent responses leading to numerous murders. Now, how is Janet connected to this item?"

Eric looks around the room, looking for a response.

"It wasn't a rhetorical question, guys."

"Sorry. I thought it was." Kenneth chuckles.

"Ok, ok. Janet knows where the item is." Eric replies, holding up his hands and smiling.

"Did you tell them where the bag is, Janet?" Mrs. Martin asks.

"Yes, I think I did."

The room falls silent again.

"So, if they know where the bag is, why did they need to bring Janet all the way to Miami? Why didn't they just go and get it themselves?" Jenny ponders.

The room falls silent again.

Eric has a distant look in his eyes as he looks out the window and says, "I think I know why." He pauses. It takes thirty seconds for him to continue, "I need to do some analysis to be sure."

"Sure of what?" Kenneth asks.

"Of the pattern."

"What pattern?"

"When I find it, I'll let you know." Eric gets up and walks over to his bags that are stacked in a corner of the room. He takes out his laptop.

Kenneth is about to ask another question, but Lisa shakes her head.

Jenny rises, "Everyone should be hungry. Let's go to the kitchen and leave Eric to do his thing."

Jenny climbs the three steps from the sunken living room to the dining room and goes through the western style swinging doors into the kitchen. Everyone slowly follows, leaving Eric, cross-legged on the rug, laptop balanced between his knees, tapping away at the keyboard.

CHAPTER 18 – I'm Serious

Marshall helps Kathy and Lisa clear the glass island breakfast table in the middle of the kitchen, and packs the dishwasher.

"That was pretty good for some what-lef food." Eric pats his stomach and leans back on his highchair.

"You criticising the food after you done wax it off?" Jenny asks as she eases herself up onto the polished oak kitchen counter that sits between the double sink and the dishwasher.

"Was that a criticism? I thought I was giving you a complement?"

"Sounds like criticism to me." Jenny says.

"Me too." Kathy agrees.

"I have to say it sounded that way to me too." Lisa points out.

"Come on. You girls are just ganging up on me. Is this another one of those gender things?" Eric protests.

"I'm sure Marshall and Kenneth agree with us." Jenny says, looking from Marshall, who is helping with the dishes, to Kenneth, who is sitting beside Eric at the island table.

"You not getting me involved in this one. I plead the fifth." Kenneth chuckles and holds up both palms in front of his face.

Marshall glances at Jenny and Kathy, while pondering the question for a moment. "No comment." He says matter-of-factly and continues to pack the dishwasher. The group enjoys the moment in laughter.

When the dishwasher is packed, the group makes themselves comfortable on the stools around the island table, with mugs of hot Milo in hand. The sun streams in through the lattice windowed wood doors that lead to the back patio and bounces off the white ceramic tiled floor. Through the doors, Jenny notices a hummingbird hovering by the hibiscus hedge that borders the patio and allows herself a smile.

Looking at Mr. and Mrs. Martin, Jenny says apologetically, "I need to go to the supermarket, and I didn't have any cow's milk, so I had to use condensed and evap milk to make the Milo. I hope it is ok."

"Tastes great to me." says Mr. Martin, and everyone else concurs.

"See Eric. That's a compliment." Kenneth says, grinning from ear to ear.

"All right, all right. I get it." Eric says, holding up his hands.

Laughter erupts again. Soon after the laughter subsides there is a loud 'bong' sound from the direction of the living room. Eric jumps up and runs to the living room and returns with his laptop.

"Good stuff." Eric has a big grin on his face.

"Have you found something?" Mrs. Martin asks, before anyone else can.

"I wrote a little application based on the Brownian motion theory implemented by Wiener's process." Blank expressions greet Eric. "It's a common way of modeling what appears to be random patterns in mathematics, economics and physics."

"English?" remarks Kenneth.

"Taking socio-economic factors and historical patterns, I looked for murder patterns that did not match my predictions and anticipated projections." Eric says, slightly deflated.

"Surely, that can't be very reliable." Mr. Martin comments. "There are all sorts of things that could cause a murder."

"A statistic median is applied to smooth out the spikes

due to normal stimuli. And I have found three hot spots over the last six months."

"Really? Great work." Kenneth compliments.

Jenny throws her hands up in the air. "I'm sorry. Maybe I'm the slow one in the room but how is this relevant to what we were discussing earlier?"

Eric looks at Jenny askance, his head tilted to one side. "I thought it was …"

"If you dare tell me that it is obvious I'm going to throw this mug at you." Jenny says, threateningly lifting the mug from which she is drinking her milo.

Eric looks at Jenny and then at Lisa. "Help me, Lisa. I can't tell if Jenny is serious or pulling my leg."

The room bursts out in laughter.

While laughing, Jenny looks at Eric, "I'm laughing but I'm serious."

This makes everyone laugh even more.

As the laughter dies down, Kenneth says, "I think to be safe you should join the dots for us."

"Ok, ok. How can I explain this?" Eric runs his hand through his hair. "Ok, ok. By nature, we are creatures of habit and consistency. There is a psychological theory called Festinger's Cognitive Dissonance Theory, which states that when ideas, attitudes and behaviours are inconsistent, it causes cognitive dissonance which in turn causes people to seek consistency to lessen the discomfort." Eric pauses and stares at Jenny.

Jenny stares back.

"Does that make sense Jenny?" Eric asks.

"Are you patronizing me?"

"No, no. I just want to make sure I'm not losing you."

"You haven't said anything yet."

"Oh, right. Yes. I guess you are keeping up." Eric shifts on his highchair, "Ok, ok. So, if we assume this theory is applicable to groups that share an interest then it is reasonable to say that if this group is willing to murder to protect this bag that Janet had, and that bag is not the end goal, then the bag leads to something that they will also be willing kill to protect." Eric looks around the table, avoiding eye contact with Jenny. There are nods around the table. "Hence, this leads me to my search for statistical anomalies in the murder patterns across the island."

"Why in Jamaica?" Kathy asks.

"They were taking the bag to Jamaica, so it stands to reason that it is connected to something in Jamaica." Eric responds.

Jenny gives Eric an approving nod.

Beaming, Eric shows the data graphs on his screen, "We have MoBay, Hagley Gap and St. Thomas. I think we are looking at Hagley Gap."

"Why do you say that?" Jenny asks.

"The MoBay spike is most likely related to a Don's girl being dissed at Reggae Sumfest, and his crew went down there to mete out some street justice. Over a two-week period twelve people were murdered. When you take out those twelve, the pattern falls back within the statistical median."

"Over an argument at Sumfest, twelve people get smoked? What madness." Marshall shakes his head.

After what feels like a respectful amount of time to contemplate the lives lost at Reggae Sumfest, Lisa says, "Ok. What about St. Thomas? That is usually a very quiet and peaceful parish. You don't usually hear about many murders there."

"Right. Some drugs washed up on shore about ten months ago. As you can imagine, the owners came looking for their goods and ten people were murdered over a period of a one month. The police also killed the drugists. When all these are removed, the distribution looks normal."

"And where is Hagley Gap?" Jenny asks.

"I guess you haven't climbed Blue Mountain?" Eric asks. "It's one of those small towns along the trail."

"We went back in our university days." Mr. and Mrs. Martin reminisce.

"This is a nice one." Eric continues, "A plane crashed in the Blue Mountains, in north-east Saint Andrew. The pilot and passenger died."

"So why is that of interest?" Kenneth asks.

"Two weeks after the crash, the case was reassigned to Busha George." Lisa says, peering over Eric's shoulder at his screen. Mrs. Martin gasps.

"Why is Busha George assigned a case so far outside of the Corporate Area?" Jenny asks.

"And it doesn't end there." Eric continues excitedly. "The crash occurred about a year ago. Over that time, there have been almost ten murders in the Hagley Gap area, which is within the vicinity of the plane crash."

"Hmm. So why is that significant? There are over a thousand murders a year in Jamaica." Kenneth asks.

Eric leans back in his highchair, "Because in Hagley Gap, there were only five murders in the previous ten years."

Jenny looks at Eric, "I guess this is what you call a statistical anomaly?"

Eric nods and mutters, "Oh yeah." Eric rubs his chin and looks at Kenneth and Marshall, "There is one more thing. The passenger who died on the plane had a scar on his head."

"Really now?!?" Kenneth exclaims. "He looked very undead yesterday."

"This is all very interesting," Mr. Martin interjects after a moment's silence, "but when can we go home?"

Instinctively, all eyes turn to Kenneth. Kenneth slowly looks around the table. He bows his head and says, "The reality is that we all can't go home until we know what this is about and find a way to resolve it."

Everyone speaks at once, and Kenneth kneels in the highchair to get everyone's attention and get a word in.

"Listen. Listen." Slowly the noise subsides. "Look. We all want to go home, but we can't. Think about it! Whoever these people are, and whatever they want, they will still be looking for us. And they are ruthless." A murmur of agreement floats around the table. "We need to find out what is in the bag, and what is on that plane."

* * *

"That's your plan?" Mr. Martin asks bug-eyed. "That's no plan, that's suicide!"

Kenneth looks around the room. His gaze rests on Janet, "Are you ok with this?" She takes a deep breath and nods resolutely. He looks at Kathy, "And you?"

Kathy looks down at her lap. When she raises her head, her eyes are welling up, "You know this is the first time since we left Jamaica that I have thought of Jeff." She bites her lip to stop it from quivering, "I worked day and night with Jeff for two years. What type of person does that make me?" She bows her head again.

CHAPTER 19 - Tokyo

Ratattat. Ratattat. Ratattat.

Guests turn from their activities to gaze at the two men in dark blue overalls and caps pushing a large luggage box across the tiled foyer of the hotel.

"Can I help you gentlemen?" The tone is cold, condescending. Her hair is tied up in a bun, and she is dressed in a white suit, the trousers falling neatly over, and hiding, her 2-inch stilettos.

"Suitcases." Marshall says, his face covered by his cap.

"Where are the passengers?" She asks, her brown eyes looking over the top of her glasses.

"Lady, how am I supposed to know that? I'm told to deliver suitcases, I deliver suitcases. I'm don't get paid to ask questions."

"Wait over there in the corner, near that potted palm tree. I'll send someone over to you." She strides away.

Marshall watches as her slender legs and firm buttocks disappear through a recessed door in the wall. Marshall pulls the box over to the palm tree and sits down in a plush leather chair. "You in yet?" He says in a whispered tone.

Eric slides behind the luggage cart and pulls out his laptop from his shoulder bag. "Almost there. It's amazing how many places like hotels don't take security vulnerability warnings seriously. It is so easy to break into one of their servers with a simple buffer overflow. Ok. Got it. We're in." Eric says without looking up from his laptop.

Approaching footsteps alert Marshall to the short, stocky,

balding man in a poorly fitting shirt and tie bustling over to them.

"Heads up." Marshall whispers. Eric hurriedly places the laptop on the floor behind the cart.

"Can I help you?" The stocky man asks. He wipes sugar from his moustache with the back of his hand.

"Yeah. Suitcases." Marshall rises and greets the man, making sure he is blocking the stocky man's line of sight to Eric.

"Which flight?"

"Tokyo, I think. Grounded for some technical issue."

"Where are the passengers?"

"Don't know."

"Let me see the paperwork." Marshall hands over a clipboard. "This looks in order, but we can't accept the luggage without the passengers."

"Ok. We'll leave it here." Marshall beckons to Eric, who starts to get up off the green tiled floor.

"Hold on. You can't do that."

"Well, we can't stand around waiting."

The stocky man stands looking at the suitcase cart and back at the front desk. "Wait here." He bustles towards the front desk.

Eric hurriedly sits down behind the luggage cart and starts working.

"You finished?" Marshall asks.

"Just adding the final touches."

"He's almost at the desk."

"Nearly."

"He's at the desk."

"Almost."

"He's looking over at us now."

"Just one more detail."

"He's reaching for the telephone."

"Finished."

The stocky man hesitates, shifts his hand from the telephone to his back pocket, takes out a handkerchief and wipes his brow as he taps away at the keyboard of a terminal. He bangs the screen a few times. He reads the screen for a few seconds before returning to Marshall.

"Ok. Sorry about the delay. The damn computer seems to be giving some trouble. I see a notification that the passengers are already here, and that these are additional pieces that were misplaced. You can put them in the storeroom. I'll show you where it is."

Marshall and Eric follow the stocky man through some lime green-coloured corridors before coming to a double door. He unlocks the door and turns on the lights. The lights reveal a ballroom with collections of suitcases arranged in a semblance of order throughout the carpeted room. The walls have shelves with more suitcases on them. Each floor-collection is surrounded by coloured rope, with a sign on a pole displaying an airline logo, city, flight number and date. He picks up a manifest off the table at the door and runs his finger down the paper.

"Ok. The Tokyo flight is over there."

He points towards a collection of suitcases behind a red rope. "Put these bags with those." He stands and watches as Marshall and Eric push past him. The phone on the wall by the door rings. "Hello. Yes. Yes. What now? How does this happen? Ok. I'll be there shortly." The stocky man hangs up the phone. "I have to go back to the front desk. I'll be back to collect you in a few minutes." He turns and closes the doors behind him.

Marshall turns to Eric, "That was you?" Eric nods. Marshall smiles and offers Eric a fist pump, "Nice."

Eric quickly opens the luggage box and Janet jumps out.

"You need to hurry. It won't be long before he is back. Do you remember what the bag looks like?"

"I think so. It was a Samsonite bag. Black. Leather. Just a little larger than a large handbag." Janet says quickly.

They hurry around the room looking at the signs beside each collection of luggage.

"These look like the most recent flight delays." Eric says, pointing to the signs as they hustle past suitcase stacks, going deeper into the ballroom.

"And it looks like the shelves are holding older cases." Marshall adds as he gets to the wall. He scans the shelves, noting the dates associated with them. Marshall points high up, towards the ceiling, "That looks like the date you were here."

"Yes, there's the bag!" Janet says excitedly, running over to the wall. She tries to jump up and reach the shelf, but it is much too high.

Eric frantically looks around the room and sees one of those library ladders leaning against the wall. He quickly wheels it over. Janet climbs up the ladder and retrieves the bag. She hurries back to the luggage box and quickly retreats into it. As they are closing the box, the door opens.

"Are you finished? I have a lot of things to attend to."

"Yes." Marshall says.

When they reach the foyer, Marshall hands his clipboard over for a signature. Then he and Eric push the luggage box out the doors and head towards their van.

"Hold on!" They freeze. "You forgot to take your copy." The stocky man hurries over, hands Marshall a sheet of paper, and turns and heads back into the hotel.

Marshall and Eric jump into the van, and do not release a breath until they drive through the hotel gates.

* * *

"What are they?" Eric is unable to discern who had whispered the question. Concerned and curious faces peer down at him as he unpacks the three boxes from the bag. Eric, still dressed in his airport overalls, empties the boxes and finds what looked like three key rings or fobs; each one has red numbers flashing on a digital display. Because of the late hour, the children are in bed, but everyone else is now assembled in the living room anxiously awaiting answers.

"Cryptographic keys." Eric says.

"What?"

"They are usually used to allow people to securely connect to internal company networks over the internet." Eric picks up one of the key fobs. In concert, everyone leans back. "It's Ok. They are harmless. See these numbers on the key? They are like a password." Eric notices the confused looks on the faces. "Think of it like this. When you want to log into your computer you use a username and password. That is simple enough, but people sometimes forget their passwords and to avoid the embarrassment of always asking for help resetting their password they write it down somewhere or they use very simple passwords." Eric notices some nodding heads. "Well, those practices are very insecure and make systems very prone to security breaches. So, devices like this help because instead of using a password, a person would enter the number on the key fob."

"But the numbers keep changing."

"Exactly. That is another great feature. Imagine you having to change your password every day?" There are scoffs and chuckles. "Exactly. Impossible for you to come up with a new password every day, let alone remembering all those passwords. Well, this little device makes it possible for your password, really a passcode, to change every few minutes. This device provides the current active number that is authorised, and then they have access. RSA were the innovators of this technology. It's a very popular solution for securely accessing internal networks."

"And this is worth killing for?" Marshall asked.

"That's the thing. These are used by thousands, if not millions of companies all over the world. So, this doesn't really make any sense to kill anyone of this." Eric responds.

"And what happens if someone loses their key?" Lisa asks.

"A new key is issued for that user. The key is tied to a user login name and password as a pair. So, the old key will be disabled, and the new one issued."

The room falls into silence.

After a few minutes, Kenneth speaks. "Let's think this through. A man gives Janet a bag. Why? What are the possible reasons why someone would give her the bag to take on the flight, considering the contents?"

After some time, Jenny offers, "He doesn't want to attract attention to the contents." Heads nod around the living room.

Kenneth continues, "What does that mean in this context?"

Everyone shakes their heads in unison.

Turning to Kathy, Kenneth asks, "Do you think the Gleaner would have any stories about any new computer security systems that were installed over the last year? Maybe this has something to do with a heist?"

"I can check. I should be able to access the server from here. Let me get my laptop." Kathy leaves the room.

"Is there anything else that these could be used for?" Kenneth asks Eric.

"They are basically a key to a lock, so they can be used for anything of that nature, but we would be speculating."

Kathy returns to the room with a frown on her face, "I can't get in. It looks like I've been locked out of the system."

"Is there anyone you can call at the office?" Kenneth asks.

"That's probably a bad idea." Eric interjects. Everyone turns to him with inquiring looks. "If the account has been locked, it is probably for that very reason, so you will call."

After a pause Kathy says, "Hold on, let me try and login to my desktop. Maybe I can get to the server from there." Kathy taps away at the keyboard, "Ok. I can get to the desktop." More tapping. "Damn! Still can't get to the server." She says in frustration.

"Let me take a look." Eric says, reaching for the laptop. He taps away for a few minutes, "Is there a way for the files from the server to be moved to your desktop locally?"

"Huh? That's what we are trying to do, isn't it?" Kathy quizzes.

"No." Eric pauses and looks up at the ceiling fan. No one says anything but just waits. "Is there a way to copy the files from the server from within the office?"

"From here?"

"No. In the office."

"How would we … Oh, I see. Ok. But you just said we shouldn't call the office. I could call Craig, my manager."

"Can he be trusted?" Kenneth asks.

"I think so. Remember he was the one who alerted me about Busha George."

"That's true. Let's give him a call."

"Hold on. I don't think that is a good idea." Eric says.

"Why?" Kathy asks.

"For one. We don't know how Busha George got your cell number and home address. Did he get it from Craig? Did he trace the call you made to Craig? Did he tap Craig's phone?"

"We don't know the answer to any of those questions."

Kenneth offers.

"Exactly. That's why we can't take the risk of calling Craig. It may lead Busha George to us." Eric says pointedly.

"I think I may have a solution. There is a young trainee in the Sports department that I could call. She joined the Gleaner in a mess. Dropped out of high school because she became pregnant and then had a miscarriage, a story I am well acquainted with. Very bright girl but just made some bad decisions. She was extremely depressed and was on the verge of being fired when we sat down and had a talk over lunch one day. I managed to help her get her head straight and her life back in order after a few months of life coaching. I don't think anyone knew about my mentoring relationship with her. It should be safe to call her."

"That sounds like a good idea. Any objections?" Kenneth looks around the room. "Ok. Let's get some rest. We can call her in the morning."

CHAPTER 20 – Don't Call My Name

Lisa holds Jenny's hand as she waits on the phone. It's a beautiful day, and the sunlight is cascading through the window and bouncing off the ceramic tiled floor.

"Yes. Hello. Can I speak with Anne Knight please?" Lisa suddenly looks very confused and flustered. "Are you sure? I know that she works there. Maybe she hasn't come in yet?"

Lisa pulls her hand from Jenny's and puts it over the phone's microphone as she looks at Kathy. Her blue eyes are wide open. Lisa starts talking very fast and neither Kathy nor Jenny can understand what she's saying.

"Whoa Lisa! Take a breath!" Jenny says.

She takes a deep breath before speaking again, "The operator says there is no one at the Gleaner by that name." Lisa whispers hoarsely.

For a moment Kathy is unsettled, "Ask for the Sport's Desk, and then ask for Anne when someone answers." she says hurriedly. Lisa follows the advice and waits.

"Hello. Yes, Anne Knight please? Ok. Thank you." A relieved dimpled smile comes over Lisa's face, and she nods at Kathy. "Hello, Anne? At last. I have someone who wants to speak with you. Hold on." Lisa hands the handset to Kathy.

"Hi Anne, it's Kathy. Don't say my name! I don't want anyone to know that you are speaking with me."

"Oh my! Ok Miss …"

"Don't call my name Anne!"

"Yes. Sorry."

"I don't mean to frighten you, but it is very important that no one knows that you are speaking to me. Also, do not tell anyone that we have spoken. Do you understand?"

"Yes. I do, and I think I know why."

"Really? What is happening?"

"The police have been here repeatedly since the shooting of Mr. McDonald. There is a lot of scaremongering going on. Mr. Bishop has had numerous staff meetings, trying to encourage the staff and assure them that this is a case of the police overstepping their authority. A lot of people are scared."

"I can assure you that I have not been involved in anything illegal."

"I have never doubted that fact, Miss ..."

"Don't call my name!"

"Yes, sorry."

"No worries. Thank you for your trust."

"You're welcome, Miss ..."

"Don't call my name!"

"I won't miss. I got it now."

"Good. I need your help as I try and investigate this. Are you up to helping me?"

There is a pause on the line, "What do you need me to do?"

"Nothing illegal or dangerous. I need some information from the server to be moved to my computer so I can access it remotely. Do you think you can do that for me?"

"Doesn't sound too hard. I guess I can do that."

"Great. Give me your cell phone number and I will text you the instructions. Text me back when you have completed the instructions. Make sure you delete the texts when you are finished. Ok?"

* * *

No one is smiling. Kathy holds tightly on to Marshall's arm. Kenneth is pensive. Eric ruminative. Jenny and Lisa are close to tears. Mr. and Mrs. Martin, sit quietly with Janet. The silence is heavy in the room.

"Are you sure?" Jenny blurts out suddenly.

"No, but I don't see any other way of us getting to the bottom of this." Kathy mutters.

"There has to be another way." Marshall offers firmly, as he thumps his thigh with his fist.

Kathy looks into his eyes, "Can you think of one?"

Marshall cannot maintain her gaze and looks down at his lap, "No, I can't, but there has to be another way." He says through gritted teeth.

"Stop saying that!" Kathy sobs. "I wish there was one, but there isn't!" Jenny and Lisa walk over, kneel and hug her. Marshall moves aside and wrings his hands as he watches the scene. Kenneth and Eric look at each. Eric shrugs his shoulders, his palms turned upwards. Kenneth nods slowly.

"Kathy is right. We don't really have any other option. We've all spent the whole day trying to find something in the Gleaner reports that will help us." Kenneth says in a resigned tone. "The only way we can all go home and feel safe is to get to the bottom of this. We don't know who we can trust until we understand how far this goes, and what it is all about."

"Unfortunately, that is the only logical conclusion, so I have to concur." Eric says softly. Everyone exchanges glances. Marshall shuffles over to the other end of the sofa so that Lisa and Jenny can sit with Kathy.

"So, when do we do this?" Kathy asks matter-of-factly. She accepts a handkerchief from Jenny and wipes her eyes.

"There isn't really anything to be gained by delaying. Busha George is still looking for us, and time is on his side, unless we find out what is going on. We might as well plan to go tomorrow or the day after." Kenneth says pointedly.

"Ok. Let's do it." Kathy says stoically, as she rises from the sofa and walks out the room.

Marshall stands and looks around the room apologetically, and then quickly follows her.

CHAPTER 21 – Laugh!

With only hand luggage, Kenneth leads Eric and Kathy from the Immigration desk towards the Customs Hall. Another two or three flights have landed just before theirs, so there is a large crowd of people assembled waiting for and picking up luggage from the luggage carousels. They skirt the crowd and head towards the Customs desks. Kenneth pauses briefly, scanning the room. He groans. There are long lines leading to all the desks. Kenneth looks inquiringly at Eric. He uses his lips to point towards the middle of the room, so they move in that direction and join a line that is almost in the centre of the room. For some time while they wait, they do not speak, but instead they each stand looking around the large room, like meerkats. The Customs Hall is a high-ceilinged, cream coloured, expansive, rectangular room with large windows close to the ceiling. These large windows allow generous doses of sunlight into the room giving the room a very airy feeling. Air conditioning units positioned below these windows labour to cool the large expanse and provide a consistent hum of background noise, adding to the din of the excited adults and children.

Occasionally, a police officer enters the Customs Hall, and Kenneth, Eric and Kathy watch the officer walk around the room until he leaves. On one such occasion, while Kathy is following the movements of a police officer, she notices out of the corner of her eye a little boy staring in her direction. The boy appears to be about ten years old, wearing a blue New York Yankees baseball cap backwards, a Derek Jeter shirt and a pair of black and blue Nike Air Jordan high-tops. The boy is intently watching Kenneth, and he has a frown on his face as he watches Kenneth. His frown grows deeper as his gaze follows Kenneth's to the police officer.

Kathy watches as the boy starts to tug at his father's shirt, while still maintaining his gaze on Kenneth. Kathy's stomach sinks and she starts to feel beads of perspiration forming on her shoulders and rolling down the pit of her back. Kathy tries to appear casual as she takes a step closer to Kenneth and Eric. Both are still watching the police officer as he walks through the passageway leading from the Customs Hall towards the Immigration desks.

The boy is now hitting his father on the arm trying to get his attention, and the father starts to notice his son's harassment. Kathy steps in front of Kenneth and Eric blocking their view of the police officer. She calmly turns her back on the boy and faces Kenneth and Eric. They both have confused looks on their faces.

"What's up?" Kenneth asks, as he leans to the right, trying to look around Kathy and follow the progress of the retreating police officer.

Kathy matches his movement. She smiles at Kenneth and Eric, and says quietly, "You guys may want to be less obvious in your interest in police officers. It has attracted the attention of a little boy who is trying to inform his father of a suspicious group of people who are carefully watching policemen."

Kenneth starts to look around.

"Don't look for him! It will be obvious that we are talking about him. Laugh as though I had told you a good joke." Kathy says. Kenneth and Eric look quizzically at Kathy. Through clenched teeth and a forced smile Kathy says, 'Laugh!'

Kenneth slaps Kathy on the shoulder, throws back his head and roars a gut-busting laugh. "Wha' yuh sey? Caan true. Tell me a nuh so." He says on the top of his voice.

"Him do what?" Eric exclaims and bends over in laughter.

"Is true! Is true!" Kathy exclaims. "Me never see nuting like it."

Now everyone is watching them. The father of the small boy looks over at the attention seeking threesome and clips him around the ear, chastising his son, and turns back to his conversation.

It takes half an hour for Kenneth, Eric and Kathy to get to the front of their line. In frustration, they watch as the customs officer for their line, a slender young man who looks very officious in the white shirt and black trousers uniform, has a very amiable conversation with a middle-aged lady with a strong head of styled white hair, wearing a dark blue business dress suit. The lady removes the jacket of the suit, revealing a white blouse with a low cut bust line, while she continues her discussion with the customs officer. They both chuckle, apparently at a joke, as the woman hands over her customs form. The officer stamps her form, and she leaves the desk without opening her large suitcases and carry-on bag. Kenneth approaches the desk when he is called. He can't help noticing a heavyset woman dragging two bulging duffel bags towards the neighbouring desk. After presenting her passport and form to the officer, she struggles to place the bags on the stainless-steel bench that extends from the customs officer's desk. A brief exchange results in her wrestling with the zipper on one of the bags. Suddenly, there is a volcanic eruption of shoes from the bag, with shoes falling everywhere. The heavy-set woman is scrambling to collect the shoes on the floor, as the customs officer stands watching with a bored expression on his face.

"Hello Mr. Johnson. You are coming in from Orlando?"

Kenneth looks at his customs officer with a blank expression and then looks back at the 'shoe flow' at the neighbouring desk.

"Mr. Johnson. Did you hear me? Mr. Johnson?"

"Sorry. Sorry. I was a little distracted. Yes, Orlando."

The officer turns and looks at the shoe scene and chuckles, "Common occurrence. A higgler bringing in her wares. They are not supposed to bring their goods as personal luggage but ship them via air cargo instead. The problem is it takes at least a day or two longer for them to get their goods that way, and it hurts their cash flow. The smart ones develop a system of shipping the majority of their goods and bringing through enough goods as personal effects to bridge the gap until those air freighted goods are cleared. This does not look like one of our regulars, so she probably doesn't know the ropes yet. She'll learn." The officer turns his attention back to Kenneth's customs form, "Anything to declare?"

"No."

"Let me take a look?" Gesturing towards Kenneth's Adidas sports bag.

Kenneth opens the bag, "Do you want me to take the things out of it?"

"Hmm," the officer peers into the bag, "no I don't think that will be necessary." He stamps the form and smiles at Kenneth. "You have a good day now."

CHAPTER 22 – Tings Rough

The wait to pick up the rental car seemed interminable. Kenneth was used to simply reading his name with a parking slot number on the members' board and driving out the car a few minutes later. He had to remind himself that it was never like that in Jamaica, so unfortunately, they had to wait for the half a dozen previous customers to be served. After their close encounter in the Customs Hall, the clock hands seem to be moving at snail's pace around the clock face. The rental company staff is professional and courteous, so Kenneth musters all his patience and control to avoid showing his frustration.

It's not their fault. It's just the system. Kenneth keeps saying to himself as they wait.

After collecting the Toyota RAV4 SUV, they do not want to waste valuable time on non-essential activities, so they quickly load into the vehicle and prepare to pull out of the Sangster's International Airport parking lot, refusing the offer to get the gas tank refilled.

"Really sorry about that, sir. The previous driver should have filled it, and our maintenance team should have picked that up and filled it before putting it back on the lot."

"Don't worry about it." Kenneth says.

"Are you sure you don't want me to fill the tank for you?" inquires the attendant in a bright yellow t-shirt and a black cap with 'One Love' stitched in green and gold, for the third time.

"No. We are in a hurry, so I'd prefer not to wait."

"It won't take long and it's not any trouble."

"Trust me. Me good."

The attendant takes a step back and smiles, "Alright, boss. Drive good."

"Nuff respek." Kenneth says as they climb into the vehicle. He gives the attendant a fist pump.

They drive in silence in an easterly direction, heading out of Montego Bay, along the north coast towards Ocho Rios. The early afternoon traffic is heavy, but it thins out quickly as they pass the Holiday Inn hotel and then climb a slight incline heading towards what Kenneth always thought of as the gateway to Montego Bay. First, on the right, the Rose Hall Great House presents a majestic and ominous pose, its brilliant and dazzling white aura inharmonious with its dark history. Like many of his classmates in high school, Kenneth had nightmares for a few weeks about that Great House after their history lessons on Anne Palmer. It took him a while to fully trust any woman after that.

Then, further long on the left, the Hilton Rose Hall hotel stands towering against the beautiful backdrop of the blue sky on the top of the hill, with white clouds cuddling the peak of the hotel towers, and the Caribbean Sea languidly caressing the shoreline and beach. For as long as he can remember, Kenneth was in awe as he drove between these two great structures, mnemonics of the city of Montego Bay.

Ninety minutes later, they skirt the outer bounds of Ocho Rios and head through Fern Gully towards Kingston. As they approached Faith's Pen, Kenneth turns to Eric and Kathy, "You guys hungry?"

"I didn't eat on the flight, so I'm famished." Eric says.

"My stomach is too nervous to eat much, but I guess I should eat something." Kathy says.

Kenneth pulls into Faith's Pen and cruises past a few of the concrete huts. "Every time I come here, I am amazed by the improvements that have been made to Faith's Pen."

"You know it was one of the bauxite companies that did

this?" Kathy says.

"Really?"

"They wanted to mine the land where the wooden shacks of the original Faith's Pen were located, so they built this upgraded version with the barber green roadway, concrete huts with running water and electricity to give the vendors a reason to move. They also offered to build the new road so that the government would approve the project."

"All and all, a win-win situation for all." Kenneth remarks. Kenneth stops the vehicle in front of 'Sonia's Hut'. Various people descend on the car.

"Yes boss. Me have boil corn, manish water, curry goat."

"Me have de business. Me have jerk chicken and pork."

"Look my way boss. Ackee and saltfish with roast breadfruit and festival."

Kenneth waves them all away as he exits the car, "Is alright. Ms. Sonia will tek care of me. Yuh nuh mind."

"How yuh gwaan so boss. Yuh caan spread round de business lickle?"

Kenneth stops and looks at the young boy who made the remark, "Why you not in school?"

"Is Saturday boss."

"Is it? Sorry. Lost track of the days of the week. Alright, bring me three cold coconut water."

"Yes boss." The young boy runs off towards his stall, labelled 'Maas HenryTings'.

Kenneth, Eric and Kathy walk up to Sonia's Hut to see what is on offer.

"Ms. Sonia. What you have today?" Kenneth calls out.

A white-haired woman appears from behind the stall. "Howdy Maas K. How yuh do?"

"Tings rough, Ms. Sonia. Rough. Yuh know how it guh?"

"Always. Well, me have some ackee and saltfish and roast breadfruit. And me also have some pumpkin soup."

"Dat sound good. Me will have all dat. No food in the soup though." Kenneth says, rubbing his stomach.

"Just ackee for me. No soup." Eric says.

"I'll just have the soup. And I'll have food with it." says Kathy.

"Boil dumplin, yam, sweet potato and coco?" asks Ms. Sonia.

"No coco." replies Kathy.

Ms. Sonia turns to Kenneth and Eric, "You want pear and fried plantain?"

"How you mean? Nuh mus." beams Kenneth.

"Is wha kinda question dat?" laughs Eric. As he waits for his food, Eric sniffs the air, "Is that jerk pork that I smell?"

"Yes, from Maas Henry hut." Ms. Sonia responds without looking up from her task of preparing the plates of food.

"Any good?"

"Yes man. Me commend it." Ms. Sonia beams.

Eric disappears, and a few minutes later comes back eating from some foil. "Ms. Sonia, you were right. Dis pork sweet." Drawing laughter from everyone.

Twenty minutes later, they are pulling away from Faith's Pen.

"Good food, cook good." Eric says and settles down in the back seat to take a nap.

"I have to admit that I feel a lot better. That soup was good. Just enough scotch bonnet pepper to flavour but not burn." Kathy remarks, also making herself comfortable in the front seat. "I think I'll take a nap."

"So, hold on! The two of you going to sleep while I drive" Kenneth asks.

"Absolutely."

"Too right."

It is not long before Kenneth can hear deep breathing from both his passengers. He smiles. He is glad that they are both getting some rest. Their mission may be very dangerous and risky, and they have to be as calm and lucid as possible. Kenneth also makes himself comfortable, but not too comfortable, for fear that he may also fall asleep, and that would not be very good, since he is driving.

Kenneth chuckles to himself.

That's funny!

* * *

Kenneth pats Kathy on the shoulder, and hits Eric on the leg.

"Wake up guys."

There are groggy responses from both of them. Kathy repositions herself in the front seat. Eric moves his leg and lets out a long sigh.

"Wake up guys." Kenneth says with more urgency.

"Are we there?" Kathy mumbles.

"No. Not yet. Police spot check." Kenneth says through clenched teeth.

Eric leans forward so that he has a better view through the front windshield. The sight of two police officers walking towards the car greets him. "The police! Were you speeding?"

Kathy jumps up. "What should we do? Should we make a run for it?" She says reaching for the door handle.

Kenneth grabs her arm, "No. It looks like a routine spot check." Kenneth takes some deep breaths, before turning down his window.

"Hello sir. Can I see your driver's licence and the papers for the car?" The police officer is a young woman with a nice welcoming smile that exposes neat, white teeth and deep dimples in her dark, round face.

Kenneth pauses, staring at the female officer, "Ah …" Kenneth splutters.

"Sir, are you ok?" The officer asks. The smile starts to disappear.

"Yes … yes. Sorry. I was a little confused for a moment." Kenneth reaches into his wallet and hands over a piece of plastic and then reaches into the glove compartment and hands over the documents for the car.

The officer looks at the driver's licence and frowns. Kenneth bites his lip. Kenneth starts to notice a thumping sound and looks around to find the source. Kenneth looks down, and behind, to see Eric's right leg bouncing up and down.

"Eric. Eric!" Kenneth says under his breathe.

"What?"

"Stop that!"

"Sorry." Eric whispers.

"Mr. Johnson." The police officer leans towards the window.

Out of the corner of his eye, Kenneth can see Kathy vigorously rubbing her hands in her jeans. He reaches out and gently grabs one of her hands.

"Yes." Kenneth says, turning to the officer.

"I need to check these. Please turn off the car and wait here."

"What …" Eric starts saying.

"Shh!" Kenneth says under his breath and gestures towards

the passenger-side window. They look out Kathy's window to see another officer standing beside the car.

"Jesus!" Kathy exclaims.

"Mr. Johnson."

Kenneth jumps in his seat. He turns to see that the female officer has returned and is now looking in through his window. "Yes."

"You live in Florida?"

"Yes, that's right."

"And what is your address?"

Kenneth gives her his Palm Beach address. The officer reads the address on the driver's licence, smiles and gives it back to Kenneth, along with the papers for the car.

"You have a good day now, Mr. Johnson."

Kathy sighs.

"Thank you." Kenneth says and starts the car.

There is a sharp rap on Kathy's window that makes everyone in the car jump. They look across to see the other officer gesticulating with his M16 rifle. Kathy's hands are trembling so much she is unable to open the window, so Kenneth uses his driver side controls to ease the window down. The officer has a big head with eyes that seem too small for his head. His large mouth curls into a sneer.

"Wha' yuh can do fi me?" He snarls.

"What?" Kenneth mutters.

"Leave someting wid me nuh. Tings rough." He says matter-of-factly.

Kenneth looks at Kathy, and then quickly pulls out his wallet. He pulls out five twenty US dollar bills, and gives them to Kathy, who pass them over to the officer. He takes them with his very large hands.

"Irie. Tek care now." He says as he quickly stuffs them into his pocket.

Kenneth slowly pulls away from the curb.

"Thank you, Lord Jesus." Eric mutters, as he collapses in the back seat.

"Amen to that brother." Kenneth responds under his breath.

Kathy sits with her hands under her thighs, rocking backward and forward.

CHAPTER 23 – Hagley Gap

They reach Whitfield Hall, a rustic lodge that has been providing accommodation to visitors for over one hundred years, just as it is getting dark. They had enough time to organize their gear and for Kenneth to take a nap before catching a ride in a Land Rover to Hagley Gap. The journey from Whitfield Hall is a short three to four miles, but they are precarious miles that cannot be traversed by a road car. This short three to four miles takes the Land Rover almost thirty minutes to traverse. Kenneth doubted whether the RAV4 would have been able to make it. This no doubt accounted for the steep US$20 per person charge for the journey. It is not a journey for the faint hearted, or the unskilled.

It is 10pm when they get to Hagley Gap and join a much larger group of people who are congregating there.

"Have you been before?" A bright eyed, young woman asks Kenneth. She is short, maybe five feet, give or take an inch or so, dark skinned, chubby-ish, but more muscular than overweight, and has short curly hair. She is carrying a massive ruck sack on her back.

"No," Kenneth smiles at her, "my first time. And you?"

"My first time too. I am so excited, but also a little apprehensive. Never done anything like this before. Hi, I'm Juliet." She sticks out her hand.

Kenneth shakes her hand and points at her ruck sack. "I'm Kenneth. Don't you think you have too much stuff? I hear it is a pretty tough climb."

"Too much huh? I just couldn't decide what to carry. I guess I got carried away. I just finished my first year of med school at UWI, and my friend Michele and I thought hiking to Blue Mountain peak would be a great way to shake off the cobwebs."

At that moment another bright-eyed young woman walks up with an equally large ruck sack on her back and hands Juliet a bottle of Pepsi. "Michele, this is Kenneth."

Michele is tall, probably somewhere about five feet seven inches tall, has a fair complexion, a slender but buxom build that she carries athletically. Two long ponytails fall down to her shoulder.

Kenneth shakes Michele's hand, "You guys could have found an easier way to shake off cobwebs than taking on such an arduous hike."

"Yeah, but there is a great saying in Brave Heart that has inspired me since I saw the movie – 'Every man must die, but not every man has lived'."

"But you're not a man."

"Huh? What?" Juliet and Michele exchange a glance and then start giggling, pointing at Kenneth.

Eric and Kathy walk up with bottles of water and packets of Ovaltine biscuits.

"What's so funny?" Eric asks, as he hands Kenneth his share of the rations. Kenneth shares the joke with Kathy and Eric.

While laughing, Kathy extends her hand, "Hi, I'm Kathy. Don't mind Kenneth. He's almost a typical man. He has a few redeeming characteristics, like a sense of humour. And this is Eric. He's a genius, so he falls outside of the ninety-nine percentile and is therefore atypical by definition."

"Hey! What did we do to become the brunt of the jokes tonight?" Eric complains.

"Don't ask. When they get into these moods, we can't say anything and win. Just smile and take it like a man." Kenneth groans. This brings more laughter and jokes from Kathy, Juliet and Michele.

The enthusiasm of the growing crowd electrifies the night air in Hagley Gap. Kenneth looks at his watch.

"Hey guys, we should be going."

Juliet looks around, "Where is your guide?"

"We don't have one."

"You're going to walk up to Blue Mountain peak by yourselves without a guide, and you've never been before?"

"Sure. How hard can it be?" Kenneth laughs nervously.

"I seem to remember someone saying earlier that it was a pretty tough climb."

"Yeah, but ..." Kenneth looks nervously at Eric and Kathy.

"We have a great guide, and I am sure he would not mind you joining our team." Juliet chirps.

"No, we couldn't do that." objects Kenneth. "Look at the number of people here. There must be over a hundred." Waving his hand at the large group of people who are mingling around the streets that are bordered by the small wood and zinc structures.

Juliet looks at Michele and chuckles, "Oh no. All these people are not with us. There must be three or four different groups congregated here. Our team is only twenty. All UWI students."

"No, there are a few lecturers also." Michele corrects.

"Oh, ok. Didn't know that. Anyway, my point is that there is no good reason why you can't join our group."

"No, we couldn't. I'm sure you had to pay the guide and make special arrangements or something." Kenneth glances at Eric, seeking help.

"Don't be silly. It's no problem." Michele suddenly points to her right, "Juliet, there's Professor Jackson. I'll go and ask him what he thinks." Michele takes off before Kenneth can object.

Kenneth looks despairingly at Eric and Kathy. They shrug.

Juliet smiles at Kenneth, "I'm sure it will be ok."

Collectively they watch Michele, thirty yards away, have an animated discussion with a short, stocky bald man, who they now know is Professor Jackson. Michele points and gesticulates while the Professor stands nodding, pulling on his Fu Manchu beard.

Kenneth leans over to Eric and whispers in his ear. "Who does that guy remind you of? I keep seeing a figure in old black and white pictures."

Without a thought Eric says, "Stalin. Only a black, stockier and shorter version."

"Ahh. Yes. I knew I had seen that mug before." chuckles Kenneth.

Michele again points in their direction and Professor Jackson, adjusting his glasses, looks over and seems to give a final nod, which prompts Michele to skip back to them with a wide grin on her face.

"You guys are all set. Prof says it is no problem and insists that you join us."

"We really don't want to be a problem." Kenneth says. "And we are planning to leave now, and it appears that your group isn't ready to leave yet."

Suddenly, there are three short blasts of an air horn.

"That's the signal that we are ready to leave. Isn't it great? We are ready to leave at the same time. It must be destiny." beams Juliet.

She gestures to Kenneth, Kathy and Eric to follow as she turns and walks towards a group that is gathering at the start of a dirt trail. As they get closer, they can read the small hand painted sign pointing up the trail saying – 'Penny Castle'. Professor Jackson is perched on an embankment doing a head count when they join the group.

"I'm glad to see everyone is in such great spirits tonight. And a beautiful night it is too." Professor Jackson looks around at the congregating group. "As we get higher up the mountain, the stars will stand out even more as we get away from the ambient light of the town. This is my fourth time, and I can assure you it is a wonderful experience and well worth the agony you are going to experience over the next six hours. As is customary, we should arrive at the peak with about two hours to spare before the sunrise, just enough time to take a nap before one of nature's most spectacular scenes that is not to be missed. The only thing I have seen that is comparable is the sunset as seen from the lighthouse of Rick's Cafe in Negril, where the purity, warmth and richness of the deep red sun disappearing below the sea on the horizon is unforgettable. You should look forward to a similarly sensational scene of the sunrise from the peak." A murmur of excitement ripples through the group. "Our party is twenty-one strong. We had two late cancellations, but, just a few minutes ago we have had three intrepid adventurers joining us. I'm going to end my address now, and pass things over to Neville, our guide."

A dark man with a small torso, but large powerful looking legs, climbs up onto the embankment beside Professor Jackson and addresses the group. From Kenneth's perspective, it was hard to tell if Neville is very tall, or if his height is exaggerated by the embankment and the fact that Professor Jackson is vertically challenged. Neville towers over the professor as he looks down on the group from the embankment. Neville speaks for a few minutes about hydration, the terrain, what they should expect to see when they get to the peak, the effects of fatigue and explains the safety procedures everyone needed to follow, encouraging everyone to be his brother's keeper.

"It is not possible for me to keep track of everyone in the group. Therefore, if you notice anyone dropping back, or notice anyone missing, please shout and we will stop and take stock of our numbers. Now who are the first timers? Please raise your hands."

Eight people raised their hands, inclusive of Kenneth, Kathy and Eric.

"Alright, you eight need to be at the front, right behind me so I can keep a close eye on you."

Kenneth groans.

"Let's get going!" Shouts Neville, as he jumps down from the embankment and purposefully strides up the dirt path. In a few strides, Neville disappears into the darkness.

* * *

Two hours into their hike, Kenneth stumbles and falls.

"Argh! Ow!"

Neville runs back and stoops by Kenneth's side.

"What happened?"

Everyone crowds around to see what has happened.

"Stand back people! Give him some room!" Neville turns back to Kenneth, "Where does it hurt?"

"My right foot is killing me. I bucked my toe on a rock. I didn't think I hit it that hard, but my foot is really throbbing." Kenneth grimaces.

"Ok. Let's take a look." Neville helps Kenneth take off his shoe and sock. Kenneth's toes look swollen as numerous flashlights shine on them. "Can you take off the other shoe so we can compare your two feet?"

Kenneth removes his left shoe and sock.

"Yup. Looks swollen." Neville looks at the shoes that Kenneth is holding. "Are those new shoes?"

"Yes. Why?"

"Ha. Don't you know that you don't buy new shoes to go

hiking, especially when you are going to travel across terrain like this? No wonder your feet are swollen." Neville shakes his head, as does everyone standing around peering down at Kenneth. Numerous 'tisks' and 'tutts' can be heard murmuring through the group.

"Ok. I guess I'm the only one who didn't know that. Can't change that now. What do we do now?" Kenneth says sheepishly.

Neville stands, shaking his head he walks around in a circle, deep in thought.

"Well? Any answers?" Kenneth asks impatiently.

"Hey, no need to get short with me. I wasn't the one to go and buy new shoes and corn mi toes." Neville snaps back.

Kenneth tries to get to his feet but stumbles and falls back to the ground. Neville reacts and starts to walk towards Kenneth. This causes the crowd to take a step back and collectively hold its breath.

Professor Jackson quickly jumps in between the two men, "Come, come. Let's not get carried away with the testosterone exhibition gentlemen."

Kenneth tries to get up again, and this time Eric pushes him back to the ground and glares at him.

Professor Jackson knells beside Kenneth and shines his flashlight on his foot. "Let me take a look at this." He takes Kenneth toes in his hand and squeezes them.

"Ow! Hey, take it easy! That hurts." Yelps Kenneth.

Professor Jackson stands, "It's obvious to me that the injury sustained has made this gentleman lame. Forward progress would be foolhardy. The prudent course of action is to find somewhere in the area to sleep tonight and make your way down the mountain in the morning."

Kenneth tries to get up again, "No. I can make it. I'm not going to stay here by myself."

Eric pushes him down again, 'It's ok. I'll stay with him, and make sure he doesn't fall off the mountain while he is sleeping." This draws laughter from the group.

"I'll stay too. I can't abandon my friends." Kathy says in between the chuckles.

"Ok. That settles it then. Are you ok finding an appropriate location for the night by yourselves? I don't want to lose any more valuable time making our way to the peak." Professor Jackson is stroking his beard.

"We'll be fine." grunts Kenneth.

At that, Neville turns and starts up the trail. The group quickly files after him. Michele and Juliet start to follow then run back. They both kiss Kenneth on the cheek before running off. The group disappears into the darkness, and soon the sound of the group and the glow of their lights are indiscernible.

Kenneth starts giggling and before long he is rolling over in laughter.

"What's so funny boss?" Eric asks, trying to suppress a smile.

"Yes, what could be so funny? You almost started a fight. Over what? Foolishness!" blurts out Kathy.

Kenneth stops laughing, tears streaming from his eyes, "Did you like my performance? I thought it was pretty good. Fooled you guys." For a moment he sits looking at the puzzled look on Eric's and Kathy's faces, before bursting out in laughter again, pointing at them and enjoying their puzzlement.

Eric and Kathy stand, nonplussed, staring at Kenneth.

Kenneth struggles to stop laughing, "You don't get it?"

"Get what?" Eric asks.

Kenneth takes up his right shoe, turns it over and shakes it vigorously. A small plastic bag filled with pebbles falls out of the shoe on to the ground. Eric and Kathy stare at the pebbles and then at Kenneth.

"You still don't get it?" Kenneth asks incredulously. "I faked the whole thing! We needed to find a way to break away from the group, so about an hour ago I stopped and put these stones in my shoe. I figured they would have no choice but to leave us and continue without us.'

"You devil!" Kathy screams and slaps Kenneth on the back.

"Ow! Hey, come on. It was the only thing I could think of."

"The fight scene was an act too?" Kathy asks, exasperated.

"Absolutely! I needed them to think that I really wanted to continue."

"Nice. Nice. I like it." Eric says and gives Kenneth a fist pump. "If we were convinced, then they certainly would be."

"That's why I didn't give you a heads up. I wanted it to be as authentic as possible."

"Really?!? I don't know how Jenny puts up with you." Kathy says, but a smile breaking out across her face.

"Don't you worry about that. Anyway, we need to find somewhere to sleep tonight, and then we can get an early start in the morning." Kenneth points out.

Eric and Kathy search the area with their flashlights. They hear Eric call out.

"This looks good." Eric waves his flashlight from a small gap in the tree line about two hundred yards back down the trail.

They pass through the gap and find what looked like an abandoned camp site. There is a small pile of stones in the middle of the site, and the ground is relatively flat, unlike the rest of the steep terrain surrounding them.

"Yes, this looks like it will do." Kenneth acknowledges.

They take out their sleeping bags, and within ten minutes they are each curled up in their bags and fast asleep.

CHAPTER 24 - Batteries

Kathy, Kenneth and Eric cautiously make their way up the path. They round a large water tower and trek for about a mile before coming to a fork in the dirt trail.

"Which way?" Kenneth turns and looks at Eric.

"Checking." Eric's head is buried in his laptop. "You would think the satellite signal would be great up here." Eric says absentmindedly. "Ok. Based on what I see here, it looks like we should take the right fork."

"You sure?"

"You want to check it?"

"Just asking." Kenneth sets off to the right, glancing up at the guineps on the large tree that stands like a sentry. The trail starts to bear downhill through thick overgrowth. A few times they have to stop to help untangle each other from prickles and shrubbery, and by the time they reach a clearing about half a mile down the hill, they each have numerous cuts and scratches. The sudden blast of light that greets them when they enter the clearing causes them to pause as their eyes adjust. The ripped vegetation and jagged soil are evidence that the clearing is artificial, and the plane wedged between the base of two trees on the edge of the precipice is further evidence of this fact.

Kenneth mops his brow and turns to Eric. "Good job boss."

They walk slowly towards the plane, warily looking around.

"Let's eat before we do anything. It will also give us a chance to think of what our next move should be." Kenneth suggests.

Kathy and Eric agree, and they retreat to the edge of the

clearing so they can sit under the shade of a tree. Although it is only 9am, the sun is beginning to make its presence felt. Kathy sinks her teeth into a bulla and avocado pear sandwich, while Kenneth and Eric set about evenly dividing a HTB spiced bun and a wedge of Tasty processed cheese that they had purchased from 'Miss Ruby's Place' when they had passed through Hagley Gap the day before. When they finished eating and washed down the food with bottles of D&G Ginger Beer, they agreed to examine the plane. It was a Gulfstream V C-37A. Kenneth turns to Eric.

"Man, you are full of surprises. Now how did you know that?" Kenneth asks Eric.

"Been taking flying lessons. Not too far away from getting my licence. We have to learn about various types of planes and their flying characteristics. This is a sweet ride, but too rich for my pocket. If memory serves me, this hauls two to three thousand kilos of cargo."

"So?" Kathy asks, looking over at Eric, while she wipes her brow with a face towel. Eric stands silently rubbing his chin, staring at the plane. "Eric?"

"Huh?"

"So?"

"So, what?" Eric looks at Kathy askance.

Kathy takes a deep breath and shakes her head, "You mentioned the weight it can carry. So?"

"Oh. Just an observation. The Cessna Skyhawk that I usually fly only hauls 800 pounds. Don't know if it is relevant." His voice trails away as he walks away from Kenneth and Kathy to look over the Gulfstream. "There are no markings on the plane."

"No what?" Kenneth asks.

"No markings. Every plane is required to carry registration markings."

"Relevance?" Kathy asks.

"Don't know yet." Eric shrugs his shoulders. "Could mean something. Maybe not."

"How come I didn't know you were taking flying lessons?" Kenneth asks as he walks around the plane.

"How come I didn't know you had a house in Palm Beach?" Eric counters.

"Touché. Touché." Kenneth says, nodding as he continues to walk around the plane. He walks to the edge of the clearing and looks over the edge of the precipice. "It's a long way down. Wait out here. I'll go do some recon."

Gingerly, Kenneth tests the stability of the plane before crawling into the fuselage through a tear in the side where the wing used to be. When he gets to the cabin, Kenneth slowly makes his way towards the front of the cabin. He opens the door and is surprised by the bright sunshine until he realises that most of the nose of the plane is missing. He is also greeted with the sight of the pilot's skeleton still strapped into his seat, the co-pilot seat is covered in blood, and Kenneth confirms that there isn't another body in the cockpit. He retreats to the cabin.

"You can come in now." Kenneth calls out.

Kenneth shines his flashlight on the path he took to enter the plane as Eric and Kathy crawl in. It does not take them long to discover what the cryptographic keys are for. Three large safes, each three feet in height, are lashed down at the back of the passenger cabin, replacing the seats that would normally be there. Despite the extensive damage to the plane's fuselage, the safes are undamaged. Each safe has a numeric keypad in the centre of the door, a digital display above it, and a large chrome handle to the right. Eric reaches into his bag and takes out the three key fobs. He lays them on the floor in front of the safes.

Eric reads one of the key fobs and tries to punch the numbers into a keypad on one of the safes. Nothing happens.

"What happened?" Kathy asks.

Eric runs his hand over his head, taking a step back from the safes. He tries another keypad and gets no response. After a pause he tries the third keypad and gets the same response.

"What's happening?" Kathy asks again.

"Hmm … I wonder." Eric says as he runs the palm of his hand over the surface of the safe.

"What's happening right now?" Kathy asks.

"I think he trying to work the problem." Kenneth offers.

"What problem?"

"I guess he will tell us when he figures it out." Kenneth says as he looks around for somewhere in the cabin to sit down. Kenneth gestures for Kathy to do the same. Kathy is about to speak again, and Kenneth puts a finger over his lips. He gestures for Kathy to relax and sit down. Kathy crosses her arms across her chest and then stands akimbo. Kenneth shrugs his shoulders, sits down and turns his attention to watching Eric.

Eric is running his fingers over the keypad and digital display. He slides his fingers over the top and the bottom of the elevated display and then he stops. He bends down and peers at the bottom of the display, illuminating the area with his flashlight.

"Ahh." Eric says.

"Are you going to tell us what is happening now?" Kathy asks.

Eric starts to chuckle, "Batteries."

"Batteries?" Kathy parrots.

"Yes, batteries. With all the technology advancements in the world, there is one thing it always needs. Power."

"Power?" Kathy says.

Eric reaches into his bag and retrieves a Swiss army knife. From it he selects a screwdriver. He works on the surface below the raised digital display. Suddenly, a small panel drops into his hand. With his finger, Eric dislodges a 9-volt battery. He holds it up for Kenneth and Kathy to see.

"Batteries. They are dead, so the lock is dead." Eric says with a grin on his face.

"Oh. Wow. So do you have any batteries?" Kathy asks.

"No. But we may be able to coax a single use charge out of the batteries so we can open the safes." Eric takes out the other two batteries. He gives one battery to Kenneth and Kathy, respectively. "Now rub the battery against your jeans. We are trying to generate heat and warm up the battery." Eric starts to vigourously rub his battery against his jeans.

Kenneth and Kathy follow suit.

"How long do we need to do this for?"

"About twenty minutes." Eric says.

"What?"

"You can take a break when you need to, but ideally, we want to warm the battery for about twenty minutes."

About twenty minutes later, Eric collects the batteries from Kenneth and Kathy and reinserts them in the digital displays. Each display comes alive and goes through what looks like a boot sequence before lighting every pixel and going blank. Eric tests each keyboard and now gets a response.

"Now we're in business." Eric says as he repositions the key fobs and watches the screens carefully. "I was hoping there was some indication of which key fob was synchronized with each safe but there isn't." He looks at Kenneth, "With the weak batteries we may only be able to open one safe before they are dead again."

Kenneth nods.

Eric takes up a key fob and clicks the button. The twelve digits flash on the screen. Eric looks at the numbers and then punches them into the first safe's keypad. The safe beeps. He moves quickly to the next safe and enters the numbers. This time they can hear the locking mechanism in the door click and clunk. Eric grabs the chrome handle and rotates it. The door swings open and Eric, Kenneth and Kathy take a deep breath. Kenneth pats Eric on the shoulder. Kathy hugs Eric.

Then their eyes are drawn to the open safe. Inside are hundreds of small, sealed plastic bags, stacked neatly so that they can all hold inside the safe. Eric pulls out one of the bags to take a closer look at the contents. Eric points his flashlight at the bag and gasps.

"I certainly did not expect this." Kenneth says.

"What are they?" Kathy asks, trying to peer into the safe. "Drugs? Is it crack cocaine?"

"No. Much more valuable. Uncut diamonds."

CHAPTER 25 – Don't Lie

"Mom, can we go down to Hollywood Mall, in Hollywood? It's near Flagler Street." Ken Jr. asks, as he watches Jackie and Jason play FIFA on the game console. Andy is sitting in his lap.

Jenny and Lisa are relaxing at the dining table, drinking cups of coffee.

"Kenny, that's an hour drive from here. Why do you want to go down there?" Jenny asks.

"There is a shoe sale on."

"Shoe sale? You don't need shoes."

"Well. Yes. Track shoes."

"Ah, I see. There are always shoe sales on, why is this one significant?"

"They are selling one of Michael Jordan's special edition Air Jordan's."

"And why do you need Air Jordan's?"

"Well, I don't need them, but I'd really like to have them."

"How much are these shoes?"

There is no answer. Jenny and Lisa look over at the kids playing on the game console. Kenny is intently watching the on-screen action while hugging Andy.

Jenny waits a little longer and then says, "Kenny?"

No answer.

"Kenny?"

"Yes, Mom."

"How much are these shoes?"

No answer.

"Stop. Stop the game." Jenny says, her voice slightly raised.

"Aw Mom. The game is …" Jackie says.

"Me seh fi stop de game now!"

"Yes, Mom." Jackie pauses the game.

Jason is about to object, but Jackie covers his mouth with her hand.

Andy is about to cry, but Kenny hugs him more closely, "Hush Andy. Hush. Please don't cry." Andy hugs Kenny back.

"Kenny Johnson, you answer me now!"

Kenny faces his mother, "They cost $200." Kenny tries to maintain eye contact with Jenny but his head soon drops.

"Two hundred dollars! For a pair of track shoes?"

"They are special edition Air Jordan's. He wore them in his last season with the Bulls." Kenny pleads. "They will be worth twice that amount the next time they are released. So, they are really a great investment." Kenny is gesticulating with one arm while holding Andy with the other.

"Kenny."

"Please Mom."

Jenny pauses and looks at Kenny. She takes a deep breath and looks at Lisa. Lisa slightly shrugs her shoulders.

"Ok young man. Tell me this. How do you intend to pay for these shoes?"

"I've been saving. I didn't spend any of my Christmas money, and I saved all the money I got for chores." Kenny says excitedly.

"And you are going to spend it all on a pair of shoes?"

Kenny glances at Jackie before answering, "No. I have saved

more than that."

"What?" Jackie says. "You told me you don't have any money?"

"What?" Jenny says, looking at Jackie.

Jackie gets up from the rug, "Yesterday, I wanted to borrow $20 to buy some makeup …"

"Some what? You told me you were going to buy some graphic pens for your art class." Jenny asks.

"Oh!" Jackie says and covers her mouth.

Jenny gets up from the dining table and walks slowly over to the living room. Both Jackie and Kenny look defiantly at Jenny.

"What have you learnt today?" Jenny asks, switching her gaze between Jackie and Kenny.

For a while there is no response or movement. Suddenly, Jason puts up his hand, "Oh, oh, I know. I know." Jason gets up from the rug.

Jenny looks at Lisa with a smirk on her face. "Yes, Jason. What do you think has been learnt?"

"Do not lie. Whenever you lie you're always found out." Jason beams. "Kenny lied to Jackie, and Jackie lied to you." Jason is jumping on the spot, "Don't lie. Don't lie. Don't lie."

"Yes. Thanks Jason." Jenny says. She looks at Jason and points to the sofa and puts her finger to her lips. Jason nods and sits down quietly on the sofa.

"Mommy, what's a lie?" Andy asks Lisa, pulling himself away from Kenny.

Lisa glances at Jenny, who nods. "A lie is another name for an untruth, baby."

Andy's face contorts into an expression of shock. His mouth and eyes are wide open, "You told an untruth?!?" He exclaims, staring at Jackie and Kenny. The defiant expressions on Jackie and

Kenny's faces melt and their chins drop to their chests.

"What have you guys got to say for yourselves?" Jenny asks after some silence. The anger is apparent on her face.

Kenny clears his throat. He looks at Jackie, "Sorry sis." Jackie looks at him and nods. He looks at Jenny, "Sorry Mom." And then he drops his head.

"Sorry Mom." Jackie says with a tear in her eye.

Jenny lets the moment sink in before she breaks the silence. "What do you think should be your punishment?" Jenny asks.

After a while, Kenny looks up, "We should be grounded for a week."

"A week? I was thinking of maybe two or three days." Jackie chirps.

"Yes, now! Spanish Town! Mama gonna to give you one whole week!" Jason starts singing on the sofa. "One whole week! One whole week!"

"Ok Jason. Ok." Jenny says. Kenny and Jackie are scowling at Jason. Jenny looks at Lisa. "I'm inclined to …"

"Before you make a decision," Lisa says quietly, interrupting Jenny, "a lesson of grace may be more powerful at this time."

Jenny looks at Lisa with a quizzical look on her face, and then she smiles and nods her head.

"You guys should be very happy that aunt Lisa is here." Kenny and Jackie look up, glancing at Lisa and then at Jenny. "Kenny, have you learnt your lesson?"

"Yes, Mom." Kenny says quietly, scratching an itch on his bottom.

"Jackie, have you learnt your lesson?"

"Yes, Mom." Jackie says, wiping her eyes.

"Ok then, let's go to Flagler Street." Jenny says triumphantly.

"What?" Kenny and Jackie say in unison.

"What? That's not fair!" Jason says.

"Do you acknowledge that you were wrong?" Jenny asks.

"Yes, Mom." Kenny and Jackie respond.

"And that you are not going to intentionally do it again?"

"Yes, Mom."

"Then, as Jesus said to the woman at the well, I say to you 'go and sin no more'. Do you remember that story?"

"Yes, I remember." Kenny says.

"What stood out for you in that story?" Jenny asks.

"That woman became the first evangelist for Jesus." Kenny responds.

"And why was that?"

"Because of the amazing love, grace and forgiveness that she received from Jesus." Kenny answers.

"Exactly." Jenny responds.

Jackie runs over to Jenny and hugs her, "Thank you Mom. Thank you. I'll never lie again. I'll never lie again." Jenny hugs her.

"Thanks Mom." Kenny says and walks over and gives Jenny a hug.

"Mommy, what's grace?" Andy asks.

* * *

Eric is able to open one more safe before the batteries fail. They confirm that the second safe also contains uncut diamonds. Eric makes a note of the safe and key fob pairs. Kenneth's phone rings, startling them.

"Hello. Hey Jenny. What's wrong babe? Why are you crying? What?!? No! When? What did they say? Oh no! How the hell did this happen? Ok, ok. We'll return immediately. Keep praying sweetheart. We'll be home later tonight." Kenneth puts his phone in his pocket. His complexion has suddenly turned sallow.

"What happened?" Eric asks as he continues to count the number of bags in one of the safes.

"They took Ken." Kenneth mutters.

"What!" Eric exclaims, dropping the bags.

"Oh my God!" Kathy shouts.

"We have to go back now."

"But I haven't finished counting the bags yet."

"It doesn't really matter. We can't take the diamonds with us, and we don't have time to hide them anywhere. Just lock it back up and let's get back."

"But …"

"Now!" Kenneth shouts, then he takes a deep breath. "Sorry. We really need to get back Eric."

Eric turns and starts repacking the safes.

CHAPTER 26 – Where Is Everybody?

Marshall is sitting solemnly under the tree in front of the house. He does not acknowledge Kenneth, Eric or Kathy when they alighted from the vehicle, he just sits throwing pebbles across the lawn. Each pebble flies across the flood lit lawn, disappearing into the darkness. The white double sash front door is ajar and the threesome run into the dark, silent and still interior of the house. They spin around looking at each other and then run back out the door.

"Where is everybody?" Kenneth shouts at Marshall.

Marshall is still slowly throwing pebbles across the front lawn. He intently watches each pebble, almost as though he is conducting an experiment, as it disappears in the distance. Marshall doesn't acknowledge Kenneth's question. Kenneth looks quizzically at Eric and Kathy. He is sure that Marshall can hear him. He is only ten yards away! Kenneth walks across the lawn and taps Marshall on the shoulder, "Hello Marshall."

Marshall falls off the gardener's stool that he is sitting on. "Wha de rhatid do yuh? Yuh no know seh man dead fi less dan dat?" Marshall glares at Kenneth as he springs off the lawn with the agility of a cat.

"I'm sorry. I thought you knew that I was calling to you." Kenneth says as he jumps back in surprise at Marshall's outburst and aggressive posture.

"Oh, I'm sorry. Me never realise seh is you." Marshall apologises, rubbing his head with both his hands.

"Where is everyone?" Kenneth asks.

"Probably upstairs." Marshall responds, before returning to

the stool. He resumes throwing pebbles across the lawn without saying another word.

* * *

Kenneth leads the way up the stairs. When they get to the top of the staircase, they turn right and walk to the end of the landing, passing the two dark guest rooms on that side of the house. Ambient light from the streetlights leaks in through the blinds covering the Edwardian windows in the hall downstairs. It is not until they are outside the main bedroom that a faint light can be seen escaping the door seams. Eric touches Kenneth's arm and points across to the other side of the house. In Ken's room, lit candles stand on his dresser. Kenneth smiles weakly at Eric, turns back to the bedroom door, and pauses before opening the door. Hesitantly, Kenneth opens the door and stands, motionless, in the doorway. Kathy and Eric look at each other. Sounds can be heard from the room, but neither of them can discern what they are. They adjust their position so that they can see properly into the room. Kathy's hand quickly comes up to her mouth to muffle any sound. Eric pats Kenneth on his shoulder and gently pushes him into the room.

As they get deeper into the room they can see that a kneeling prayer circle surrounds the bed. Jenny and Lisa were kneeling on one side of the bed, with Jackie, Jason and little Andy between them. Mr. and Mrs. Martin and Janet are kneeling on the other side of the bed. A bedside lamp is the only illumination in the room.

"Oh, heavenly Father, give us strength. Protect our Kenny." Jenny whispers.

"Yes, Jesus." Mrs. Martin says.

"Give him strength, Father." Lisa says.

"Protect my baby." Jenny says.

Kenneth and Eric collapse at the head of the bed. Kenneth is shaking, Eric is heaving. Kathy flops into a wicker chair in the corner of the room, pulls her knees up to her chest, and buries her head in her lap.

"Have your guardian angels protect our Kenny, Father." Eric manages to say.

"Yes, sweet Jesus." Jenny whispers.

"Gentle Jesus. Please bring my big brother home." Jackie says.

"Yes … oh my baby." Jenny sobs. Kenneth crawls on his hands and knees around the bed and hugs her.

Jason hugs his mother as she cries, "Don't worry Mommy. God will help Daddy, uncle Eric and uncle Marshall outsmart these bad people and bring Kenny home."

CHAPTER 27 – Give Me Back My Son!

Jenny opens the curtains. Light floods into the room like a wave crashing against the rocks of a virgin shoreline. The all-night prayer vigil had eventually ended when everyone was physically and emotionally exhausted at about 5am. Most, excluding Mr. and Mrs. Martin, had been too tired to go to their rooms and had simply fallen asleep on the carpeted floor of the master bedroom. Jenny looks around the room and a faint smile crosses her face before she remembers why they are praying, and then she feels like her heart is being ripped out of her chest. As Jenny is standing by the window holding her chest she is distracted by a periodic tapping sound. Looking outside, Jenny shakes her head. Marshall is still sitting on the lawn throwing pebbles at the front wall. The pebbles that he has thrown throughout the night have landed by the wall and formed a small, neat pile against the wall, reminding Jenny of a mole hill. Each pebble that he now throws hits the top of the pile, bounces off and rolls down the side of the pile. Sometimes it causes a mini avalanche, and other pebbles join in and roll down the pile. Jenny doesn't know how long she has been standing at the window watching Marshall lob pebble after pebble towards the pile by the front wall until she notices a dampness on her chest. She looks down and sees that her t-shirt is wet from the tears she can now feel running down her cheeks. She looks out the window again and Marshall is still throwing pebble after pebble.

Movement causes Jenny to turn around. Kenneth is tiptoeing between the prostrate bodies towards her. She glances at the gold hands of the driftwood clock on the wall. Seven o'clock. They had drifted off to sleep only two hours ago. She looks up at Kenneth, and she can see the pain in his eyes. They embrace.

"I know." Jenny tells him. "I know."

They hold each other tightly.

* * *

Eric and Marshall sit on the ledge of the oak veneer bookshelves that lined two walls of the study. Kenneth is sitting behind his desk in his leather chair, while Jenny and Lisa counterbalance each other on the arms of the Kenneth's chair. Mr. and Mrs. Martin stand by the door, and Janet is sitting on the edge of the desk.

They are all waiting, in silence.

Although the window is open and a cool breeze is drifting into the room, it still feels warm. A dog woofs as a garbage truck makes its way down the street. Everyone stares at the phone when it finally rings. Kenneth gestures to Mr. and Mrs. Martin to close the door.

"Hold on. What about the kids?" Lisa asks nervously.

"I'm sure they'll be ok." Jenny says. "They're playing on the game console."

"Just in case, I think I better stay with them. Plus, I don't know if I can do this. I'm sorry." Lisa gets up and hurries out of the room.

"I'll help." Mrs. Martin offers and closes the door behind her as she leaves.

Jenny squeezes Kenneth's free hand as he reaches for the hands-free button on the phone on his desk.

"Hello."

"Mr. Johnson. Do I have your attention?' A voice with a clipped South African accent fills the study.

"You haven't given me any choice. Is my son ok?" Kenneth

says.

"Of course he is. I'm not a monster Mr. Johnson. I'm not in the business of hurting children, but I needed to make sure that you are very attentive."

"I want to hear his voice."

"Of course you do."

The wait for Kenny to come on the phone is interminable.

"Hello? Daddy? Are you there, Daddy?" Kenny's voice burst through the speaker.

"Yes Kenny, I'm here. How are you?"

"I'm ok, but I want to come home now Daddy. I don't like it here anymore."

"Kenny, this is Mommy. Are they treating you ok? Are you hurt in any way?'

"I'm not hurt, I just miss you guys, and Jackie and Jason. I had a Wendy's burger for lunch, but I am getting hungry now."

Jenny leans forward and grips the phone with both her hands, "Do you know where you are, sweetheart?" She whispers into the phone.

There is silence on the line for a few moments, "Please tell Jason to make sure that Relgalf does not lie in the mud puddle in the back garden. By the link fence. He does it to try and stop the fleas, but it will mean I have to bathe him when I get home. I know it's bizarre."

"What?" Jenny looks at Kenneth, who shrugs his shoulders and looks at Eric, who shakes his head.

"Kenny, what are you saying?" Jenny presses.

"Pigs, Mom. No, I think I'll have Taco Bell next. No, I know, I'll have Burger King, a huge Whopper … What? Mom, I have to go now."

"No, no. Kenny? Kenny!" Jenny shouts into the phone.

"Hello? Mr. Johnson? Are you satisfied?" The clipped South African voice says over the phone.

"Yes. What do you want?"

"I want what is mine. I believe you have something that is mine."

"Oh! And what would that be?"

"Mr. Johnson, please no games. You know what I am talking about."

"Spell it out for me."

"I prefer to keep things obtuse."

"Obtuse?!? You listen to me you bastard. Give me back my son."

"Of course."

"Give me back my son!" Kenneth stands up, shouting into the phone.

"Mr. Johnson."

"Give me back my son!" The veins in Kenneth's temples are bulging.

"Mr. Johnson!"

"Give me back my son!"

Click.

"Give me back my son!"

"Hello?" Jenny says into the phone.

"Give me back my son!"

"Kenneth! Kenneth! He has hung up!" Jenny grabs Kenneth and hugs him.

CHAPTER 28 - Relgalf

"We don't have a dog. Especially one called … what was the name?" Kenneth lifts his head and looks at Jenny.

"Regaf?" Janet offers.

"No, that doesn't sound right." Kathy says.

Eric has his eyes closed, "I think it was Relgalf." He opens his eyes, looking for affirmation from everyone else.

"Yes. That sounds like it." Jenny says.

"What the hell is a Relgalf?" Kenneth asks.

"It seemed to me that Kenny was sending a message to Jason. He said – 'please tell Jason.' Maybe we should ask Jason what this is about." Eric offers.

"Good idea." Jenny says as she runs out of the study. She returns a few minutes later with Jason, with Jackie, Mrs. Martin, Lisa and Andy in tow. Jenny leads Jason by the hand around to the front of the desk. She shoos Kenneth out of the way and puts Jason to sit in the leather chair at the desk.

"Guess what?" Jenny says to Jason.

"What?" Jason asks, his legs swinging aimlessly from the chair as he wiggles his bottom towards the back of the chair, trying to get comfortable.

"We just spoke to Kenny."

"Really? Why didn't you call us so we could speak to him?"

"Yeah! Why didn't you allow us to speak to him?" Jackie chimes in.

"Well, he had to hang up suddenly, so we didn't get a chance to call you. But he did leave you a message, and we need your help to understand it." Jenny says as she reassuringly rubs Jason's arm.

"Will you let me speak to him if he calls back?" Jason grumbles.

"Maybe. We are trying to find out where he is so we can go and get him." Jenny says soothingly.

"Ok." Jason frowns, "so, what is the message?"

"He said Relgalf mustn't lie in the mud in the back garden." Jenny says.

"Ah, a code! Trust Kenny" Jason says excitedly.

"A code?" Kenneth says.

"Yup. We play games with codes all the time. It's our way of speaking without anyone else understanding what we are saying." Jason beams. "Tell me what he said."

"That was it, wasn't it?" Jenny says, turning to Kenneth.

Kenneth shakes his head, "No, there was more. I think you had asked him if he knew where he was."

"Yes. I asked him if he knew where he was and he said something about a dog."

Jason shakes his head, "I need more than that." Jason looks around the room, "does anyone remember exactly what he said?"

Mr. Martin lifts his hand, "I think I recall the whole conversation." Everyone looks at him. "I used to teach English Literature, so I tend to remember things like this." Kenneth nods his head. Mr. Martin recounts the conversation verbatim, as Eric scribbles the words on a flipchart in the corner of the office.

Jason looks up in the ceiling, "Pigs. Hmm, that means that he is using Pig Latin, at least one version of it. There are different versions of Pig Latin. The most popular one takes the first letter or syllable of all words and puts it at the end of the word."

"Really?" Kenneth says.

"Yup. For example, 'please help me' would be 'easepl elphe eme'."

"And you understand this?" Kenneth asks, looking at Jason and Jackie quizzically.

They giggle, "Of course. We use it in school all the time. Takes a lot of practice though." Jackie answers. "Kenny probably didn't use this version because you wouldn't understand, and it would be too obvious to the bad men that he was using a code."

Jason continues, "The other version inverts a whole word."

Eric moves the flipchart to beside the desk so everyone can see it. "The only word that sounds wrong in this context is RELGALF." He underlines the word and then tears off the top page and sticks it to the wall. Eric writes 'relgalf' on the flipchart and inverts it. 'FLAGLER'. You kids are geniuses!"

"Awesome. So, we know he is somewhere on or near Flagler Street." Kenneth says with a smile, leaning closer to Jason. "What else?"

Jason beams, "We don't have a link fence in our back garden. So, that means that he is using word links to try and tell us where he is."

"Word links?" Kenneth asks. "You mean linkages?"

"Yeah, I guess." Jason says haltingly.

"Links? Linkages? You mean associations?" Jenny asks.

"Yes. That's the word." Jason says.

"Word associations. Ok, let's take a look at what Kenny said and see if we can work out what the word associations are." Everyone reads the script on the torn off sheet of paper stuck on the wall.

"Bwoy, where did you learn to write?" Marshall asks.

"Hey, as a mathematician I only learned how to write numbers. Never had to write words." objects Eric.

"Your handwriting is as bad as a doctor's." Marshall quips.

"Can you read it?" Eric asks.

"Just barely."

"Good. Well shut up and let's get down to the business of figuring out where to find Kenny." Eric responds, then turns and smiles at Marshall.

Everyone stands huddled around the sheet of paper on the wall.

"Is that an 'e'?"

"Is that a 'f' or a 'j'?"

"Ok, ok. Let me rewrite this so we can avoid all the questions and Eric doesn't get upset." Kenneth says. Kenneth rewrites the message on the flipchart in block letters.

PLEASE TELL JASON TO MAKE SURE THAT RELGALF DOES NOT LIE IN THE MUD PUDDLE IN THE BACK GARDEN. BY THE LINK FENCE. HE DOES IT TO TRY AND STOP THE FLEAS, BUT IT WILL MEAN I HAVE TO BATHE HIM WHEN I GET HOME. I KNOW IT'S BIZARRE. PIGS MOM. NO, I THINK I'LL HAVE TACO BELL NEXT. NO. I KNOW, I'LL HAVE BURGER KING, A HUGE WHOPPER.

Kenneth turns to Marshall, "Is that more legible?"

"Absolutely. I can stop crossing my eyes now."

Laughter breaks out in the room. Even Eric is laughing. Everyone stares at the words, trying to understand what they mean, hoping they will lead them to Kenny.

After several minutes, Kenneth looks at Jackie and Jason, "Anything?"

Jason shrugs his shoulders, "I think this one is for you

grown-ups."

Jackie shakes her head, "Kenny has put together a real doozy. You're going to have to pull a George to solve this one."

"Pull a what?" Kenneth asks.

"A George. Don't you know what a George is?"

"No." Kenneth looks inquiringly around the room at all the adults, each shaking their heads in bewilderment. Kenneth looks at Jackie.

"How can you not know what a George is? Well, let's see, how can I explain this? I thought everyone knew what a George was."

"Jackie, can you just tell us what you are talking about." Kenneth says as patiently as he can manage.

"It's like a different way of doing things." She looks around the room expectantly at all the faces but is greeted with blank looks. Jackie scratches her head. "Oh, I know!" She gets up and walks up to the flipchart. She draws a vertical line and then connects a horizontal line to the bottom of that line. She writes the letter A at the top of the vertical line, "If someone wants to travel from this point A, to B," she writes a B at the open end of the horizontal line, and a C at the point where the two lines met, "they would normally travel along these two lines, passing through C." She turns and looks at everyone. They all nod in unison. "A George, would be to travel along this line." She draws a straight line directly from A to B, forming a triangle. She turns triumphantly, with a broad smile on her face. The smile fades as everyone has a blank expression on their faces looking at the flipchart. "Don't you get it?" she asks exasperated, throwing her hands in the arm.

"No." Kenneth says.

Eric gets up and walks to the flipchart, "I do." He whispers. He stands in front of the flipchart for a few moments, and then turns to the group, "Thinking outside of the box. That's what a

George is." He smiles at Jackie. He pats her on her head. "I get it. Thanks Jackie."

Jackie beams and walks back to Jenny and sits down beside her. Eric stands looking at the words. He starts drawing circles around some of the words and connecting them with lines. Kenneth starts to speak, but Lisa waves at him and puts her finger over her lips. After a few minutes, Eric whistles.

"Jenny, your kids are smart. I wonder who they take after?" He chuckles, turns and looks at Jenny and Kenneth. "Do you have a map of South Florida around?"

"Yes, I think there is a map in the car. What do you mean, who do the kids take after?" Kenneth says while gesturing to Jason to go to the car and get the map.

"Because they are geniuses." Eric laughs, drawing laughter from the group.

Jason returns with the map and gives it to Eric. He drops the map on the floor, falls to his knees and opens the map. Everyone gathers around the map. Eric runs his finger over the map.

"I thought so. Wow! Dis bwoy good." Eric looks up beaming.

"What?" Jenny asks.

Eric looks at her with a large smile on his face, nodding his head slowly.

"Bwoy! Stop smiling like a cheshire cat and tell us where my bwoy is!" She says and slaps Eric on the shoulder.

"Ok. Ok." He points at a spot on the map.

"What is that?" Kenneth asks.

"That is Flagler Dog Track."

"How are you sure that Kenny is there?" Jenny asks.

"Because in addition to this being the location of the Dog Track, this is also the address of Flagler Flea Market!"

"So?" Jenny says.

Eric points to the words on the flipchart, "he lies in the mud to keep away the fleas … I know it's bizarre." Eric says.

"I don't get it."

"Another name for a market is a bazaar." Eric says triumphantly.

"Wow! Kenny is smart." Jason comments.

"How can we be sure?" Kenneth asks.

"I bet if we checked, we would find Wendy's, Burger King and Taco Bell restaurants in the area. Probably within a street or two." Eric offers.

"That should be easy enough to check. Let me call directory assistance." Kenneth reaches for the phone. After a few minutes and a few questions, he puts down the phone, "There is a Burger King and Taco Bell on NW 37th Avenue, and there is a Wendy's on NW 7th Street, all within a five-minute walk of Flagler Dog Track," he looks at the map and points, "in fact, they are across the road." Kenneth looks at Eric and nods, who acknowledges likewise. Kenneth takes Jenny's hand in his and kisses it. He looks Jenny in the eyes, "Let's go and get our son."

CHAPTER 29 – Help!

Kenny sits nervously. *Will they understand the clues?*

He gets up and walks to the window and looks out over the scene below. Men and women were trotting around with very thin athletic looking dogs on leashes. Kenny shouts and bangs on the glass.

"Help! Help!"

No one looks up. No one notices.

How can they not hear me? Someone's got to notice!

Kenny tries to pick up a metal chair, but it does not budge. He looks down and realises that the chair is bolted to the concrete floor. He looks around the room and notices that everything is bolted down, all the tables and the chairs.

Everything is bolted down! Who bolts down everything? What kind of place is this?

Incongruously, a wooden chair stands in the corner of the room. It keeps attracting Kenny's attention, and as he stands there looking at the chair he wonders why it looks out of place. Suddenly, he looks around the room.

All the other furniture in the room is metal!

Kenny quickly walks over to the chair. It is not bolted down! He picks it up and carries it to the large expanse of glass that fronts the room in which he is being held.

Let's see if they notice this!

Kenny picks up the chair and swings it violently at the glass. The chair disintegrates against the glass, with shards of wood and splinters flying back into the room. He looks on in despair.

How am I going to get out of here? Daddy! Daddy, where are you? Please God. Help them to understand my code.

Kenny's attention is drawn to the door as it slides open slowly.

"Hey kid. What do you want to eat?" A large man, with tattoos running down both arms stands in the doorway.

Kenny thinks about rushing the door to try and escape, but the man's forearm is bigger than both Kenny's thighs, put together!

"Come on kid. How hard can it be to figure out what you want to eat?"

Kenny considers the question.

CHAPTER 30 – You Think This Is A Game?

The expressions are stern, the eyes cold, the jaws firmly set. They are all dressed in black. Black slacks, black long-sleeve shirts and black wool skull caps. Kenneth turns around in his seat so that he can address Eric and Marshall at the same time in the dark.

"Let's go over the plan again."

"We've already gone over the plan a dozen times." Eric says.

"Yes, I know. But this is my son. I don't want any mistakes."

"Kenneth is right. I'll start first." Marshall offers. They each talk about their role in the plan. As they conclude, Kenneth's cell phone rings.

"Hello."

"Mr. Johnson. I trust you have now calmed down."

"It's him." Kenneth whispers and puts the phone on speakerphone. "I'm still angry, but I'll talk with you now."

'Excellent. Let's get down to business. I want what is mine, and then I can give you back your son.'

"Ok. How do we do this?"

"I will pick up the package from your home and then will inform you where to pick up your son."

"No way! I don't want you anywhere near my home. And how would I know my son will be safe after you get what you want?"

"You don't. And you don't have a choice."

"I have an alternative plan."

"Oh? Why would I be interested in an alternative plan?"

"Do you want your key fobs or not?"

There is silence on the line for a few moments. "Ok. Tell me your plan."

"There is a baseball game taking place right now at Joe Robbie stadium. I can call and book tickets that can be left at the box office for you to pick up. Take my son with you. When you get to your seat, you can call me, and I'll tell you where you can find the key fobs within the stadium. When you get the key fobs, I'll go and pick up Kenny from the seat."

Once again, there was silence on the line for a few moments.

"Ok. That's sounds reasonable."

"Good. Call me when you are leaving so I can arrange for the tickets in good time."

The line goes dead.

"Well? What do you think?" Kenneth peers at Eric and Marshall.

"He bought it." Marshall says and Eric nods.

"Let's get set-up." Kenneth says.

Grim faced, they open the doors of the Navigator and get out in unison.

* * *

The phone vibrates. Kenneth glances at Eric, who is sitting in the back of the Navigator, and points at his ear as he walks away from the vehicle. He turns and looks at Eric, who gives him a thumbs up. Kenneth reaches up to a button on his headphones and presses it. "Hello?"

"I am leaving now Mr. Anderson."

"Hold on." Kenneth presses the button again, switching to the closed circuit comms. "Eric, do you have him yet?" Kenneth asks, walking across the parking lot, away from the Navigator.

"It's coming. The triangulation will take about 30 seconds. You have to find a way to keep him on the line for that long."

"This wasn't part of the plan!"

"I know. I know. The stadium is causing some interference with the signal."

Exasperated, Kenneth turns and looks across the expansive parking lot, "Marshall, do you see anything?"

"No. I don't see any movement in my direction."

Kenneth's heart sinks, "I'll try and hold him. Thirty seconds?"

"Yes, I think so." Eric breathes.

"You better be right." Kenneth fingers his headphones, switching back to his cell phone. "Hello?"

"What the hell is going on?'"

"I was checking on the tickets."

"This doesn't feel right. Did you get the tickets?"

"No. Not yet. Let me check again." Kenneth pauses. "Is that ok?"

"Go ahead. I'm waiting."

Kenneth fingers his headphones again. "Well, Eric?"

"Not yet."

"How much longer?" Kenneth almost shouts into the comms.

"I don't know. It's not working the way I expected. Something is blocking one of the signals and stalling the triangulation."

"Jesus Christ!"

"I'm sorry Kenneth. I'm trying everything."

"Try harder!" There is silence on the line. Kenneth takes a

long breath. "I'm sorry. I know you are doing all that you can. How much longer do you need?"

"Another thirty seconds?"

"I'll try."

"I'll go and do some scouting around the grounds." Marshall chimes in.

"No. Stick to the plan." Kenneth snaps.

"I can help by looking around."

"Stick to the plan!"

"He won't see me. I'll be back before you know it."

"Marshall!" There is no response. "Marshall!" Still no response. Kenneth sighs, "Eric, please! As fast as you can. Please!"

"I'm trying."

Kenneth fingers his headphones. "Hello?"

"I'm getting tired of this, Mr. Johnson."

"Not much longer now. They said they were having some trouble with the credit card authorization system, so there is a delay. I'm sorry. I'm working on this."

"Make it quick, Mr. Johnson."

Kenneth switches lines again. "Eric. Tell me you have something."

"Yes. Only a few more seconds. Hold on! I got it! He is in the northwest corner of the lot, walking away from us!"

"Marshall!"

"I'm almost there already!"

"Eric! Move the car around that side of the lot!"

"On the way."

Kenneth fingers the phone, while jogging north across the lot, around the large expanse of buildings. "Hello?"

"Yes, Mr. Johnson."

"We are all set now. You can pick up your tickets at the ticket office. They will be there in my name. The password to get the tickets is stones."

"You have a sense of humour, Mr. Johnson, despite the situation. I like that."

"Right. Well just make sure that …"

A large trumpet blares over the tannoy loudspeakers on the top of the dog track. "Welcome ladies and gentlemen to tonight's meet at the Flagler Dog Track!"

Kenneth fumbles with his phone, trying to engage the mute. He turns the corner of the building to see the South African standing looking down at his phone. Then he looks up at the top of the Dog Track building, in the direction of the loudspeakers. He stands motionless.

"Mr. Johnson!" He screams into the phone. "You think this is a game! You think this is the Hardy Boys?" He holds up his phone and shouts, "Where are you Mr. Johnson? No more games!"

Kenneth hesitates. He isn't sure what to do. "Marshall? Are you near them yet?"

"Almost. I can see him now."

"Can you see Kenny?"

"Not really. They are in the shadows. I can't tell how many of them there are, or which one is Kenny. I'm going to try and get closer."

"Mr. Johnson!" The South African's voice is shrill.

Kenneth quickens his pace, weaving between the vehicles in the lot. He removes the earpiece in his ear.

"Mr. Johnson!"

"Here I am." Kenneth steps out from behind a pickup truck

about fifty yards away from the South African.

The South African spins around. His eyes are wide. "You think this is a game?" He stretches his arm behind him and pulls Kenny from the darkness and pushes him to the ground before him. "You think you can outsmart me?" The South African reaches into his jacket and pulls out a gun and points it at Kenny.

"No! No! Surely, we can work something out!" Kenny screams as he runs forward.

"The time for that is over now."

Suddenly, there is a sound behind the South African. A large heavy-set man stumbles out of the darkness holding the back of his head. Blood is running down his neck. Marshall bursts out of the darkness holding a samurai sword over his head. Before he can lower the sword, the South African side-steps him. There are two flashes of light followed by loud explosions and Marshall is thrown to the ground. He does not move.

"What is wrong with you amateurs? You don't get it, do you?" The South African strides forward and stands over Marshall, glaring at Kenneth. "This is not a game. I don't play games." He looks down at Kenny who still lying on the ground, looking up in terror at the South African. "I tried to be reasonable, but I guess you have to feel pain before you do as you are told." He aims the gun at Kenny and fires. Kenny's head rocks back and hits the ground with a sickening thud. Blood quickly pools under his head.

"No!" Kenneth screams and sprints across the fifty-yard distance and drops beside Kenny. "No! No!" He is having trouble seeing Kenny's face as the tears well up in his eyes.

* * *

"No! No!"

"Kenneth! Kenneth!"

"No!"

"Kenneth!'

Kenneth can feel himself being shaken. He opens his eyes, and in the soft white light hue of the desktop lamp he can see Jenny's sleep veiled eyes staring at him, concern written across her face.

"Kenneth? Are you ok?"

Kenneth raises his head from the desk and looks around the room, confused.

"Sweetheart, are you ok? You were screaming on the top of your voice." Jenny strokes his face.

Kenneth points towards the flipchart with his chin. The flipchart has a diagram of the Flagler Dog Track on it, with notes and formulas scribbled around it.

"The plan. Let's call off the plan. We have to find another way."

CHAPTER 31 – Scorpion?

Kenny sits looking at the Whopper. He nervously picks up the coke and takes a long swig through the straw.

Maybe if I eat the fries and drink most of the coke first, the reaction will be less.

He squeezes the ketchup over the fries and eats them one at a time, warily eyeing the Whopper. Five minutes later he has finished all the fries and half his coke, and Kenny again sits looking at the Whopper. The door opens and the tattooed man with tree trunks for arms pokes his head into the room,

"You done yet kid?"

"Not yet. I'm about to eat my burger."

"Hurry up kid."

"Come back in ten minutes and I should be done."

Ten minutes later the tattooed man returns.

"Jesus! Jerry! Jerry! Oh shit!" He rumbles into the room and kneels beside Kenny. He glares down at Kenny.

"What is it?" A slender black guy strolls into the doorway. "What's all the racket about? The boss warned us to make sure to keep the noise down."

"It's the kid. He seems to be sick."

"Oh fuck! What the hell?" The black guy trots into the room and stoops beside the tattooed guy. "Do you know what's wrong with him?"

"How the hell would I know? Am I a doctor?"

"Hey, I was only asking. Is he breathing? He looks kinda

blue?"

The tattooed man puts his index finger under Kenny's nose, "Yeah, he seems to be, but …" He puts his ear to Kenny's chest and then close to his nose. "He seems to be having trouble breathing. His heart is racing like he was in a race or something."

"He looks a lot fatter than he did earlier, like he's swollen up, like a mud fish." Jerry comments.

"Jesus! Oh shit! You don't think he was stung by a scorpion? I hear people swell up when stung by scorpions?" Tattooed guy asks.

Jerry jumps up on the table, "Scorpion? You see a scorpion?"

"No. Do you?" Tattooed guy also jumps up and climbs, less nimbly, onto a chair.

"No fool!" Jerry exclaims, slapping the tattooed guy on the shoulder. Jerry climbs off the table and stoops beside Kenny. "I thought you … oh never mind. What do you think is wrong with him?"

The tattooed guy gingerly gets off the chair, looking suspiciously around, and kneels beside Kenny, "I don't know, but it sounds like he is having trouble breathing. I think we should call the boss and ask him what we should do."

Sighing, Jerry reaches for his phone. He paces from side to side as he gesticulates while speaking on the phone. He hangs up and looks down at Kenny, "The boss says we should leave him."

"What? He could be dying?"

"Boss says we should pack up our stuff, wipe the place clean and get out."

"But, but he's only a kid."

"You want to call the boss and tell him that?"

The tattooed guy looks down at Kenny, "No. I guess not." Slowly, he rises to his feet. "I guess we better do what the boss says." The tattooed guy heads for the door.

"Where you going?" Jerry asks, as he starts wiping down the surfaces of the room with a handkerchief.

"Got to take a leak. Be back in a second." As the tattooed guy leaves the room and hurries down the corridor, he reaches for his phone. "Hello? Yes, I need an ambulance at the Flagler Dog Track. A boy has collapsed and seems to be having trouble breathing."

* * *

"He's in here!" The police officer calls from the room. The paramedics wheel in the cart and kneel beside Kenny.

"Do you know what happened here?" The first paramedic who entered the room asks. He is a tall black guy in his thirties.

"No. There was a 10-38 call, about a boy who was having trouble breathing and collapsed. It was deemed suspicious because it was anonymous. I was asked to come and case the premises to make sure that you guys were ok and had backup."

"D, his esophagus appears to be swollen." The second paramedic says as she examines Kenny. She is Hispanic, broad hipped and in her early forties. "His vitals are very weak. His system seems to be shutting down."

"Looks like some kind of allergic reaction." D says as he opens Kenny's shirt and notices the red blotches on his torso, and the swelling of his lips and around his mouth.

"If we don't do something he could be dead in a few minutes."

"Yeah, but the problem is that we don't know what antigen to use because we don't know what he is allergic to."

"You see any bees around? Scorpions? Ants? Anything that can sting him." The female paramedic asks as she looks around. The police officer shines his flashlight around Kenny, searching the floor, under and around the table and the chair. They all crawl around on their knees searching. "Anyone see anything?"

"Nothing." D offers.

"Naw. Only these food wrappers." The police officer calls.

"What food wrappers?" D asks, quickly turning towards the officer.

The police officer reaches into the trash bin and takes out a brown Burger King bag and a Coke bottle. D and the female paramedic exchange a glance.

"Sesame seeds!" They say in unison.

"But surely with such a violent reaction he would know that he has this allergy and not eat sesame seeds?" The female paramedic pauses.

"J, it's our only clue. Do you have any other ideas?"

J plays with her brunette ponytail for a few short moments and shakes her head. "Let's go for it. Call it in."

D reaches for his radio handset, "Mercy General, we have a boy possibly in his early teens; appears to be suffering from anaphylactic shock. BP thready, breath shallow, esophagus closing, and allergic dermatitis. Please advise stat."

"What's the cause?" a crackly voice asks.

"Possibly sesame anaphylaxis."

"Possibly?"

"We don't have a lot to go on here. That's our best guess."

"Heartbeat accelerated and lips swollen?" Crackles the voice.

J puts her stethoscope to Kenny's bare chest and nods.

"Affirmative."

"Hook up the patient to a heart monitor. 0.3mg of epinephrine and monitor."

"Roger." They work rapidly to put Kenny on a stretcher, place white discs on his chest and arm with cables running to a heart-monitoring machine. J quickly takes his blood pressure while D prepares the epinephrine injection. D checks with the female paramedic, "You ready J?"

J nods without looking up from the heart monitor. D injects Kenny. J watches the monitor intently and after a minute takes his blood pressure again.

"No improvement in his BP."

Suddenly, Kenny starts convulsing violently.

"Violent convulsion!" shouts D into the radio.

"One milligram of epinephrine!" Crackles the voice.

D quickly prepares the new dosage, while J holds Kenny. D applies the injection. Kenny coils into a fetal position as the convulsions subside.

"BP is settling. Heart rate is falling." J places the stethoscope on Kenny's back and listens. "Breathing is improving." J allows herself a smile.

"Mercy General, we are heading in with the patient. He has stabilized."

"10-4. Good job."

CHAPTER 32 – John Doe

"Mr. Johnson. Time to act. No more games, no more discussion."

"Can I speak with my son?"

"No. Let's get this transaction completed and I will call you and tell you where you can pick up your son."

"But …"

"Enough! I'm tired of this shit! Listen carefully. There is a pawn shop on the corner of NW 7th Street and NW 30th Avenue. Put the keys in a sealed brown manila envelope addressed to Winnie Nelson. Give the envelope to the proprietor and go back home. I'll call you when I have my keys."

"The pawn shop will be open this late?"

"It's open. How many keys do you have?"

Kenneth pauses for a moment.

"Don't lie to me Mr. Johnson."

"Three."

"Good. Put them all in the envelope. Hurry Mr. Johnson. The clock is ticking, and your son may not have much time left. Oh, one more thing. I want to remind you that we still want to keep this between us, that means, no police."

* * *

Why hasn't he called back? Has he harmed Kenny? Why hasn't he called? Call you bastard! Kenneth mind is going crazy running through the worst case scenarios and the what-ifs he should have explored.

Out of the corner of his eye, Kenneth notices Eric watching him. The room is dark, with the only light source coming from the TV. Images flash across the screen from the CNN news feed. Despite the poor and intermittent light, Kenneth tries to make eye contact, but then realizes that Eric is gazing, not watching him. Eric has one of those distant looks in his eye.

"Eric. What's up? What's on your mind?"

Eric slowly focuses on Kenneth. "I've been mulling over what Kenny said. Something has been bothering me."

"Shoot."

"He seemed to focus a lot of time and effort on what he was going to eat."

"Yeah. I thought we agreed that was to give us a frame of reference. Help us isolate the location."

"It could be …"

"But you don't think so?"

"Well, no. Think about it. He already said he had Wendy's, then he said he was trying to decide between Taco Bell and Burger King. Why bother to say that he was going to have a huge Whopper? What is the relevance of that? What message is he trying to send us?"

Kenneth sits for a moment, looking at Eric. He lifts his legs up and rests them on his desk. Suddenly, Kenneth pushes himself up. His chair slips and he crashes to the floor. Footsteps can be heard running towards the study by the time Kenneth jumps up.

"Jenny! I know where Kenny is!"

* * *

Kenneth and Jenny rush into the Emergency Room of Mercy

General. They frantically read the signs and hurry to the reception desk. A middle-aged woman, in her white nurse's uniform with blue trim looks up from the desk.

"Yes? Can I help you?"

"I called earlier, and you said you had admitted a John Doe boy who had suffered from sesame anaphylaxis? We are his parents. At least we think so, we pray so." Jenny blurts out.

The nurse checks a chart, leafing through sheets of paper. "He has been moved to Intensive Care. Second floor. The elevator is to your right. I'll call the nurse upstairs to let her know you are coming."

Jenny squeezes Kenneth's hand as they hurry to the elevator.

"O God, please let it be him." Jenny whispers as they wait. The wait is unbearable as the elevator doors slowly open and close behind them, as Jenny impatiently keeps pressing the number two button. The elevator doors have barely parted before Jenny darts out into the corridor, leaving Kenneth behind, as he has to wait for the doors to open a little more for him to get through. Kenneth arrives at the desk to hear Jenny being told that the boy is in room 5, and she shots down the corridor, bursting into the room.

"No!" Jenny exhales.

Kenneth enters the room to find Jenny bent over at the waist hugging herself. A low primeval groan escapes from Jenny. Confused, Kenneth looks up to see a small Hispanic looking boy with a cast on his left arm sitting up in bed. Sitting beside the bed is a woman with a white scarf tied over her hair and glasses perched on the tip of her nose. She looks up from a book that lies between her and the boy, with a startled look on her face.

"Digame?" The woman says.

For a moment, time seems to stand still for Kenneth. He looks from Jenny to the woman and boy, and back to Jenny.

"Que pasa?"

"Ah, lo siento. Ah, hablas ingles?" Kenneth sputters.

"Poco. Muy mal."

"Ah, donde estas?" Kenneth says.

"Que?" The woman said, a very confused look on her face.

"Ah. El numero?" Kenneth says, pointing to the floor and around the room.

"Ah, si. Es habitation cuatro." The woman says, smiling.

"What? Cuatro?" Kenneth whispers. He hesitates for a moment, then says, "Jenny. Jenny, we are in the wrong room. This is room number four. The nurse said five." He puts his arm around Jenny and guides her towards the door. "Muchas gracias." He calls over his shoulder as they go out the door.

Kenneth stops at the neighboring door and takes a deep breath before gently pushing it open. Through the crack that he has created he cannot see anything but darkness. His heart drops into his stomach, but then he notices a small flashing red light on the far side of the room. He hugs Jenny a little closer and pushes the door further open. They slowly make their way into the room. Kenneth stops and fumbles around on the wall, feeling for the light switch. Finally, he finds it and turns on the light. The darkness recedes suddenly, and there, lying on the bed, with tubes and wires hanging from him, is Kenny!

CHAPTER 33 – We Love You Son

Jason taps Kenny on his leg. Kenny doesn't acknowledge the tapping as he is giggling at a joke from uncle Eric and uncle Marshall. Jason waits patiently for a lull in the conversation, as everyone in the room seems to have something to add to the joviality.

Mommy and Daddy look so happy, Jason thinks, looking into their eyes. Jason chuckles as he watches aunt Lisa hold her side as she laughs at yet another joke from uncle Marshall.

Pinkish light bounces off the ceiling as sunlight floods the room through the window and reflects off the petals of the white and pink carnations that are sitting on the windowsill. Jason reflects on his father's words when he had placed the vase on the sill.

"These colours were chosen for a reason Kenny. Pink stands for a mother's love, a love that is as great as any love you will experience on this earth." Kenneth had paused to look at Jenny. He reached for her hand and squeezed it, which caused Jason to choke up a little. He had to hurriedly rub his eyes so no one would notice that they were moist. "The white signifies pure love and good luck. As you know I don't believe in luck, except to say that luck is the residue of design, but no purer love is there than that of a parent for their child, as God shows us in his love for us. We just want you to know that we love you son."

"Whoa!" Jason is jolted back to the present by Kathy's exclamation. "Stop Marshall! Stop! I can't laugh anymore." Kathy says, as she wipes her eyes with a tissue.

"But it nuh done. We a walk pon dis deserted road somewhere in the Blue Mountain range and we a dead fi get home. Lawd have mercy pon we! How we a go get home? Den, out of de darkness, we see one man, so we call to him, meanwhile we a huddle together for warmth. We call to him and ask,

'*How you get to Papine pon a Sunday?*' Him look pon we like we mad. '*You see me in Papine pon a Sunday?*' We are speechless. Is this man mad? We look at each other in complete bewilderment. '*Eh! Eh! You see me in Papine pon a Sunday? Cho! Uno lie like what, and uno foot dry like jackass corn. You better tek foot and run before me chop you.*'

Den dis madman pulls one lass long like mi arm from somewhere, me no know where. Back foot! We never stop run till we reach the foot of the mountain!"

The whole group bursts out in an uproar. Kenneth laughs so hard he falls off his chair. Lisa is already on her knees. Kathy stops trying to dry her eyes, and cries freely. Eric is bent at the waist gasping for air.

Jason taps Kenny on the leg. Kenny rolls over in his bed, away from everyone else to face Jason.

"What's up little bro?" Kenny smiles at Jason.

Jason leans forward, resting both his elbows on the bed, "I heard you almost died?" Jason whispers.

"What was that, Jason? I didn't hear you." Kenny says, tilting his head towards Jason.

"Did you almost die?" Jason asks a little louder.

"What? Speak up little bro. Wha'ppen to you? Yuh voice get kidnapped?" Kenny snickers, proud of his little joke.

Jason frowns, "Did you almost die?" He says loudly.

The laughter stops suddenly. Jenny audibly gasps. Lisa and Kathy both bring their hands up to their mouths to stifle a similar response. Kenneth starts to respond, when Jenny puts her hand on his arm. He turns to her, and she shakes her head. Kenny pulls himself up in the bed and looks at his brother askance.

"I mean, did you see God, or any of his angels, or heaven?" Jason rattles off, oblivious to the change of the mood in the room.

"Oh yeah, I saw the archangel Michael." Kenny's expression becomes grave, "He said that if you give me any trouble he was going to come and zap you when you are sleeping."

"What?!? Mom!" Jason exclaims.

"Kenny!" Jenny chastises.

"Ok, ok. I'm sorry. Just joking." Kenny reaches over and pats Jason on the head.

"That's not funny." Jason whines.

"Yes, you are right. I'm sorry." Kenny smiles reassuringly. He beckons to Jason to come and sit beside him. Jason nervously glances at his father, who nods. Jason climbs up on the bed and sits beside Kenny. Suddenly, Kenny flinches and grabs his stomach, "Ow!" He rolls over violently, into a fetal position.

Jason jumps off the bed, "What? What did I do? I'm sorry! I'm sorry!"

Jenny rushes to the bed, "Kenny! What's wrong baby?" She strokes his head.

Kenny starts shaking.

"Oh, dear Lord. Kenneth, call the nurse, he is having a seizure!"

Kenny rolls over, gulping for air. "Hahaha, did you see Jason's face?"

Jenny slaps Kenny, wiping the laugh off his face. "Bwoy! Yuh crazy! Yuh know you nearly give me a heart attack!"

"Sorry Mom. It was just a joke."

"Joke! Bwoy! If you weren't in that hospital bed already, I would put you in here."

"Sorry Mom." Kenny says sheepishly, noticing the disapproving looks from everyone in the room. He looks over at Jason and gestures to him and pats the bed again. "Come on Jason. What do you want to know?"

Jason gingerly climbs onto the bed, this time sitting on the edge of the bed. "I just wanted to know if you saw God."

Kenny stifles a smile and is about to respond, when Jason interrupts him, "I wanted to find out if you had a chance to tell God thanks for sending you back to us, otherwise I will tell him when I say my prayers tonight."

Kenny, like everyone else in the room, struggles to hold back the tears.

* * *

"I'm sorry Mr. and Mrs. Johnson, but you have to leave now. Visiting time ended a few hours ago, and your son really needs to get some rest, so he is ready to go home tomorrow."

A young nurse stands at the door surveying the room that is littered with Papa John's pizza boxes and two-litre Coke and Pepsi bottles. Everyone groans, collecting all the food and drink packages and containers as they prepare to leave.

"I'm sorry folks. I've been as lenient as I can, but you have been here all day. Little Kenneth needs to get some rest."

"Bye Kenny." Eric and Lisa hug and kiss him.

Andy waves enthusiastically.

"See you tomorrow little man." Marshall and Kathy hug and kiss him.

"Tomorrow big brother." Jackie says, waving as she moves towards the door.

"Yeah, see you tomorrow." Jason says, stopping to give the young police officer outside the door a high five.

Jenny kisses Kenny on the forehead, "See you tomorrow

baby." She gives the police officer a stern look as she leaves the room.

"Don't worry ma'am." His youthful face beams a reassuringly warm smile, "Your son will be kept safe under my watch."

Jenny's countenance softens, "Thank you."

"Sweet dreams little man. See you tomorrow." Kenneth says and gives Kenny a hug. "We'll pick you up after we finish the interview at the police station. Ok?"

"What? You have to talk to them again?"

"Yeah. Today we only gave them a little information. They said they understood our desire to spend time with you after this ordeal. So tomorrow we have the real interviews with them."

"Ok. Bye everyone." Kenny calls to the group as they exit the room.

CHAPTER 34 - Contrition

"Mr. Johnson, I am an experienced detective of 30 years. You really expect me to believe this story?"

Kenneth is exasperated. He glares at the short, potbellied, grey-haired imbecile sitting across the table from him.

This is a waste of time!

The detective reminds Kenneth of a mafia crime boss, instead of a police officer.

"You want me to believe that someone kidnapped your son because of something you had? What's this something that's so valuable for this someone to go to so much trouble? How did you come by this item? Where is the item now? Where are these individuals who took your son? Why was your son not delivered to you instead of left to die in a dirty room at a dog track? Who called the ambulance?" The detective spits the questions at Kenneth like a machine gun, his grey-blue eyes seemingly trying to burn a hole in Kenneth.

This is crazy! Now I am the villain!

"The pawnshop. You said you went there at about 7:30 last night."

"Yes. It took me about an hour to get there after the phone call."

"The owner said he closed the store at six o'clock."

"What?"

"Your story has more holes in it than Swiss cheese." The detective smirks.

Think! Think!

Kenneth wrings his hands and smiles sheepishly.

Think contrite. Think contrite.

Kenneth bows his head and takes a deep breath. Kenneth finally speaks, keeping his eyes down and his chin pinned to his chest.

"I'm sorry. You're right. I should have known I would not get away with it." He pauses and runs his hand over his hair. "I, I … it was my wife."

"What? Now you're telling me your wife did this?" The detective bellows, his belly bobbing up and down above the table, like a beach ball on the shallow seashore as the waves lap the sand.

"No. No. I mean … let me try and start again. I caught my son smoking pot and I slapped him around the head, and we argued. He ran out of the house in a huff."

"So, what has this got to do with your wife?"

Kenneth looks up slowly.

Think contrite.

"My lawyer and accountant have been telling me for months that my wife plans to divorce me. I did not believe them, but when this incident happened, all I could think of is her taking my kids away from me, citing that I am an incompetent father."

"You lost me." The detective gets up and sits on the edge of the desk and scratches his head. He wobbles precariously for a moment before gripping the desk with his hand.

Think contrite.

"It was one of my son's friends, or so-called friends, that called me and told me what had happened. He said he had called an ambulance, but they were too scared to hang around when Kenny collapsed. He apparently got carried away and forgot about his allergies."

"Go on." The detective says quietly, eyeing Kenneth carefully.

"I decided to make up this story so my wife would not blame me, and maybe, somehow, if she is thinking about leaving, she would have a change of heart."

The detective sits silently for a moment and looks at Kenneth.

Think contrite.

"Have you spoken to your wife about this? I mean about her leaving?"

"No. I have been too terrified to even contemplate the idea. We have three wonderful kids, and I don't know what I would do if she left. Everything I have done, everything I have worked for is for her, and my children." A tear rolls down Kenneth's cheek. He quickly wipes it away.

The detective shakes his head slowly, "I could lock you up for wasting my time like this, do you know that?"

"I'm sorry. I panicked."

"You rich people are so stupid. More money than sense." The detective says as he pushes himself up from the table. The interrogation room door opens, and a uniformed officer enters with a phone.

"Phone call for Mr. Johnson." The officer's hat is pulled low over his eyes, and he turns and leaves the room after putting down the phone.

Kenneth picks up the handset, "Hello."

"Mr. Johnson. I said you should not speak to the police."

Kenneth holds his breathe.

"You people really must learn to listen." Click.

"Who was it?"

"Just my wife asking if I was ok. She didn't think I would be down here for so long." Kenneth pauses, "Can I ask for a favour? I know I am not in a position to do that."

The detective stops at the door and turns to face Kenneth. He pulls up his trousers after they have slipped below his very large belly, "What?"

"Can I ask that you leave the officer at the hospital till I get there, just to keep up the pretense a little longer, so that I can ease into explaining this to my wife. I don't want to alarm her." Kenneth pleads.

The detective stands still for a moment, looking down at his shoes, assuming that he can see them below the expanse of his stomach. "I guess it can't hurt anything. Sure, I'll do that." He looks up and wags his finger at Kenneth, "Now listen to me, I don't want to see you again anytime soon, Mr. Johnson. Get the hell out of here."

The detective waddles out the door and disappeared into the chaos of the police station.

CHAPTER 35 – What Was That About?

"You're not serious?" Eric asks incredulously, as he fills his mouth with sui mien noodles.

"This thing goes a lot deeper than we thought." Kathy whistles.

Kenneth looks across at the children's table and nods at Kenny, who has a big grin on his barbecue-soiled face, as he picks up another rib from his plate. Jackie is sticking her red tongue out at Jason, who seems to be trying to show Jackie his tonsils, and Andy is laughing hysterically at whatever Kenny has said, while simultaneously trying to sip from the very tall straw poking out of his glass of soda. Janet stretches across the table, and in hushed tones she exuberantly relates a story to the group. Suddenly, Kenny falls off his chair, howling. Jason chokes and has coke dripping from his nose as he giggles. Jackie wipes Jason's face while grunting a laugh. Andy cackles and claps his barbecue-covered hands gleefully.

Kenneth smiles at the scene. "How did we get into this mess?" He asks as he turns back to the group sitting at the adult's table.

"We are sorry to have brought this down on you." Mr. Martin says.

Kenneth snaps his head around to Mr. Martin, "No, that didn't come out right. That wasn't what I meant."

Marshall interrupts, "Well I don't know how we got here, but I'm going to get some more of those snow crab legs while I still can."

He gets up from the table and heads towards the buffet.

There is a collective chuckle, and everyone follows suit, joining the various long lines to the serving stations for this Thursday's special All-You-Can-Eat buffet. The Golden Dragon is one of the family's favorite restaurants, and they try to visit whenever they are in the area. Kenneth is the last to sit down at the table after he has to pause and apologise to a very slender woman, in what looks like bed slippers, for elbowing a crab claw off her plate as he passed her. She accepts his apology with a smile and eases herself into her chair behind her brim-full plate. As Kenneth enjoys another mouthful of barbecue ribs, he looks around the two tables, smiles and gives Jenny a kiss on the cheek.

"Hey, not with those barbecue lips." Jenny playfully complains and wipes her cheek with her napkin.

"So, what next?' Eric asks as he finishes his beer and sits back in his chair.

"How about we just kick back and watch some movies on Netflix." Kenneth offers.

"No, come on. You know what I mean." Eric says in a hushed tone, as he leans forward, resting his elbows on the table as he eyes Kenneth, "Where do we go from here? We seem to be at an impasse."

"Yes, you have a point. To be honest, I don't know." Kenneth looks around the table, "Any ideas?"

"Kenneth," Jenny says softly, "why can't we just go home?"

Kenneth looks around the table, trying to read everyone's face, before looking into Jenny's eyes, "Is that what you think we should do?"

"Yes. I'm tired, and we almost lost our son. We should go home."

In the corner of his eye, Kenneth notices a red paper or cloth lantern hanging from the ceiling, with a gold dragon etched on each of its four sides, seemingly swaying slowly from side to side in unison with the heads nodding around the table. From the vantage point of their table at the back of the restaurant, Kenneth is able to survey the whole dining area of approximately twenty plus tables. "I guess the only question to answer is whether it is safe to go home or not."

"Is it?" Marshall prompts.

"That's what I was asking." Kenneth says.

"No. I meant, is that the only question?"

Kenneth slumps back in his chair, "What do you mean?"

"Why did we come here in the first place?" It is Marshall's turn to lean forward and examine the faces of everyone at the table. "Need I remind you all that Kathy's partner was murdered?" He points at Kenneth and Jenny, "I mean, you guys were chased by persons unknown who may actually be the police to rhatid! Like you were criminals!" He points at Mr. and Mrs. Martin, "Your daughter was kidnapped, and she can identify the people who did it."

"But surely that is behind us now? We have given them what they wanted." Jenny pleads.

"Yes, we are no longer a threat to them." Mrs. Martin rebuffs.

"They may have what they want, but not where they want it." Eric says reflectively. This causes everyone to pause. All eyes settle on Eric. "It's common sense. The diamonds are in Jamaica, but that is not their final destination. They can't legally move them, and we are possibly the only threat to them being able to successfully smuggle them into the US."

Kenneth notices the bed slipper clad woman making her way back to her table with another mountain of food on a plate. *Where does she put it all?* Kenneth wonders for a fleeting moment.

"We know too much."

Kenneth looks around the table. "What?"

Kathy repeats herself, "We know too much. That is why

they will still be after us."

"But what do we really know?" Jenny asks. "We don't know who is behind all this. We don't know any names. We don't have any real evidence." She searches the faces around the table, "I mean, you heard what Kenneth just said, the police didn't believe his story." She gestures in the direction of Mrs. Martin, "The police would not help you find Janet. Even if we talked, who would listen to us? They have nothing to fear from us."

"Jenny does have a point. Maybe that message will filter back home and Busha George will leave us alone. We can't prove anything against him." Mrs. Martin offers.

"This is a mistake." Marshall says brusquely.

"Eric? You brought this up. Lisa?" Kenneth turns to them.

Eric looks at Lisa, looks down at the table and takes a deep breathe. "In contradiction to what I said earlier, we would like to go home. Without a plan, we seem to be here in limbo, and maybe we can get more done there."

"What is wrong with you people?" blurts out Marshall.

"What would you have us do, Marshall?" Kenneth asks, exasperated.

"Let me help. I have connections."

"We discussed this already."

"But I can help. Look at where we are, doing it your way."

"So, what do you suggest? Slit the throats of all those involved?" Bursts out Kenneth. Jenny gasps.

"Come on. That's a low blow." Marshall protests.

"How about shooting a few people. One barrel, no, maybe both barrels of a twelve gauge?"

"Ok. That's enough now." Marshall hisses.

'Oh, I know. Maybe we can vent all our frustrations by bludgeoning some people to death. That will really work."

Lisa puts her hand over her mouth.

Marshall glares at Kenneth. He opens his mouth and then pauses. He clenches his fists and slowly pushes his chair back and starts to stand. Kenneth tries to jump up from his chair, but Jenny grabs his arm and pulls him back into his chair. Kenneth tries to pull himself clear, but Jenny holds his arm with both of her arms.

"Yuh waan some a dis?" Kenneth hisses at Marshall.

Marshall thumps the table. Everyone and their plates jump in unison. People at neighboring tables start to look over to see what is happening. Marshall looks around and notices the curious onlookers. He stands up to his full height and walks towards the exit.

"What was that about?" Kathy asks, looking frantically from Kenneth to the retreating Marshall.

"He hasn't told you?"

"Told me what?"

"I think it best if he tells you."

"Tell me what?"

"Talk to Marshall about it. It is not my place to say."

"Argh!" Kathy jumps up from the table and hurries after Marshall.

CHAPTER 36 – Oh

Twenty years ago

"You going to UWI?" Kenneth asks. He takes a swig from his Red Stripe as he looks out at the waves breaking gently against the beach.

"Nah. Not for me." Marshall responds.

"Why not?"

"People like me don't belong in places like that."

"What are you talking about? Anyone can go. Access is based on merit. You get the grades you're in." Kenneth puts his beer down on the beach and focuses on Marshall.

"I didn't apply." Marshall says sheepishly.

"I don't get you. I'm sure you will get the necessary grades. You made sixth form look like a breeze. Why don't you want to go to UWI and get a degree?"

"Those of us who live below Cross Roads sometimes have different priorities."

"What the hell does that mean?"

Marshall sighs, "It takes money to go to university. And I have to help put food on the table."

"Oh."

Kenneth and Marshall sit quietly, sipping their beers. After some time, Kenneth breaks the silence.

"How is your mom doing?"

"She working two jobs to put me and Jeremiah through high school." Marshall says with a grim expression on his face.

"Oh." The awkward silence hangs over them again for a while. "And how is Jeremiah doing?"

Marshall's face lights up, "Dat bwoy going to be somebody. I don't know where he gets his smarts from, but I am very proud of him. He came first in his class last year."

"He is in second form now?"

"Yes. He wants to be a doctor or a lawyer. Or his latest thing is to be a lawyer who deals with medical malpractice, combining the two things." Marshall laughs. "He's been reading some medical journals that have highlighted some cases in the US. He wants to help and protect those who are unable to help themselves. I asked if there was money in that and he told me that everything is not about money." Marshall laughs again.

"He's young and idealistic."

"That is the truth."

They share a laugh.

"So, what do you plan to do then?" Kenneth asks.

"I've been thinking about that. The Civil Service is taking on young people and offering them training and will pay for you to go to university. With my A-Levels I should be able to get a job, I can help Mom, and then I can get a tertiary education that is funded by the government."

"Hmm … that's."

"What?" Marshall snaps.

"That's, that's a good plan." Kenneth says, nodding his head.

"Oh. Thanks." Marshall says. They fist pump and then watch the waves breaking on the beach in silence.

"So, what about you? Are you going to UWI?" Marshall asks.

"I haven't decided yet. I did apply, but I also applied to the US Navy."

"What?!? Why the hell would you want to do that?"

Kenneth hesitates, "I read a recruiting flyer when I was in the US last year and I became enamoured with the idea of being a Navy aviator or a special ops operator in the Seals."

"Are you mad? Those flyers are designed to hook the gullible. Nothing in them is real. And everything in the movies is fantasy. All they want is more warm bodies to send on their crusades. It's all propaganda."

"Yeah," Kenneth mutters, "but the Seals are also tasked with going into tough places in the world and helping those who are unable to help themselves. Kinda like what Jeremiah wants to do." He then says with more conviction.

"Hey, if you need to believe that bullshit to justify your decision, go for it."

"Come on. That's not fair. That was a low blow." Kenneth objects.

"Ok, ok. My bad."

They both pick up their beers, sip them and watch the waves.

"So, when would you be leaving, if you are going to join the Navy?" Marshall asks.

"Their semesters are the same as a regular university. So, I'll probably leave during the summer to settle in and figure out my options."

"Oh." Marshall sips his beer.

"I could also go to UWI first and then join the Navy. I haven't decided yet." Kenneth says thoughtfully. Marshall nods. "And when would you start working in the Civil Service?"

"I have already been offered a provisional job, depending on my results. I'll start on probation right after we break for summer holidays. My results will come out at about the same time as my probation ends."

"Oh." Kenneth sips his beer.

As the sun begins to set, Kenneth and Marshall fist pump.

"One love my brother." Kenneth says.

"Nuff respek." Marshall responds.

They man-hug and part to go their separate ways.

CHAPTER 37 – De Bwoy Fall Asleep?

Still twenty years ago

Marshall left the office much later than normal. He has really enjoyed his integration into the Civil Service training program. As part of the program, he has been rotated through The Office of the Prime Minister, Ministry of Finance and Ministry of Education, and he has found the experience fascinating seeing how policy is created, formulated, and executed on the ground and makes a difference in the lives of the everyday citizens of Jamaica.

On this evening, he enjoyed his journey home on the bus, probably because it was empty due to the late hour. He was humming the strains of Bob Marley's 'No Woman no cry' as he walked down his lane. It had been playing over the radio on the bus and now he can't get it out of his head. But as he approaches his home, he knows that something is wrong. He can see that the front door is ajar, and the house is in darkness.

Jeremiah should be home from school by now. Marshall thinks. *And where is Mom?*

Marshall slows his pace as he gets closer to the house. He tries to listen for any sound from the house but the loud music coming from his neighbour opposite and the loud TV from his neighbour to the right, Maggie, makes it impossible for him to discern any sounds from his house. He looks towards the house opposite.

Damn it, Keshane! Why does he always have to play his music so loud?

He peers through a gap in the drawn curtains in their neighbour Maggie's house. It sounds like the evening sport's report being blared out from her TV.

Why is it so loud?

Immediately, Marshall draws back from his inquisitive glare, as he catches a glimpse of a topless Maggie, in only her panties, playfully running around her living room being pursued by a naked, well-endowed and aroused man, that he doesn't recognise.

I guess Maggie's children are not home this evening.

Marshall smiles briefly before returning to the mystery at hand. He can now see that the lock on the front door has been broken. He stops by the door and listens. After not hearing anything for a few minutes he enters the front door gingerly. He slowly walks through the small living room, unsuccessfully trying the lights, and then passes through the small kitchen. He doesn't find anything, not even dinner on the stove.

What is going on?

He shares a bedroom with Jeremiah, which was added as an extension on the original one-bedroom house. This extension was added to the kitchen. So, Marshall exits the kitchen and steps into his bedroom. The room is in darkness, so he tries to turn on the lights, but they don't work. He reaches into his pocket, pulls out his cell phone and uses it to illuminate the room. He sees Jeremiah sitting at his desk, with his head resting on his books.

De bwoy fall asleep? Him supposed to be studying!

Marshall strides over to the desk and slaps Jeremiah on his back.

"Hey bwoy! What yuh doing sleeping?"

The blow causes Jeremiah to fall to the floor. Confused, Marshall points the light at Jeremiah. He stares at Jeremiah's face, but his brother's eyes are unrecognisable. Then Marshall notices a red line across Jeremiah's neck, and then he understands what is wrong with his brother's eyes. They are lifeless. Marshall drops his phone, cries out and falls to his knees. Marshall is frozen. All he can do is stare at his brother. Then he scrambles across the wooden floor to his brother, in hope. As soon as he touches Jeremiah, he knows there is no hope.

"Mom!?!" Marshall shouts.

He jumps up and stumbles through the kitchen and living room to his mother's bedroom. He tries the lights, but they do not work. He swings his phone into action. The bedroom is a mess with clothes and furniture strewn across it. The bed is dishevelled and then he sees his mother, naked on the bed. Her neck has also been cut, and the bed sheet is covered in blood. Marshall then notices the blood around her crotch and the widespread orientation of her legs. Marshall violently turns and throws up against the wall.

Marshall doesn't know what happened after that. He only becomes aware of what is happening when he is looking up to see Maggie looking down at him on the floor. Her eyes are red, and he can feel the tears dripping on his face. She hugs him tightly, and then Marshall can hear the hurried footsteps and excited voices throughout the house. In his dazed state, Marshall tries to look around and strangely feels some relief.

O good. They fixed the lights!

* * *

One year later, Marshall receives a visit from two police officers at the Office of the Prime Minister.

"Mr. Monroe. Can we speak with you please?" Says the officer standing in front of Marshall's desk. Everyone in the office is looking over at these two persons in suits.

"What is this about?" Marshall asks.

"I think you would prefer to discuss this in private, sir." Says the taller and thinner of the two.

Marshall looks around the office of technocrats. He shares

the spacious office with ten other people, each with large stacks of file folders on their desk.

"Ok. Follow me."

Marshall leads the two men to a room with the label 'meeting room 1' on it. He turns on the light and closes the door behind the men. Marshall invites them to sit around a meeting table for six with padded chairs around it.

"Can I get you gentlemen anything to drink." Marshall asks, as he walks over to the small fridge in the corner of the room. There is a tray of glasses on a table beside the fridge.

"Just water." Says the shorter, darker man. The taller man simply nods.

Marshall pours two glasses of water, gives them to the men and sits opposite them. "How can I help you gentlemen?"

After gulping down the water, the taller officer addresses Marshall, "We found the men who killed your mother and brother." He says matter-of-factly.

"Really! That's wonderful. I will finally see justice." Marshall says, wringing his hands.

"Well, justice was already meted out." Says the shorter officer.

"Really? I don't understand."

"We found them dead."

Marshall bows his head and is silent for a few moments, "I won't pretend that I am sorry." He says, raising his head and holding a steady gaze with the officers.

The two officers exchange a glance.

"Aren't you interested to know how many there were? How they died? Where we found them?" The tall officer asks.

Marshall thinks for moment. "Not really. It makes no material difference to me."

This time the officers huddle and whisper to each other. "We think that for completeness we should give you a full report of what we have found in our investigation." The officers observe Marshall as he processes this statement.

Marshall bows his head again. "As you wish." He says eventually.

The officers look at each other again.

The taller officer gets up from the table. "I think better when I walk around." He says.

Marshall nods.

The taller officer begins, "We found the bodies along the Port Royal main road, on the beach. There were five young men. Their throats were cut, and they were castrated." He stops pacing and looks at Marshall.

Marshall smirks. Both officers look at each other.

"Mr. Monroe. Are you smiling?" The short officer asks.

"Am I?" Marshall shakes his head. "I was just thinking that karma is a bitch."

The officers exchange another glance.

"It seems that your brother stood up for a boy at school who was being bullied by the younger brother of two of the dead men. The word is that your brother gave the bully a real beating. Your brother's killing was retaliation."

"And my mother?"

There is silence for a moment, "A crime of opportunity." The officers say solemnly and quietly.

Marshall lets out a sob and then composes himself. He looks at the two officers. "Thank you for letting me know. Is there anything else?"

"Aren't you going to ask who killed the men?"

Marshall shakes his head, "As I said, karma is a bitch."

The officers look at each other, "The thing is, we don't know who killed these men. Do you?" The shorter officer asks.

Marshall maintains a steady gaze with the officers, "No. And I don't care. They got what they deserve. Maybe there is a God after all."

The officers hold Marshall's gaze. "We do hope you have nothing to do with these murders, Mr. Monroe."

Marshall gets up from the table, "Once again, I'd like to thank you gentlemen for informing me. I really do appreciate it. If there is nothing further, I need to get back to work."

The two officers rise from their seats. "We will be watching you, Mr. Monroe. We now have five murders to solve instead of two, and we are good at what we do." The taller officer says. "You take care of yourself." The officers leave.

Throughout the rest of the day Marshall is unable to concentrate on his work, and over the next week it is noticeable that he is being monitored by the police officers. The monitoring is relentless and obvious.

How am I going to stop these people from harassing me?

The following month, Marshall goes to the National Stadium to watch Jamaica play a Concacaf Nations League football match against Mexico. The pre-match buildup includes a helicopter fly-by of the Jamaica Defence Force Air Wing and then the playing of the National Anthem by the Military Band. Then it hits Marshall.

The next day, Marshall signs up to join the Jamaica Defence Force.

CHAPTER 38 – Don Gorgon
Ten years ago

Lieutenant Jones strolls into the temporary command centre that has been setup on the adjacent road from the crime scene. He sees two tall, slender Jamaica Constabulary Force officers, in their dark blue field gear, standing around a table covered in maps.

"Gentlemen. I'm Lieutenant Jones from second battalion, JDF Regiment, special operations." Jones shakes the hands of the two officers.

"Hi. I'm Deputy Superintendent Smith, and this is Inspector Stephens of the Narcotics Division."

"Speak to me." Says Jones.

DS Smith responds, "Thanks for your prompt response. Two of our detectives were following up on a lead in connection with some homicides in the area. It seems they stumbled on to a drug house. My officers and some civilians have been taken hostage in the house. There was some gunfire and there are two casualties, one civilian and one of my officers. High Command does not want a blood bath or massive property damage. They suggested we work with you on a more precise extraction."

Jones nods his head and looks at the grim expressions on the JCF officers' faces, "We are the tip of the spear." He says looking down at the map. "Thank you for withdrawing your vehicles, as we requested. It helps to reduce the tension and gives us more latitude in our operations. We want them to think the officers were alone. What do we know about inside?"

"We believe there are five suspects in the house. Also, five hostages and our two officers." Inspector Stephens responds.

"And the layout of that house is similar to this one?"

"Yes."

"Ok. Give me a second." Jones picks up a map, walks outside to a heavily tinted, military green, Toyota Land Cruiser. He climbs in the vehicle. "This one is messy." He hands Marshall the map.

Marshall takes the map and analyses the layout of the house.

"What do you think, Sarge?" Jones asks Marshall.

Marshall rubs his chin, "Lieutenant, I don't see a stealth entry as an option." Marshall peers into Jones' eyes.

"Don Gorgon?" Jones asks.

Marshall nods.

Jones shakes his head. "Are you sure about this? You may not walk out of this one if it goes wrong?"

"Do we have a better option?" Marshall asks. "We may end up with two dead officers and five dead civilians if the hostiles decide they have no escape route."

Jones nods.

"Do we know whose crew this is?" Marshall asks.

"Corporal?" Jones says to the driver of the Land Cruiser.

"We're checking that now. We should have news soon." The corporal says. "Hold on, something coming through now. Looks like it is the Medina cartel in Columbia. Word is this is a trans-shipment point not a cookhouse. We should be able to make a shadow call to get you inside. A shipment should have landed in Miami yesterday, and it didn't arrive. We can piggyback on that. There was a call this morning, and we can expand on that."

Marshall nods, "Send me the transcript."

"Roger that."

Thirty minutes later, after reading the transcript of the call, Marshall picks up the satellite phone and dials.

"Who dis?" Marshall hears over the phone.

"Who dis? Who the bomboclawt is this?" Marshall says.

"Dis is Peanuts."

"Peanuts, where is Saw?" Marshall asks.

"Him in the other room."

"Put him on the phone." Marshall says.

"Hold on. Saw! Saw! Someone want talk to you."

"Who dat?" Saw asks.

"Me nuh know." Peanuts says.

"So how you a call me fi talk?" Marshall hears some muffled sounds and then, "Who dis?"

"What the hell happened to the shipment?" Marshall asks.

"What? Who dis?" Saw asks.

"Saw. You supposed to ask me for a codename. It doesn't matter who you are talking to. If I tell you who this is I will have to kill you. Do you understand that?"

"What? Who the fuck is this?" Saw says defiantly.

"I'm going to ask you one more time. Listen carefully. The codename is bird-watch, so you know this call is legitimate. Now, what happened to the shipment yesterday and why hasn't it been sent today?" Marshall says slowly and firmly.

"And I asked, who the fuck is this? Who do you think you are talking to?" Saw shouts.

Marshall sighs, "Saw. Are you sure you want me to tell you who this is? I am enroute and will be there within the hour."

"You damn right I want to know who I'm talking to. I don't recognise this number or your voice."

"This is Don Gorgon." Marshall says quietly.

"What?" Saw whispers. "Me did hear seh you was dead."

"Rumours." Marshall says matter-of-factly. "I'm going to be there within the hour. You better be able to tell me what the bloodclawt is going on."

"Yes, yes, sir Gorgon."

Marshall hangs up and looks at Jones. "All set Lieutenant. You better go and keep our JCF friends calm and at arm's length."

Jones nods and jumps out of the Land Cruiser.

"Corporal, let's go and get ready." Marshall says to the driver.

"Roger that." The Corporal says as he starts the car.

* * *

An hour later, a black BMW with heavily tinted windows cruises up to the drug house. Marshall and the Corporal, dressed in full black, with black baseball caps and dark glasses, get out of the car and stroll casually, past four Mercedes and a Porche parked in the driveway, up to the front door. Marshall knocks on the door. The front door opens, and a rotund, brown skin young man opens the door.

Marshall speaks before the young man, "Peanuts?"

The young man hesitates. His expression is one of surprise. "Yes."

"I called earlier. Saw is expecting me."

Peanuts steps back and holds the door open. Marshall steps inside.

Marshall points to the Corporal, "He's with me."

Marshall keeps on his dark glasses so he can scan the layout without anyone noticing his eyes. The house is a simple three-bedroom house with a living, dining and kitchen open plan, with the three bedrooms leading off this open plan to the left.

Marshall can see that the civilian hostages are huddled in the rear bedroom with a man, with a gun on his hip, sitting on a chair by the door. The injured officer and civilian are sitting on the floor in the dining room, right outside the bathroom and the middle bedroom. And to the rear, beyond the rear bedroom, Marshall can see a number of green duffle bags, maybe ten, sitting in what looks like a washroom at the rear of the house.

Two men are sitting at the dining table playing cards. Some dirty plates have been pushed to the edge of the table to make space for the cards. Their guns are lying on the table. Out of the corner of his eye, Marshall sees movement and a large, athletic, dark man approaches him from the front bedroom.

"Don Gorgon. Me sorry fi disrepek yuh earlier." Saw says as he approaches.

Marshall waits until Saw is right in front of him, facing him. "Saw, what did I tell you when you asked me who was on the phone?"

"Ahhmm," Saw rubs his chin, "Me no remember." Saw doesn't look at Marshall.

Marshall whips a 6-inch black carbon steel Commando knife out of its sheath on his waist, and puts it under Saw's chin before Saw is able to blink. Marshall looks around the house at each of Saw's men. The men are frozen in shock as they watch Marshall's knife at Saw's neck.

"I said I would kill you if I had to tell you who I was. Do you remember now?"

Saw's eyes are wide open, and he tries to take a step back.

"No, no. What yuh doing? If you step back, I will push this through to the back of your neck. Yuh hear?" Marshall says firmly.

Saw takes another step back.

"Saw. Did you hear me?" Marshall asks.

Saw takes another step back.

Marshall moves quickly, taking two steps towards Saw. He thrusts his knife into his throat. Saw's eyes get wider as the knife is plunged into his throat. Marshall pushes the knife into Saw's larynx and then slides the knife across Saw's jugular vein. Saw's hands clutch his neck, trying to stop the flow of blood from his neck and hold his neck together.

The men at the dining table reach for their guns. Marshall pulls his gun from his waist holster. He shoots both men centre mass in their chests with two shots each. Corporal shoots Peanuts in the head.

The man sitting by the bedroom where the hostages are being held grabs the nearest hostage who is a young woman in a pair of jeans and a red polo shirt, with a UHWI logo on the chest. He stands up with woman and points the gun at her temple.

"Me will shot her! Me will shot her!" The man screams as he wraps his free arm around her neck. The woman is sobbing quietly.

Marshall slowly walks towards the man.

"Me will shot her!"

"You know who I am?"

"Me will shot her!"

Marshall stops and calmly stares at the man.

"Me will shot her!"

"What's your name?" Marshall asks calmly. He is careful to slowly drop his arms by his side. Marshall hides his gun behind his leg.

"Me name Clemont." The man says. His hand that is holding the gun is shaking.

"Clemont. Do you know who I am?"

Clemont nods his head slowly, "You is de Don Gorgon."

"I'm glad you know that. So, what you think will happen if you kill that woman?"

Clemont stares at Marshall, then looks at the woman, and then stares at Marshall. His eyes then drift around the house, looking at all his comrades who are now dead. His eyes rest on Saw, who has bled out on the living room floor. Slowly, his grip on the woman loosens until she pulls away and runs towards Marshall. Suddenly, realising that the woman is no longer in his grasp, Clemont raises his gun. Marshall shoots him in the head twice.

"Corporal, secure the location." Marshall says calmly. The Corporal hurries around the house checking all the doors and the rooms.

Marshall makes his way over to the injured police officer and civilian, after seating the woman in the red polo shirt in the sofa in the living room.

"How are you both?" Marshall is surprised when he gets close to the officer. It is one of the officers who had visited him at the Office of the Prime Minister five years earlier.

"We are ok." Says the civilian, a middle-aged man with greying temples. "I'm a doctor and they allowed me to treat both wounds. They are through and through wounds."

"Wait?" Says the officer. "Aren't you Mr. Monroe?" He asks wearily. "I never forget a face."

Marshall kneels beside the officer, "Isn't karma a bitch?" he whispers in the officer's ear. Marshall takes a step back and smiles at the officer. The officer returns a faint smile and nods at Marshall.

Marshall gets up and heads for the front door, "Corporal, call the lieutenant and wind this up."

CHAPTER 39 – I Want To Go Home
In the present

Silence. Even the children are quiet. Occasionally, the clink of cutlery against crockery disturbs the uneasy noiselessness. Jenny touches Kenneth's arm and points to the orange juice carton. He reaches over and gives it to her. Everyone watches as the orange liquid swirls into Jenny's glass, the morning sunshine bouncing off its undulating surface. Andy drops his fork. It clatters across the ceramic tiles. Everyone jumps. Lisa glares at Andy, and he starts to sniffle.

"Why are you crying?" Jackie asks.

"I'm not crying." Andy hurriedly wipes away a tear running down his cheek.

"Yes you are. You're a real crybaby." Jackie says.

"No I'm not."

"So why are you crying?"

"I'm not."

"Lawd give me strent! Stop it!" Jenny shouts. She slams her glass down on the table. Everyone suddenly sits up. "Dis is madness! Is what a gwaan? Is what we pussyfooting round fah?" Jenny points at Marshall, and slaps Kenneth on the arm. "Man up!"

Kenneth rubs his arm, "But …"

"Man up! Yu hear me!"

"But …"

"Now!"

Kenneth looks across the table at Marshall. They hold eye

contact for a few moments and then Kenneth nods his head slightly, pursing his lips. Marshall nods his head curtly.

"Good. That's that. Kids, go watch TV, we adults need to talk." Jenny says firmly.

"Last one to the living room is a rotten apple!" Jason shouts as he runs out of the kitchen. Jackie and Andy race after him.

"Hey, that means you too mister." Jenny points towards the door with her lips.

"Aw! Can't I stay? I'm almost a teenager." Kenny pines. Jenny glares at him. Kenny slowly pushes himself away from the table and reluctantly stands up. He looks pleadingly over at his father. Kenneth shrugs his shoulders and nods towards the door. Kenny shakes his head, his chin drops to his chest and he makes his way towards the door with his shoulders slumped.

"Kenny." Jenny calls.

"Yes." Kenny spins around, his eyes wide in expectancy, his posture suddenly erect.

"Close the door when you go out."

"Yes Mom." Kenny says with a large sigh, and with slumped shoulders exits the dining room. The glass door slowly clicks shut.

Jenny glares around the table. "I want to go home. How do we make that happen?" No one speaks. "Well? Someone must have a thought."

"Sweetheart ... Marshall has a point. Is it safe?" Kenneth says softly, haltingly.

"I've been thinking about that." Marshall quickly interjects. Everyone looks at him in surprise. Marshall rubs his chin thoughtfully, "Maybe we can call Jay? He should be back from England by now. He can tell us what the climate is like and do some sniffing around for us. They may not have made any links between him and us, since he was away, so it should ok." Marshall looks inquiringly around the table. Everyone nods enthusiastically. Kenneth picks up the cell phone and dials. "Hey Jay! How you doing? How was your trip?"

"Jesus Christ, Kenneth! I've been calling all over the place trying to find you! Why haven't you been answering your phone? Where the hell are you?"

"We are still in Florida. We haven't been able to get to the bottom of our problems in JA, and the things got worse with Kenny being kidnapped."

"What?!?" Jay exclaims.

"We got him back safely, thank God. I'll tell you all about it when we see you. Right now, we want to come home, but we don't know if it is safe to do so. Do you have a sense of what is happening down there?

"Well, I'm glad you called, because there are some serious problems down here."

"Oh? Wha'ppen?"

"There was a fire at your house last night!"

CHAPTER 40 – I Don't Want To Go

Kenneth sits looking straight ahead. A taxi swerves violently in front of the Navigator and screeches to a halt. The back door flies open, a pencil thin man in a grey suit and wire rimmed glasses jumps out of the car with a briefcase and suit bag, and sprints towards the glass double doors, leaving the taxi door open.

"What are we doing?"

Kenneth looks over at Jenny. The windscreen wipers screech their way across the drying windscreen.

"It's for the best. We discussed this already."

"But I don't want to go."

The windscreen wipers screech again.

"It will relieve the pressure. The kids will have a great time."

"It doesn't feel right for us to be enjoying ourselves at Disney while you guys are working."

The windscreen wipers groan.

"I explained this to you already. Please Jenny. Don't make this any harder than it is. I need you to be strong. I need your strength."

Jenny sits silently for a moment, "I'm scared Kenneth."

"I know sweetheart. So am I."

"I don't want to leave you."

"I need to know that you and the kids are safe." The windscreen wipers squeal across the windscreen. Kenneth reaches forward and flips the lever to turn them off. "You need to go now so I can go and park."

"Why is Marshall coming with us?" Jenny asks.

Kenneth takes a deep breath, "He's not."

"But he also has a bag packed, and I heard him telling Kathy goodbye when we were leaving the house."

Kenneth sighs, "He's going back home."

"Oh! Why?"

Kenneth looks away. A blonde-haired boy pulls away from a woman, and with a vacuous smile on his face runs along the pavement. He is only able to run a few yards before crashing into a large suitcase being pulled along by a woman dressed in a floral print dress and an incongruous sun hat. A perplexed expression on the boy's face is quickly supplanted as his mouth distends to give everyone full view of his teeth and tonsils. The woman, probably his mother, quickly arrives at his side and a small crowd, including the floral dress clad woman engulfs the child, obscuring Kenneth's view.

"Kenneth?"

Kenneth looks at Jenny, but he can't maintain eye contact with her.

"No! No, Kenneth."

"We need all the help we can get." Kenneth says sheepishly. In the background, Randy Crawford cries out the refrain of 'Knockin' on Heaven's Door' on the radio.

"How much did you give him?"

"Fifty thousand."

"Jamaican dollars?"

"No."

"US dollars? Kenneth! We don't need this type of help. Not this way."

"I, we, can't do this alone. Marshall knows the streets better than any of us. And I trust him."

"Kenneth."

"I do. I trust him." Kenneth reassures Jenny.

Kenneth reaches out and pulls Jenny towards him and hugs her tightly. He feels her tears running down his neck as he holds her. They hold each other for a few minutes, until there is a sharp, loud rap on Jenny's window that makes them both jump. A police officer peers in through the window and gestures with his thumb. Kenneth kisses Jenny on the cheek. Jenny wipes her eyes with the back of her hand, opens the door and steps out onto the pavement.

"I'll park and meet you at the check-in desk." Kenneth says. Jenny slams the door and turns towards the terminal.

* * *

Kenneth, Eric and Kathy wave as Mr. and Mrs. Martin, Janet, Jenny, Lisa, Kenny, Jackie, Jason and Andy disappear through the security checkpoint and head towards their gate. They stand, watching. It is several minutes and several hundred people later, before any of them speak.

"Have we done the right thing?" Eric asks quietly.

Kenneth turns to him, "I hope so."

"And Marshall?"

Kenneth sighs, "I pray so."

CHAPTER 41 – Ital Soup

Marshall waits patiently. He sips his Red Stripe and looks at his watch. Twelve forty-five. He thinks about taking another sip but decides to put the bottle down. It's his second beer, and he needs to keep his mind clear and sharp. From his position at the back of the room, Marshall carefully observes each person sitting in 'Debbie's Soup Kitchen'. Everyone seems to be genuinely enjoying his or her lunch. No one is taking any notice of Marshall. Debbie saunters over to Marshall.

"Yuh ready fi order now?"

"Yuh 'ave any ital soup?"

"Only de pepper pot."

"Dat mean seh no pig tail in it, right?"

"Is what yuh ask fah? No ital soup."

"Yes. Sorry. Me will 'ave a bowl of de pepper pot."

As Debbie leaves, an athletic woman, dressed in a black skirt and white blouse, sits down.

"You're late."

"The traffic was terrible. I thought you were dead."

"Yeah? Where did you hear that?"

"Rumours."

Debbie comes by with a large bowl and places it in front of Marshall. She looks at the woman. 'Is what yuh want?'

"I'll have a red peas soup and a diet coke."

Debbie turns lethargically and makes her way slowly across the wooden floor of the gully-side restaurant. They do not speak until Debbie brings the second bowl of soup, a glass of ice and a can of diet coke. As they eat their soup, Marshall explains what he wants in hushed tones. Marshall keeps his eyes up, surveying the room as he speaks, occasionally fanning away a fly.

"You realize that if we're caught, they won't find our bodies."

Marshall nods slowly and puts a clump of dumpling in his mouth. He washes it down after a few chews with a swig of beer. "So, we don't get caught."

"How much?"

"I thought an opportunity for revenge would be reward enough."

"The medical care and funeral costs wiped me out. I still need to eat."

"How much you want?"

"Twenty thousand."

"Wait! Is how much yuh a eat so? Yuh a nyam! Five thousand."

"Fifteen."

"Seven five."

"Twelve thousand five."

"Seven five."

"Ten thousand."

"Seven five."

The woman pauses looking Marshall in the eye. "We talking 'bout green backs, right?"

Marshall nods curtly. She sits back in her chair, folds her arms and nods, with a satisfied look on her face. "How do I get paid?"

Marshall takes a brown envelope out of his pocket and slides it across the table. The envelope is neatly folded and sealed.

Marshall sits back and folds his arms across his chest. The woman quickly picks up the envelope and slips it into her handbag. Her expression is one of irritation.

"How do I contact you?"

"There's a number in the envelope. Use that."

"Yuh sure of yuhself."

Marshall shrugs, "When?"

"A day, maybe two."

"Good. I'll wait for your call." Marshall takes out four five hundred Jamaican dollar notes and drops them on the table as he gets up. "Lunch is on me." He pauses before leaving and bends to whisper in his lunch guest's ear. "Before you think about betraying me, remember how your brother suffered. And who was responsible for his suffering." He walks away without looking back.

CHAPTER 42 – Rae Town

'It wasn't me.' Shaggy sings through the 15-foot speakers. Marshall walks past a speaker and his heart seems to adopt the same beat as the bass rhythm coming from the speaker tower, which initially disorientates Marshall. He pauses to get used to the feeling. It has been a few years since Marshall had been to a street dance, and he had forgotten how loud and intense the sound is.

"Rae Town! Give it up for Stone Love!" Selector Craven shouts into the microphone. The thousand strong crowd roars. Hundreds of uptown people flood to Rae Town every Sunday night for the weekly street dance, but tonight there are possibly thousands because of the presence of the Stone Love sound system. Craven continues to spin some new tunes, mixing in original dub rhythms that makes the crowd roar with delight. Marshall stops by an old lady, with strong features and dark eyes, sitting on a stool beside a large steaming pot sitting over a small coal fire.

"Mother, what you have?" Marshall asks.

"Caaan soup."

Marshall nods his head, and the old woman, her head wrapped with a calico cloth, prepares a cup of corn soup for Marshall. The wooden door behind her creaks as a younger woman steps out in skintight jeans and a glittering gold halter-top. Until the door opened, Marshall has noticed the wooden shack, with its corrugated zinc roof and louvered windows. Marshall estimates that there couldn't be more than two or three rooms within the walls of the shack. The younger woman pauses and looks over Marshall from head to toe, and back again, and then steps past the old lady, who Marshall surmises must be her mother, or more likely her grandmother, based on the strong resemblance and strong features they shared.

"Is what time yuh a come back?"

"Me no know Mamma. When tings done." The younger woman pauses and turns to the old lady.

"Memba yuh 'ave wok a marrow. Yuh nuh fi tek de massa wok fi granted."

"No worries Mamma. Me will be back early." A broad smile flashes across the younger woman's face, revealing a gold tooth, "Marci! Gal, is wha you a wear!" And she runs off to hug a heavy breasted woman, wearing what looked like a painted on full body suit to Marshall.

Marshall strolls around, soaking up the atmosphere and taking deep breaths of the sea air, pan chicken and roast corn. He sips on his cup of corn soup surveying the crowd. A very sexy woman with shoulder length bleached hair in a silver 'batty rider' and sheer halter-top blouse stops in front of Marshall and dances a dub with him.

"Look me up anytime sweetness. During the week you can find me at Lee's Fifth Avenue, in the underwear section. Anytime up to 5pm." She blows him a kiss and slithers away.

Marshall buys a Dragon stout and decides to take a seat on the knee-high sea wall. He waits patiently, scanning the crowd. A Rastafarian, with a plate of food in hand, stops a few yards from Marshall to talk with someone he apparently knows. Marshall watches as he skilfully simultaneously talks and shoves rice into his mouth. Then the rastafarian pauses and picks up a piece of jerk pork and starts stripping the meat off the bone.

Humph! Is one rent-a-dread! Marshall thinks.

The dread throws the stripped bone on the ground, sparking a fight between two mongrel dogs. The fight continues until it disrupts the rastafarian's discussion.

"Is wha' do yuh dawg?" The rastafarian kicks out at the dog nearest to him, catching the dog on the hind leg, causing the dog to run off yelping with a limp. The other dog retreats behind a sky juice cart and settles down to eat the bone.

Marshall takes another swig from his Dragon and slowly walks towards his bare-chested target. Marshall casually leans against the speaker and takes another swig from his stout.

"You Johnny Thomas?" Marshall says, just loud enough for Johnny to hear above the music. Thankfully, legendary selector Wee-Pow has taken over from Craven, and is now spinning R&B oldies. Marshall's ears have thankfully stopped ringing.

"Who wants to know?" Johnny asks.

"A friend. A friend who has a business proposal for you, and a chance for some revenge for those." Marshall gestures towards two keloid circular scars in Johnny's right shoulder.

"Revenge? Yuh mad! Yuh know is who do dis?"

"Yup."

"Me was lucky fi get wey wid mi life. Dat is enough for me."

"Oh? And what about Pringle? You just gwine forget 'bout him?"

"How yuh know 'bout Pringle?"

"Nuh worry 'bout that."

Johnny looks around and steps behind the speaker boxes. Marshall follows him. "Is who yuh? Is wha' yuh really want?"

"As I said, I am here to offer you a business opportunity, and to sweeten the pot, I am also offering a chance to get back your own for Pringle."

"Wha' kinda business? Me not into nothin' illegal, yuh know. Me done wid dat now. It nearly kill me, and is dat kill Pringle."

"Dat is not what killed Pringle. It was betrayal and greed that killed Pringle, and dat nuh right. Justice demands that someone pays for that."

"Humph! Justice! Is wha' dat? We ghetto people no get no justice. Dat is fah de rich uptown people. Dat is not fi we."

"So you saying you not interested?"

"Will it cost me anything to listen?"

"You still work at Caymanas?"

"Yeah. Only day I not at the racetrack is Sunday."

"I need some Ketamine."

"You mad! Dat stuff is always under lock and key. The vets guard it closely."

"I'm sure you can find a way, and you will get paid."

"How much?"

"Not so fast. You in or out?"

Johnny thinks about it for a while. "Yup. I'm in. How much?"

"Two bills. Green backs."

Johnny's expression does not change. He eyes Marshall for a moment. "What's in this for you?"

"Revenge."

Johnny thinks about it and a sneer slowly creeps across his face. "How much is a dish served cold worth to you?"

Marshall doesn't respond.

"Me figure it worth more than two large ones." Johnny studies Marshall. "Me seh it worth at least ten bills."

Marshall doesn't say a word. He takes a final swig from his Dragon, puts down the empty bottle and starts to walk away. "It was nice doing business with you."

"Wait. Where mi money?"

"What money? I gave you a price and you didn't accept it. So, we have no deal. I'm sure I can find someone else to do this for me."

"Wait! No. Ok, ok. Let's talk."

"What is there to talk about?"

"Come on. Nuh do me so."

"I told you my price."

"Ok. Say yuh give me five bills. Me have two baby mother, and dem waan fi send de pickney dem a prep school."

Marshall rubs his chin. "For five bills, I need you to also make a call for me."

"A call? To who? Bout what?"

Marshall explains.

"What?!? Yuh mad?!?"

"Five large ones if you make the call, otherwise, two."

"Come on. Why yuh chuck it so?"

Marshall turns and starts walking away.

"Ok. Ok. I'll make the call."

Marshall lifts his shirt and pulls a brown envelope from his out of his waist. "The instructions for the phone call are in there." Marshall steps closer to Johnny and whispers in his ear, "I would advise you not to talk to anyone about this. The next scar will probably be between your eyes, and that one won't heal."

CHAPTER 43 – Six Love

Marshall slams four dominoes on the table, "Bow! Six love!"

The other dominoes jump, and Marshall and his partner exchange a high five. The recriminations start between the other pair as they discuss who had played poorly to allow this to happen.

"Pardy, is wha' kinda shot dat yuh did play? How you can go push blank back to him? Yuh nuh see sey me beat blank."

"Is either me give him de double blank, or me release de double six."

"So you never have nuh deuce?"

"No P."

The beaten pair rise, "What you guys drinking?"

"Whites and milk." Marshall says. Marshall's partner asks for a rum and coke.

"Jerk chicken and festival also?"

"Yeah man." The opponents leave the table to get the drinks and food.

"What you doing with yourself since you left the Office of the Prime Minister?" Marshall's partner asks.

"This and that. Trying to stay out of trouble." Marshall says. "I hear you worked on the new cellular network, as one of the senior statesmen of the telephone company."

"Yeah, they had sent us on six weeks training in Miami on this new system. Pretty archaic if you ask me. The technology out of Europe is better."

"Enjoying it?"

"I guess. Pay still sucks. A lot of guys have been leaving over the last two years, going into the IT companies. The pay is much better, although you lose a lot of freedom, as it is not as easy to do roasts."

"You still doing dem tings?"

"Of course. How else can I afford to go on vacation to the US each summer? Need to earn the airfare and pocket money for the family."

"Ha." Marshall leans across the table, and says in a hushed tone, "Tell me something?"

"Sure, what?"

"Are the cellular phones as easy to tap as the landlines?"

"Easier. It's amazing. That's why I said the system was archaic. I know that there are more secure systems around, but the one we are implementing now isn't very secure."

"You can also block calls?"

"No problem."

"So, if I need you to tap a number for me, could you do it?"

"Sure. Who is it? Some old flame you trying to keep tabs on?"

"No." Marshall indicates that his partner should lean closer. Marshall whispers in his ear.

"What? Are you crazy!"

"Shh. You don't want to attract attention to yourself over this."

"I can't do that."

"What if I made it worth your while? Pay for your vacation."

"How much?"

"Five large ones."

"That's not worth my while."

"Green backs."

"Whoa!" His partner sits back in his chair. "It means that much to you?"

Marshall nods. "No questions asked. No trace left behind."

"Deal."

Marshall takes a brown envelope from his back pocket and slides it across the table. He looks around the room at Jerry's Jerk Centre, "Where's the food?" Marshall calls.

CHAPTER 44 – Indisputable and Irrefutable

George Albert bites into his patty and swallows a mouthful of cream soda. A blob of hot meat escapes from the patty and drops onto his thumb, causing him to swear and quickly suck the meat off his burning thumb. In between bites, he watches as the workmen empty the truck of the sand, and he feels a wave a pride as he surveys all before him. The foundation of the house is now almost complete. He is beginning to make sense of the chaos that has concerned him for so long. It has taken months, and a few hundred thousand dollars to blast the rock and clear the land so they can begin building. It has also taken the architect months to complete the design of his new house, and for the plans to be approved so that the contractor can start work. He had hoped to have finished the house by now, but they are now months behind schedule and way over budget. He chuckles to himself.

Who cares about budgets when you have such a steady flow of money coming in. He chastises himself. *Need to be frugal. No point in wasting the money.*

He turns and looks out on the scenery below. To his left, he enjoys the green, rolling Warieka Hills, and on his right he watches the sun bounce off the numerous red and white roofs of the houses in the flat expanse of Portmore and Caymanas Estates. In between these two landscape contrasts are the skyscrapers in New Kingston, beyond them the landmark Bank of Jamaica and Scotia Centre buildings on the Kingston waterfront, and in the distance the Norman Manley airport leading out to the shimmering blue Caribbean sea.

Beautiful!

All this hard work has been worth it. He can move his

mother and girlfriend into the house when it is finished. They will be safe here, with a state-of-the-art security system planned. Although who is going to be bold enough to touch the house of Busha George? He chuckles again, but his smile disappears when his cell phone rings. Slightly agitated that anyone would call him during his lunch hour, Busha George takes his phone out of his pocket.

"Speak."

"Mr. Albert?"

"Yes. Who is this?"

"This is Ms. Brown calling from the Inland Revenue Department."

Busha George almost chokes on his patty. He starts coughing and spluttering.

"Mr. Albert? Are you ok?"

Busha George takes a quick sip of his cream soda. "Yes, yes. I'm ok." He coughs again. "How can I help you?"

"We would like to speak with you at your earliest convenience."

"Oh? What about?"

"You have been selected for a tax audit."

"What?" Busha whispers. He sits down on a rock beside him.

"Yes, we periodically do audits of people who work in government service, and your name came up."

"Why?"

"To be honest, I'm not sure of all the details. What I do know is that an account that is somehow linked to you came to our attention and it was red flagged. A preliminary investigation raised some questions in our compliance department, and it was sent over to us."

"What?"

"When can we meet? I'm sure it is just a misunderstanding that we can easily clear it up, but we need to go through the formality. I'm sorry for the inconvenience."

"What?"

"I'm sure it won't take long. Can we meet next week?"

"Ahh … can it wait until the following week? I'm working on a case now that I expect should be closed by then and that should free up some time."

"Certainly. It can wait until then. Should I call your office to finalize?"

"Yes, please do that."

"Great. We'll see you then. Sorry for the inconvenience."

The line goes dead.

* * *

Ms. Brown relaxes in her chair and takes a deep breath. She looks around the office nervously as she picks up the card lying on her desk. She surreptitiously pulls a cellular phone from her desk and dials the number that she reads from the card.

"Hello."

"It's done." She says into the receiver.

"Ok. Thanks."

Marshall hangs up and smiles.

* * *

After hanging up, Busha George sits with the phone to his ear for a few seconds.

Jesus Christ! Bomboclawt! A tax audit! How the hell did this happen! There is no way I can justify this house on my income. Fuck! What am I going to do? Jesus Christ? Dem a go tek wey mi money! What am I going to do?

Busha George absentmindedly watches the activities around him. The sand truck is now empty and starts to make its way down the makeshift driveway that has been made to allow the trucks to enter his lot of land. Some of the sand is already being shoveled into a cement mixer, as masonry work continues on the foundation of the house. An idea occurs to Busha George. He unlocks his phone and dials.

"Hello."

"I have a problem." Busha George relates his last conversation.

"Stupid! Hoe kon jy toelaat dat dit gebeur?"

"What?"

"Sorry. How could you let this happen?"

"I did exactly as you said. I don't know how this happened."

"So, what do you want me to do?"

"We need to get all the diamonds out now, in the next week, and I need to move my money also."

"That will be risky. A single courier cannot carry everything that is left to come up."

"I'll travel too. I can make the arrangements to move the balance. It will also give me an opportunity to move my money. I need your help to hide the transactions."

"You can get that much through security?"

"Do you know who you are talking to?"

"Ok. I'll set it up. I'll let you know which flight to book on." The line goes dead.

* * *

Eric looks at the screen and nods his head. A smile forms across his face.

"What?" Kenneth asks. "Did it work?"

"Oh yeah!"

"Ok. I'll catch the next flight back home. You sure you don't need me here?" Kenneth asks.

"You set up the meet?"

"Yes."

"Then I'm good."

"And you're sure you have to stay here?"

"Probably. The firewall traversal will be easier from here than there. More red flags are likely to popup from an IP address is Jamaica, which means I then need to use a VPN to mask my IP, which should work, but that is one less thing I need to worry about when I am here. I'll catch a flight as soon as I'm finished."

"Ok. See you then." Kenneth picks up his bag and heads out the door.

* * *

"Do you know what you are asking me to do?" Her eyes are steady, her hair neatly gathered in a tight bun, her unpolished nails perfectly manicured, her clothes immaculately arranged, not a wrinkle to be seen. Her dark uniform contrasts with the gold eagle, anchor and musket insignia, that she proudly wears on her chest.

"Yes." Eric says matter-of-factly.

"We would all go to Leavenworth, and they will throw away the keys."

"Yes."

"Are you sure you want to do this?"

Eric matches her gaze. "Kenneth said you could help."

She bows her head and gently fingers the insignia on her jacket. "Commander Johnson asks a lot."

"Major Hernandez. Commander Johnson said your father was one of the best and loyal persons he had served with."

"And you are sure that there is Federal involvement?"

"That's Kenneth's assessment."

She sighs, "How do I contact you?"

Eric scribbles on a pad, tears off the sheet and passes it to her. "Call this number."

She looks at the pad, "Where is this?"

"Best if you don't know." Eric puts a plastic bag on the table. "Use this when you call. Don't use your home or office phone."

She looks in the bag. "And what do you plan to do?"

"The less you know, the better, but rest assured that it is nothing detrimental to National Security. I think Kenneth's track record speaks for itself in that regard."

She nods reflectively.

"Just call when you have followed the instructions I have given you."

She nods again. Eric gets up and leaves.

* * *

"Kenneth. You ask a lot."

Kenneth leans forward. "Yes, I know Mr. Prime Minister."

"I cannot move, unless you provide me with indisputable,

irrefutable evidence."

Kenneth thought about telling the PM that those words are synonyms but thought better of it. "I understand, Mr. Prime Minister.

"I cannot embroil the Office of the Prime Minister, or my government, in any business that appears politically biased or motivated, or if there is any suggestion of impropriety."

"I understand."

"How are you so sure?"

"The GPS data from the plane is irrefutable."

"Explain the plan to me again."

Kenneth opens an executive notepad, "Allow me to do some white boarding."

The Prime Minister of Jamaica leans forward studiously, as Kenneth pulls out a whiteboard pen.

* * *

Eric picks up the vibrating phone.

"Yes."

"We're good to go. Make the call." Kenneth says.

"Ok." Eric hangs up and takes a deep breath.

CHAPTER 45 – It's A Go

Kenneth knocks on the door and waits. Eventually, he hears a yes. He pushes open the door.

"Excuse me sir. You asked to be informed if things were proceeding as I had explained."

"The monitor is up?"

"Yes sir. In the conference room as you requested." Kenneth replies, and hurries back to the conference room. The Prime Minister enters, with the Commanding Officers of the JDF Air Wing and the 2nd Battalion. Kenneth snaps to his feet at attention, and salutes.

"At ease Kenneth. You're not in the service anymore." The Air Wing CO smiles and extends his hand to Kenneth.

"Sorry sir. Habit." Kenneth shakes the hands of the COs and sits down.

"What am I looking at?" The Prime Minister asks as he sits down and looks up at the 80-inch monitor on the wall.

Kenneth reaches over to the conference telephone system, un-mutes the phone, and turns up the volume button. "Eric, can you explain what we are seeing please?"

Eric's voice crackles through the speaker, "We believe the team on the left of the monitor is a foreign extraction team tied to the smugglers. On the right is the JCF Special Squad team led by Busha George. They are both approaching the crash site."

"How far out are they?" The Prime Minister asks.

"The foreign team is about two kilometers away. The Special Squad team is about four kilometers away."

The Prime Minister looks at the Air Wing CO and nods. The CO picks up the second phone on the conference room table. "It's a go."

CHAPTER 46 - LZ

Busha George holds his team for long enough to confirm his suspicions.

Humph! Dem tink seh me a eediat. Dis is my land!

He holds up his hand and signals to his team.

* * *

"Damn!"

The South African pulls out his handkerchief and wipes away the perspiration. The scar still stings when sweat gets into the recesses.

"Come on! Hurry it up! We don't have all day." He shouts at his team. The men stuff the duffel bags efficiently, using a human chain to pass the plastic bags of diamonds from the fuselage to the duffel bag packers a few yards outside in the clearing. Every five minutes, a man inside the fuselage will exit soaked in perspiration. His light green shirt, now dark, and he will be replaced by the next man. It is not long before all the men have their shirts off, hanging them from tree branches, their muscular frames glistening in the sunshine from their exertions. It takes them an hour to pack the six duffel bags.

"Ok men. Fifteen minutes to rehydrate." The South African shouts.

* * *

Busha George holds up his index finger to his men. His men start checking their weapons and hydrating themselves. Busha signals, his men get up slowly, never taking their eyes off their targets. Busha and his men exit the underbrush, and Busha strolls confidently into the clearing, his gun trained on the South African.

The South African chokes on his water. "George! What the fuck are you doing here?"

"Yuh right to be surprised. I could also ask you the same question. What are you doing here?"

"We, we …"

"Cat got your tongue Simon?"

Simon stops and looks at the posture of Busha George and his men. "George. What's going on?"

"I'm wondering the same thing." Busha George gestures towards the duffel bags with his head, "When were you planning to let me know that you moved the diamonds?"

"I tried to call you, but you wouldn't pick up, so I had to make other arrangements."

"Really. It's funny you should say that, because I got an interesting call from an informant, and he predicted that you would be here, and that you would say that. Now how did he know that?"

"George." The South African laughs nervously, "What are you suggesting?"

"Who said I was suggesting anything?"

* * *

"Can you zoom in and confirm the identities?"

"Yes Mr. Prime Minister." Eric says over the loudspeaker.

The screen changes resolution and the next frame shows Busha George sneering at the white man with the keloid scar across his head, who is dressed in army camouflage fatigues.

"Ok. I am satisfied." The Prime Minister looks at the Air Wing CO, "You can give the green light."

The CO picks up the phone, "Green light in sixty seconds."

* * *

"Tell me Simon. How did you expect to get those bags off this mountain without my protection?" Busha asks calmly.

"I was going to call you when we got back to our HQ."

"You know what my informant told me? He said this was your LZ."

"LZ? What the hell are you talking about?"

"Well. I say we wait a few minutes and see if my informant is right or not. What do you say?"

"This is nonsense." The South African starts to move.

"No. No. No.' Busha George raises his gun. "Take a seat Simon and get comfortable. We'll wait here for five minutes."

"But …"

Busha turns to one of his men and says calmly, "Sergeant, if he moves again, shoot one of his men." Busha smiles at Simon, "You know it's funny. I always knew that one day me was going corn you. I just don't know if that day is today."

Simon, the South African slumps back into a sitting position. He surveys his men, and the position of Busha George's men. Their situation is not good, but at least there is no chance of this site becoming a Landing Zone.

Five minutes has almost passed, and Busha George looks at his watch. He is starting to relax. Another minute and they will start to make their way down the mountain. He starts to wander over towards his sergeant when the unmistakable 'chub chub' sound drifts towards the clearing. Simon has a look of shock and terror on his face. Simon's men instinctively scramble in the direction of their weapons.

Simon shouts, "No!"

Busha George shouts at his men, "Kill dem!"

Simon looks Busha George in the eyes, pleading. Busha smiles at him raising his free hand. Simon breathes a sigh of relief and motions to his men to relax. Busha George raises his Glock semi-automatic pistol and shoots Simon between the eyes. The fire fight only lasts seconds. Simon's men are dead after the first volley of bullets from the Special Squad unit.

"Grab the bags!" Busha George shouts.

* * *

"Lay down covering fire as soon as the birds come over the trees." The Air Wing CO says into the phone as he watches the live pictures on the monitor.

The helicopters are greeted by gunfire as they appear over the trees. Their first volley of 50mm bullets kills a quarter of Busha George's team. The next volley of bullets kills another two. Busha George raises his arms high above his head, and his surviving men follow suit.

CHAPTER 47 – Ask Not

Jean Michel Mbozi surveys the eager and hungry faces in front of him. He must focus so that he doesn't smirk or smile or show signs of overconfidence. He takes a deep breath.

"Back in 1961, US President John F Kennedy made a statement to the people of America - 'Ask not, what your country can do for you. Ask what you can do for your country.' At that time, in that place, that was the appropriate rallying call to a people who needed to unite and work together to build a nation. We need to build more than a nation; we need to build a continent. Our continent is the bedrock of civilisation, our continent was once the richest on the planet, our people were once the thought leaders of the world." Mbozi pauses and looks around the conference centre hall, appearing to establish eye contact with as many as he can, as far back in the hall as he can, "But what of today? Our continent is the home to the poorest countries in the world. Death, pestilence, famine and war are synonymous with our continent, and our people are denied the simple right," he pauses again and scans the room. He leans forward, closer to the microphone, and everyone in the room leans forward, and Jean Michel has to catch himself again, to avoid a smile from slipping out. Speaking softly, he adds, "the simple right of opportunity."

Applause starts to break out throughout the hall, but Mbozi raises a hand, and the applause dies down. With a stern countenance, he allows his voice to return to its normal tone.

"My compatriots, I say to you today that this must change," he thumps the podium, "and it will not change by our people asking what they can do for their country, but by their leaders ushering in a new era of vision, partnership and integrity. An integrity that demands that our people must be seated at the table first, before their leaders; that our people must eat and drink first, before their leaders; that our people must reap the fruit of their land and their labour, before their leaders." His voice steadily grows in volume. "So, I say today, ask not what you can do for your country, but what your leaders can do for you!"

The 4,000-strong audience rises in unison with thunderous applause throughout the entire conference hall. The United African Congress Conference banners hanging from the balconies of the second-floor sway in concert with the rumbling sound of the pounding feet. President Mbozi steps back from the podium and bows deferentially, clasping his hands in front of his chest.

CHAPTER 48 - Naivety

It has been a long, but a rewarding day. Jean Michel revelled in the adoration from the conference delegates after his rousing speech. He enjoyed it all the more when he was told that the delegates represented more than 200 million people from all parts of Africa. Now, he is sitting in the back of the car, being driven to his hotel. His young attaché, Davide Osothe, spins around in the front seat with a broad smile on his face.

"Mr. Mbozi, your speech was astonishing. I was told that the last time the conference stood and applauded like that was when Nelson Mandela spoke. That was more than twenty years ago."

"Thank you, Davide. The response has been very flattering. Being compared to Mr. Mandela is beyond my wildest dreams." Jean Michel nods.

"Typical sentimentality. Can you eat sentimentality?" Anniesse Mensa asks, shaking her head in the seat beside Jean Michel in the spacious and comfy S-series Mercedes. "What damn good is that?" The small diamond in her nose twinkles, even though it is evening, and the car windows are heavily tinted. Davide is fascinated by the thought that the diamond somehow matched Anniesse's mood.

"Being a great leader is not sentimentality." Davide says defensively.

"Let's examine that thought. Mandela? Died poor. Ghandi? Died poor. Truman? Died poor. Churchill? Died poor. Do you want me to name any other great leaders?" Anniesse nose seems to flare as she makes her point, which makes the diamond twinkle even more.

"But they each inspired a generation of people, a nation to do more, to fulfil their potential and to fight against the odds." Davide counters.

"You see. You are making my point for me. Sentimentality. You know who is not dying poor? Gates, Musk, Zuckerberg, Bezos, Jobs. Do you want me to go on?"

"Apples and oranges." Davide says dismissively.

"I'm not talking about fruits you fool! I am talking about money!" An exasperated Anniesse says.

"And I am talking about making a difference in the lives of people. Our people." Davide responds defiantly.

"And you don't think these men that I mentioned have made a difference in the lives of people? Which phone do you have in your pocket? Which app did you use on your phone to talk to your children this morning? What computer did you use to help craft Jean Michel's speech? Which word processor application did you use on your computer? Which cloud storage did you use?"

"Again, apples and oranges. I am talking about policy and legislation that shapes a country, not technology that only the rich and privileged use."

"You naïve fool! Without technology a nation cannot move forward. A continent cannot move forward without technology. That is why Africa is floundering behind. And how can you be so hypocritical to criticize the privileged while seated in a one hundred thousand US dollar car, and wearing a one thousand US dollar suit."

Before Davide can respond, Jean Michel says calmly, "Anni, can both not be true at the same time?"

Both Anniesse and Davide pause. It takes a moment for Anniesse to regain her composure.

"Jean Michel. I am here to protect you against the naivety of people like Davide."

"Hey, that's not fair. I am part of this great team to help our leader forge a great new path for our people." Davide objects.

"Ok, let me put it this way, Jean Michel. I want you to be properly renumerated for the wealth that you generate for our country, just as executives of large corporations are renumerated for increased value that they deliver to their shareholders."

Jean Michel looks at Davide, "That sounds reasonable. Doesn't it?"

"There is many a slip between lip and cup. This sounds like there is too much room for too many slips." Davide offers.

"Double talk. Straight talk please." Anniesse says. Her captivating, light brown eyes are on fire. "Because that almost sounds like you are accusing me of something. Are you accusing me of something, Davide?"

Davide looks nervously at Jean Michel, then Anniesse, and back at Jean Michel, "Mr. Mbozi, I took another look at the contract we signed a year ago in the Congo with that American, Johnson. The seller of the diamonds is not our government but a private company. I checked with our Commerce and Mining ministries, and there is no record of such an agreement. There is no record of us working with this private company."

"Oh, Davide. You shouldn't have done that." Jean Michel says quietly.

Davide has a confused look on his face until the knife from Anniesse is plunged into the base of his skull, and his expression becomes vacant.

"Don't get any blood on the upholstery." Jean Michel says softly.

Anniesse holds the knife in place while pushing Davide's body forward in the front seat, so he slumps forward. "Kali, go straight to the underground parking garage of the hotel. My people will take care of the body." She says to the driver.

Jean Michel looks at Anniesse, "Did you have to kill him?

He was a very good attaché. The best that I have had. Good help is so hard to find."

"I don't think we had a choice. I told you it was a mistake to involve him in this deal."

"It gave us a veneer of authenticity and trust. People really gravitated to him because," Jean Michel smiles, "of his naivety."

Anniesse and Kali chuckle.

"Tell me," Jean Michel says, "what has happened to my diamonds?"

"We heard that there was a plane crash in Jamaica." Anniesse starts.

"Where?" Jean Michel asks, surprised.

"Jamaica. The plane was apparently blown off course by a hurricane. The team was trying to retrieve the diamonds, but we haven't heard from them."

"And my money?"

"The Americans say they will not pay until they receive the diamonds."

"But we delivered the diamonds to them in the Congo. It was their responsibility to get them to their market. Why are we being punished for their incompetence?"

"Because they can." Anniesse spits. "They know we can't do anything about it, or so they think."

Jean Michel casts an admiring look at Anniesse, "Sounds like you have a plan?"

"I am working on it. Rivers know this; there is no hurry. We shall get there some day."

CHAPTER 49 – Where Are My Diamonds?

Busha George coughs, splutters, and fights to catch his breath as water streams down his face. His eyes spring open, but he quickly shuts them as they hurt from the bright light shining in his face. He tries to turn his face but finds that he is restricted. Constricted. He is confused but is having trouble clearing his head and organising his thoughts. A fly lands on his nose, and he tries to move his right hand to brush it away, but he can't move his arm. He tries to move his left arm and cannot move that arm either.

What the hell a gwaan?

Busha George begins to realise and understand that he cannot feel his extremities. Panic rises from the pit of his stomach.

Calm down! Got to think.

Busha George breaths slowly and deeply. He then tries to feel and move his fingers and toes. Slowly, he begins to become aware of his body and its position. He can feel cold metal around his wrists, and he begins to feel the cold, wet, hard floor under his bare feet. He tries to open his eyes, but the bright lights still hurt his eyes.

"Mr. Albert."

Busha George is startled by the female voice. He had not heard anyone enter nor had he sensed the presence in the room. "Yes. Who the hell is that? Where am I?"

"Who I am is not important. Where you are is also inconsequential."

Cluck. Cluck. The footsteps are slow. Slow. Measured. Deliberate. The echo in the room makes it difficult to be sure from which direction the steps are coming, but it does help Busha realise that the room is small.

"What do you want from me? Where are my diamonds?"

"Ah. A man of my own heart. To the point. So, you are working for Mr. Johnson?" Her accent is African.

"For Mr. Johnson? Lady? Yuh know who me is?"

"Deflection. You disappoint me. I am not interested in who you are. Just answer the question."

"Mr. Johnson. That Jamaican fool tried to get in my way."

"Jamaican? Mr. Johnson is American."

"What? Woman. What the fuck is wrong with you? Stop playing games. Let me down."

"Where are my diamonds?"

"Woman, let me down."

There is silence. Busha can hear that the stiletto footsteps are now moving away from him. The blazing light is switched off. It takes a moment for Busha George's eyes to adjust to the dim light, but he soon notices a table in front of him, illuminated by a lamp. A monitor sits in the middle of the table. The monitor flickers into life and Busha George can see himself on the screen. It was not long before Busha George realises that he is watching a video of the scene at the plane crash site. He watches as his team killed Simon's team, and see his men run and retrieve the duffel bags. The monitor then goes blank.

"I'll ask you again Mr. Albert. Where are my diamonds?"

"Where the hell did you get that from?"

"That is immaterial. Where are my diamonds?"

"Lady. I think that video shows that the diamonds are now mine." Busha waits but doesn't get a response, nor does he sense any movement. "Look lady, maybe we got off of the wrong foot. Let me down, and I'll split the diamonds with you."

The woman walks within view of Busha. The woman is athletically built with strong but subtle, attractive features, and she has a small diamond in her nose.

"Mr. Albert, have you ever heard the term - death by a thousand cuts?"

"Are you trying to scare me? Do you know who I am?"

"Historians say that the Chinese used that form of torture as late as 1905. They cut their victim with extremely sharp knifes, and it took as long as three days for them to die."

"Lady, I don't scare easy. And when I get down from here, you and Mr. Johnson will regret this."

"You know that it is said that they usually cut out the eyes of their victims first, because it enhanced the mental agony." The woman says calmly. She pushes the table with the monitor away and wheels another table into view. The table has a selection of knifes arranged on it. Busha eyes the knives suspiciously.

"I have tried to reason with you, but now you are resorting to threatening me. You are either very stupid or," she pauses and looks at Busha askance, "you know I can't think of what the alternative would be. I guess you must be stupid."

Busha watches as she starts to pull on surgical gloves. She wheels another table within view. This has a small coal burner on it, with some red-hot skewers resting in the fire.

"What are you going to do?" Busha asks nervously.

"Where are my diamonds, Mr. Albert?"

"I don't know. I don't know where I am, or who you are."

"That is immaterial. I just want to know where my diamonds are."

"I don't know."

She picks up a long blade, which has a wooden handle. She quickly approaches Busha and cuts a three-inch shallow wound in his chest. Busha shouts in surprise. She turns, puts down the knife and returns with one of the red-hot skewers, and cauterizes the wound. Busha screams.

"Did I mention that I have spent some time perfecting the Chinese methods? My record is four days. After that amount of time, the subject is willing to tell me their life story." She chuckles. Her white teeth are neat and even. "One man even proposed to me. But that was just before I removed his testicles. So, I had to decline." She laughs.

"Listen. I have money." He watches as she returns with a smaller knife. The tone of Busha's voice rises. "I have a Swiss account with five million US dollars in it. You can have all of it."

She makes a two-inch incision in Busha's thigh that makes him wince. He looks down and can see blood slowly seeping from the wound.

That wasn't too bad. Busha George thinks. *Maybe her bark is louder than her bite.*

He almost smiles as he watches the woman slowly walk away. His eyes open wide as he watches she approaches with a skewer that glows red in the dim light.

She licks her lips as she watches the whites of Busha George's eyes expand alarmingly as the skewer gets closer and closer to his thigh. She cannot hold back the emotion and squeals in delight as Busha George releases a guttural scream when she closes the wound with the skewer.

"Fuck! What do want to know?" Busha pants, "I'll tell you anything."

"Je sais que vous, Monsieur Albert. I know you will." She smiles.

CHAPTER 50 - Betrayal

Kathy observes the scene dispassionately. She is surprised at her ambivalence, but under closer scrutiny during a later moment of introspection, she will realise that her exhaustion and relief deadened her senses.

"How did you know?"

Kathy turns to see a group of inquisitive, wide-eyed colleagues staring at her.

"I suspected something was wrong when the South African turned up alive and well, when he was reported as having died in the plane crash. I had a friend examine our server, and we found that Craig had changed the original story. Further investigations uncovered links between him and Inspector Albert."

"Where is Busha George?" One of the reporters asks.

"No one has seen him since the encounter on Blue Mountain." Kathy says absentmindedly.

They watch as Craig Bishop, Kathy's boss, is taken away in handcuffs.

* * *

"Mr. Johnson, how did this happen?"

"We are looking into it now Mr. President."

"What do we have so far?"

"Well, it is inconclusive at the moment, sir."

"Let me hear it."

"Well, the trail ends here."

"What? Inside the Oval Office!"

"No, sir. Inside the White House."

"You are saying that not only was one of our satellites repurposed without our knowledge, but there was a security breach within the White House also?"

Mr. Johnson touches his tie, "We are still looking into the matter, sir."

"Mr. Johnson, no other president may have been able to get rid of you, but mark my words, I will surely dislodge you if you can't satisfactorily get to the bottom of this matter. Do I make myself clear?"

"Yes, Mr. President." Using his little finger, Mr. Johnson scratches behind his ear.

CHAPTER 51 – Closest To Nowhere

Kenneth is sitting on the balcony, away from everyone else, enjoying some Bob Marley music. He is listening to the strains of 'Heathen'. Occasionally, he hums along to the tunes as he looks out across the treetops below. He gazes up at the deep, cool, pure blackness of the sky that is simply beautiful, and soothing. He smiles as he overhears Eric deliver the punch line of a joke that has everyone in stitches.

The stars really are bright up here. He thinks to himself, sipping from his glass of Drambuie. Jay had brought back a bottle from England on his last trip.

"Beautiful, isn't it." Jenny says as she gracefully slides into his lap.

"Yes." Kenneth kisses Jenny on her cheek and hugs her.

"How did Jay find this place, all the way up here?" Jenny eventually asks.

Kenneth thinks for a moment, "I think he said that a couple of years ago the Gorge was blocked, and he decided to drive the Red Hills route instead of going through Spanish Town and Sligoville. If I recall, he said he was enchanted by the natural, undeveloped and unspoilt locality."

Jenny chuckles, "That sounds like Jay."

Kenneth laughs, "Yes. He then started coming up here regularly, looking for a place where he could build a house."

"Cooper's Hill is a bit too far though."

Kenneth sips his drink.

"The closest place to here is nowhere." Jenny says reflectively.

They both start to laugh.

"Mom!" Jason runs out onto the balcony. "Mom, it's not fair!"

"What's the matter, Jason?" Jenny asks.

"They're watching a scary movie and won't watch something I can watch!"

"What are they watching?"

"Gremlins. And they have these little monsters in it, and I'm scared."

"Go and call your brother and tell him to come here." Jenny sighs.

"Kenny!" Jason screams.

"I said go and call your brother, not stand here and shout."

"Ok." Jason disappears through the sliding doors.

"You guys ok?" Jay appears.

"Great, man." Kenneth says. "The meal was fantastic. You cook it all?"

"Most. My mom did the sweet potato pudding and the ginger beer."

"One day, some woman is going to be very lucky to have you." Jenny smiles at Jay.

"Yeah. Need to stop all this traveling first. There always seems to be someone somewhere who needs security consulting or training."

"When are you on the move again?" Jenny asks.

"Got a request yesterday to join a team in the UAE next week. I think they are bidding for a conference or a global sporting event, or something like that, and they want some consultation to work out the security costs that should be included in the bid. For some reason I am leading an Italian team." Jay shrugs his shoulders at the quizzical expressions on Jenny and Kenneth's faces. "I haven't worked that part out yet."

"So how long will that take?"

Jay shrugs, "Maybe two weeks or a month."

"Wow! And you are ok being away for so long?"

"Mi dà l'opportunità di lavorare sul mio Italiano"

"What?"

Jay laughs, "One advantage is that I get to learn new languages."

"Now you're beginning to show off." Jenny says and they all laugh.

Suddenly, the lights go out.

"Hey!" are the cries from the living room.

"Mom! The movie switched off!" Is the cry from the basement.

"Uncle Jay is going to fix it in a minute. Hold on!" Jenny shouts back.

"Sorry, guys! I don't know what happened." Jay goes to the edge of the balcony and looks around, "It doesn't appear to be a power cut. The streetlights are on. I'll go check the fuses in the basement. There's a kerosene lantern on the coffee table and matches in the draw under the TV. I'll be back in a few minutes. Shouldn't take long." Jay starts for the basement.

"That won't be necessary." A voice says from behind them. "And please. No sudden moves. I don't want to have to shoot anyone before I'm ready."

Busha George is standing in the doorway, his silhouette lit by the moonlight.

CHAPTER 52 – I'm Sorry

Busha shifts his position on the wooden stool. All the lights are on in the open plan space that covers the kitchen, dining and living rooms. He leans back against the breakfast counter between the kitchen and dining room, so that he can get a clear view of the children that are huddled on the living room floor by the sliding patio door. One of the little runts is sniffling. The oldest child starts to hush him when he notices Busha George watching them. Busha glances at the women who are tied together on the opposite side of living room, and his gaze finally settles on the men who are handcuffed to the carved wooden banister dividing the dining room from the sunken living loom. Busha looks at his watch and adjusts his position again.

Where the hell are those guys? Busha wonders.

Andy sniffles. Kenny hushes him, whispering in his ears as they sit on the tiled floor.

"Shut up!" Busha George shouts at Kenny, making Andy sniffle louder. Busha jumps off the stool and menacingly strides across the dining room in the direction of the huddled children.

"You stay away from my children!" Jenny shouts, tugging at the rope that has tied her to Lisa and Kathy. Busha ignores her.

"You know what I want to know?" Kenneth asks in a measured tone that belies his simmering anger.

Busha stops and swivels to face Kenneth. His face is twisted in an ugly sneer and his eyes are wild and on fire.

"How the hell did you escape custody?"

"That's what you want to know?" Busha says incredulously.

"Tell me. We had you locked down. How the hell did you get out?" Kenneth asks.

The anger seems to ebb away from Busha as he considers the question.

"You know, I have no idea. Can you believe that? One minute I am in Up Park Camp. I guess my team and I were too good for Central Lockup." Busha chuckles at his own joke, oblivious to what anyone else thinks, "and then I find myself in some kind of torture chamber with this African woman from hell. Fuck! She wants her diamonds real bad. No idea where I was or how I got there. I'm guessing I was drugged because I don't remember a thing. That bitch tortures me and then I wake up in my house with a message stapled to my chest – 'Get me my diamonds!' You have to hand it to the bitch; she is persistent and concise."

"So, what do you want with us?"

"What do I want? How yuh mean, what do I want! Yuh know how much trouble yuh cause me? Yuh know how much pain me suffer?" Busha George waves his gun at Kenneth. "I have used up a lot of good will and money. Yuh cost me plenty."

"This is about money?"

"Money! Is wha'pen to yuh? Yuh a eediat? Yuh nuh hear what me seh?"

"What?"

"Me deyah fi get me pound of flesh and enjoy it too. To get me payback. Take a good look." Busha lifts his shirt, exposing numerous keloid wounds across his chest abdominals, and back. "And, in case you never understand me earlier, the bitch that do dis ... she want back her diamonds."

Kenneth bites his lip, "Please. You can take as much money as you want. Please don't hurt my family."

Busha laughs, "Uno no get it, do yuh? Me a wait fi weeks fi dis yah opportunity. Yuh presented it to me pon a platter by coming up here in de hills. No one will hear yuh screams up here."

"So what are you waiting for?" Kathy asks defiantly.

"No rush. Me want back me money and de banks nuh open til de morning, so we have a lot of time to have some fun. Me have some bredren pon dem way who would love to get a piece of you, sweetie." Busha lets out a raucous laugh.

"Now!" Jay shouts. Jay, Eric and Kenneth all pull in unison. There is a loud crack as the wood banister shatters, and they all fall to the floor.

"Bloodclawt! Oh no yuh don't!" Busha shouts. Eric is the closest to Busha George. Busha quickly strides forward and kicks Eric in the head. Eric falls with a grunt and is motionless after his body hits the floor. Lisa screams and Andy starts crying loudly. Jay jumps up and bull-rushes Busha, ramming him in the midriff. They crash into the breakfast counter. Busha screams in pain. Jay bounces off him and lands in a heap on the floor. For a moment, Busha is disoriented. Jay tries to get up, rocking backward and forward vigorously, but his handcuffed hands make it difficult for him to get his feet under him. Kenneth finally manages to free himself from under the dead weight of the unconscious Eric and tries to hurry across to help Jay. Busha quickly jumps up to a squatting position, aims and fires. Kenneth instinctively rolls to his left, but the bullet hits him in the shoulder, throwing him backwards. Kenneth is unable to control his body and his head crashes into the wall, falling in a heap.

By now, Jay has regained his feet, he moves quickly and aims a vicious kick at Busha's head, but Busha manages to tilt his head at an angle, so he only gets a glancing blow on the side of the head. Busha's ear turns a dark shade of red before he hits the floor. Jay charges forward, but Busha manages to prop himself up on an elbow. There is loud explosion. Jay coughs, his stride suddenly becomes halting before he drops to his knees. Time stands still, as Jay looks down at his chest. He turns to look at Jenny, Lisa and

Kathy and mouths, "I'm sorry."

A drop of blood drips from Jay's dangling lower lip. Jay slowly closes his eyes and falls forward, his head crashes into the tiled floor as he makes no attempt to break his fall.

CHAPTER 53 – He's Dead

They hear the engine noise before the lights hit the roof of the living room. The sound gets louder as the lights move across the roof, until they then descend towards the floor and disappear. The engine noise is replaced by voices and the distinct sound of slamming car doors.

"Yeow! Busha? Weh yuh de?" A shout comes from outside.

Busha George walks to the patio glass door and slides it open, "I'm up here." He shouts. "Go round de back. De grill open." Busha walks back into the living room with a devilish smile on his face. "I hope you ladies are ready to party."

* * *

Marshall knew something was wrong when he drove up and saw all the lights out. He slowed down and pulled under a tree to observe and listen. Then he sees Busha George walk out on to the balcony.

Bomboclawt! Busha George! Dem was supposed to lock him up and throw away the key!

He watches Busha George and notices him talking to three men who have just alighted from a car.

"I'm up here. Go round de back. De grill open." Marshall hears Busha George shout down to the men.

Oh shit! This looks bad!

Marshall waits for Busha George to go back inside and then he sprints through the open lot adjacent to Jay's house, deftly dodging between trees and bushes.

Damn it! If only I had walked with my gun!

Marshall reaches the back of the house before the three men. He watches the men from behind a large breadfruit tree, as they nonchalantly approach the grill to the carport where Jay has parked his pickup. Marshall assesses the men quickly. Based on his gait, the guy on the left has a weakness in his right knee; the guy in the middle is the biggest, and fittest, with no obvious weaknesses; the guy on the right is overweight, which probably means some weakness in his back. The absence of light works to Marshall's advantage as he quickly and quietly approaches the men, his focus on the big guy. When he is about five paces away from the men, the big guy seems to notice the movement in front of them and stops. Marshall quickens his pace and crouches. He kicks the guy on the left in the side of his right knee, and there is a satisfying crack and collapse of the joint under Marshall leg. Before he can scream out in pain, Marshall jabs him in the throat. The man grabs his throat, and only guttural sounds escape his open mouth.

Marshall then ducks and weaves out of the way of punches thrown by the big guy, he quickly drops to one knee while sweeping away the legs of the overweight guy on the right. With his opposite arm, Marshall guides the torso of the overweight guy, so he falls backward with his back landing across Marshall's braced thigh. Marshall uses the arm that he has across the overweight guy's chest to bend his back as he falls so he lands with an arched back over Marshall's horizontal thigh. Marshall can feel the crack and then the expulsion of air from the overweight guy's lungs. He quickly rolls overweight guy off his leg on to the ground and swivels to face the big guy. Marshall punches him in the groan twice, which brings his head down, and Marshall then uses his arms to bring big guy's head down to meet his upward propelled knee. Marshall's knee crashes into the bridge of big guy's nose and he crumples to the ground.

* * *

Busha waits for a few minutes and then walks to the door and calls out, "Yeow! Where are you guys?" There is no sound for a few seconds. "Hey! Wha'ppen?" It takes a few more seconds before there is a barely discernible response.

"Coming. Stopped to take a piss."

"Bomboclawt! How yuh so nasty? Toilet up here, yuh know. Cho!" Busha exclaims. He walks back into the living room. He loosens his belt and nods towards Kathy. "Me have someting fi yuh." Busha says with a wide grin on his face.

"And so do I!"

In shock, Busha turns to see Marshall bounding across the room. It only takes him three strides to reach Busha. Marshall hits him with a metal pipe and the thwack sound explodes off his head. Blood splatters across the wall as Busha is thrown off his feet, and his shoulder hits the floor first. Amazingly, Busha still holds onto the gun and manages to get off one round that catches Marshall in the hand, causing him to drop the pipe. Marshall stamps on the gun-toting hand. There is an audible crack as Busha's wrist collapses under the violent impact of Marshall's boot. Marshall slams his other boot into the side of Busha's face. A tooth and the gun clatter across the tiles towards the kitchen, and more blood splatters across the floor. Despite being prostrate, Busha reaches into his waist with his good hand and tries to pull out another gun. Marshall kicks him in the stomach.

"Oouuff!" Accompanies the expulsion of wind from Busha's lungs, but he still clutches on to the gun.

Marshall kicks Busha again. Busha's gasp partially masks the sound of his breaking ribs, and he loses his grip on the second gun. Marshall quickly kicks the gun across the room, and as it clatters across the floor, Marshall swings his boot again into Busha head.

Busha struggles to get up to his knees. Marshall looks around and quickly runs over and picks up the pipe that had rolled into the corner of the dining room. With a wide arching swing, Marshall brings the pipe down on Busha's head. He drops to the floor like a sack of potatoes. Marshall swings the pipe again, and again, and again. Busha doesn't move. Blood splatters on to Marshall as he swings the pipe again.

"Marshall."

Marshall swings again.

"Marshall." Kathy calls to him again.

Marshall swings again.

"Marshall!" Kathy shouts.

Marshall stops and looks at Kathy, the whites of his eyes shining brightly against his dark complexion. His eyes are like saucers.

"He's not moving. I think he's dead." Kathy says.

Marshall looks down at Busha, and back at Kathy. Kathy beckons to Ken Jr, and he hurries over and loosens the rope fastening Kathy, Jenny and Lisa. Jenny and Lisa hurry over to Kenneth and Eric. Kathy runs towards Marshall who is statuesque over Busha George. She takes the pipe away from Marshall and rests it on the floor, and then reaches down to check for a pulse on Busha's neck.

'He's dead.' She reassures everyone.

Marshall looks down at the body, bemused, and then he starts to shake. Kathy pulls Marshall away from the body and hugs him tightly.

CHAPTER 54 – Why?

Handkerchiefs are in ample supply, wiping teary eyes and mopping damp brows. The voices are robust in song, and the sermon is inspirational and delivered with passion, but the expressions are somber. Mr. and Mrs. Jefferson sit composed in the front pew, comforted by their three other children, along with John I and John II, Jay's great grandfather and grandfather, and Jay's grandmother. Other family members unfamiliar to Kenneth occupy the next three pews. Jay's closest friends, including Kenneth, Jenny, Eric, Lisa, Marshall and Kathy, sit in the pew behind the family, and Jay's unit from the Royal Marines are sitting in the row behind Jay's close friends. The service is beautifully conducted by the Jefferson family's Baptist minister, who proudly related how he had the pleasure of baptizing Jay only last year.

Later, outside at the graveside, everyone stands and watches, transfixed as the coffin descends slowly into the ground. There is no sound, no breeze, no movement, until the first shovel of dirt is thrown into the grave and thuds onto the casket. Mrs. Jefferson is visibly shaken by the sound, and she can't hold back the tears any longer.

Her loss of control is the catalyst for an avalanche of emotion that thunders into the hole in the ground. There is wailing and shouting. Jay's grandmother stumbles forward and falls to her knees as she tried to throw her handful of dirt into the grave. Her black, wide-brimmed hat falls from her head onto the ground. One of the gravediggers bends down, picks it up and passes it to a young boy, of maybe ten or twelve years old, who is smartly dressed in a black suit, and who is bravely trying to hold back the tears.

"Whoee! Whoee! Jesus help me! Mi baby dead! Whoee! Lawd help me Jesus!" Grandma Jefferson cries.

Two of her grandsons try to help her up, but she shrugs off their hands with a slap, and wails on her knees. Suddenly, Mrs. Jefferson's legs buckle and two of her sons rush forward and grab her before she falls. The crowd behind them parts like the Red Sea as the young men try to lead Mrs. Jefferson away from the graveside but she refuses to go. Her angry glare informing them that she is adamant that she is staying.

"Abide with me, fast falls the eventide; the darkness deepens, Lord with me abide …" the minister starts to sing.

Slowly, the wailing subsides, as people start to sing. A cloud passes in front of the sun, offering some relief from the intense midday heat, accompanied by the puff of a cooling breeze.

"… Through cloud and sunshine, O abide with me …"

The singing increases in volume as the cloud passes by and the sun returns with a vengeance.

"Mercy Jesus!" Mr. Jefferson mumbles as he stoops to pick up a clump of dirt and to throw it into the rapidly vanishing hole in the ground. Mr. Jefferson briefly loses his balance, and he lands on his hands and knees. For a moment the singing stops, as everyone watches Mr. Jefferson stare at the grave from his knees. The gravediggers wait. Mr. Jefferson's head drops and his body shakes.

"… where is death's sting? Where, grave, thy victory? I triumph still, if Thou abide with me …" The minister resumes, leading the gathering through the song.

"Why?" Mr. Jefferson throws back his head, as he shouts angrily at the heavens while the gathering tries to sing. "Why did you take my son?" He shouts. His daughter stoops beside her father and hugs him.

"… Hold Thou Thy cross …" The gathering sings.

"Why?" He shouts.

"... Shine through the gloom, and point me to the skies ..." The song continues.

"Answer me! Why?" One of the sons, the older of the two who has been holding up Mrs. Jefferson, indicates to his sister that she should go and be with their mother. He kneels beside his father and hugs him.

"In life, in death, O Lord, abide with me." The song ends and the congregation falls silent.

"Why?" Mr. Jefferson whimpers, holding on to his son.

The children help Mr. and Mrs. Jefferson to stand, and the family hugs as they watch the gravediggers continue to fill in the hole in the ground. Within minutes, the hole is no more. Squares of grass are patiently and carefully placed over the mound of dirt by the gravediggers, after which the gravediggers slowly and quietly retreat. In silence, the congregation stands, staring at the corrugated patch of grass.

Later, as the congregation starts to filter away, Mrs. Jefferson beckons to Kenneth.

"Mrs. Jefferson is calling me." Kenneth says quietly to Jenny, as he steps away.

Mrs. Jefferson takes a few discreet steps back from the family as Kenneth approaches her. She takes Kenneth's arm when he gets beside her and guides him out of earshot of the family.

"Thank you for coming Kenneth."

"I would not have missed for the world, Ma'am."

"I know. John spoke very highly of you. He loved you like a brother."

Kenneth doesn't know how to respond, so he remains silent.

"Kenneth." Mrs. Jefferson looks Kenneth firmly in the eyes.

"Yes Ma'am?"

"Find the person responsible for my son's death."

"We did Ma'am. He'd dead."

"No. I know about Busha George. I want the person who Busha George answers to. Busha George is just a street thug. I want the person who sent Busha George."

Kenneth stares at Mrs. Jefferson.

"Do you understand me, Kenneth?"

"We will bring them to justice, Ma'am."

"Kenneth. I know what you and Jay did while you served. I know you were both the tip of the spear." Mrs. Jefferson takes Kenneth's hand and squeezes it. "I want you to be that razor sharp sword for me, and separate the flesh from the bone, to remove that cancer that has infected the body and is causing it to die." Mrs. Jefferson glances at the grave. "Has caused it to die."

Mrs. Jefferson's looks deeply into Kenneth's eyes.

"Do you understand me, Kenneth?"

"Yes, Ma'am."

CHAPTER 55 – I Love You
A few days after Jay's funeral

"Bye Dad!" The kids shout as they run through the door.

"You have the car keys?" Jenny shouts after the kids.

"Yes, Mom."

Jenny pushes her head into the study. "Dropping the kids at school."

"Come here." Kenneth calls. Jenny strolls into the study. Kenneth hugs and kisses her.

"What was that for?"

"I love you." Kenneth says as he holds Jenny.

"And I you."

"Can't you just say, I love you."

Jenny smiles, holds Kenneth's face in both her hands, "Kenneth Johnson. You are by far the most complex, contradictory, scary, cunning, kind, caring and softhearted man I have ever met. You are my heart and soul, my friend and the adoring father of my children. I love you more than you can imagine, and I shouldn't have to tell you, because you know it in your heart."

Jenny gives Kenneth a soft and tender kiss. Jenny pulls away as the kiss becomes very moist. Kenneth's eyes are closed, and tears are rolling down his cheeks.

* * *

"How are the repairs going?" Eric asks as he licks the rum and raisin ice cream running down the side of his waffle cone.

"Good. The contractor that Marshall recommended is doing a really good job, and it's given us a chance to do some remodeling, which we had thought about doing for some time now but never got around to doing. Would you agree, Jenny?" Kenneth responds as he shovels a spoon of guava ice cream in his mouth.

Jenny doesn't respond as she shares a joke with Lisa.

"Jenny?" Kenneth prompts.

"Huh?" Jenny turns away from Lisa with a wide grin on her face. "What was that?"

"Eric is asking about how the repairs are progressing. They're doing a good job, aren't they?" Kenneth says.

"Yes, dear." Jenny responds and turns back to Lisa, giggling at something that was said.

Kenneth and Eric inquiringly look over at Lisa and Jenny who are giggling incessantly on the neighbouring bench.

"Is what sweet dem so?" Eric asks Kenneth.

"No idea."

Another laugh bursts from Jenny and Lisa. Kenneth and Eric look over and smile. The two couples are relaxing in the afternoon sunshine on the grounds of Devon House, enjoying ice cream.

"Here they come. Here they come." Lisa says excitedly.

"Who?" Eric asks.

Lisa points across the grounds, and she hugs Jenny enthusiastically. Eric and Kenneth squint, looking into the distance beyond the numerous trees and blended Caribbean and Georgian architecture of the Devon House Mansion, beyond dozens of other people who are also enjoying the serene surroundings, to see a couple walking hand in hand across the lush grass towards them. It takes at least five minutes for Kenneth and Eric to agree that it really is Kathy and Marshall. When Kathy and Marshall finally arrive, Kathy is glowing, and Marshall has an impish smile on his face. Lisa and Jenny look like they are going to burst.

"Well? Well?" Jenny says.

"Well, what?" Kenneth and Eric look at each other in confusion.

Kathy says, "Yes."

Jenny and Lisa scream, jump up and give Kathy a huge hug. The three women are jumping up and down, screaming.

Kenneth and Eric look at each other. Then they look at Marshall. "Dude! What is going on?"

Marshall just stands there, looking at the women jumping up and down.

"Can someone please tell us what is going on?" Eric says, exasperated.

The women stop jumping up and down, stare at Kenneth and Eric, and start laughing and pointing at them.

"You guys are so stupid." Jenny says, still laughing.

"What?" Kenneth says, defensively.

"You silly billies." Lisa says, "Marshall asked Kathy to marry him, and she said yes."

Kenneth and Eric look at each other, and then at Marshall. They jump up and give him a massive bear hug.

"Whoa! Yes!" Kenneth exclaims.

"Awesome, dude!" Eric shouts.

Hugs are exchanged, tears are shed, and there is much laughter.

"Finally, dude. What made you finally ask?" Eric says, with an arm around Marshall shoulder.

The smile on Marshall face fades. He looks at Eric and then

scans the faces of everyone in the group before resting on Kathy's. "I almost lost you all. I almost lost Kathy." Marshall's eyes become moist. "It made me realise how much I love you guys. How much I love Kathy."

Kathy breaks away from Jenny and Lisa and walks over to Marshall. "I love you too."

EPILOGUE

Jean Michel looks around the table at his cabinet. He taps the table while he thinks about how to respond. He slowly focuses his attention on the mining minister.

"Please repeat what you just said. I want to be sure that everyone heard what you just said." Jean Michel says.

The mining minister looks at his notes and clears his throat, "A preliminary audit of our diamond stock suggests that one or more tons of diamonds may be missing." The minister adjusts his black pencil thin tie. Even though the room is air conditioned he takes out his handkerchief and mops his brow.

"One or more?" Jean Michel queries.

"The audit was preliminary." The minister clears his throat again. "It was a surprise audit."

There is a murmur of discussion around the table.

"Silence please." Jean Michel says calmly. The murmur subsides. Jean Michel gets up from his seat and slowly walks around the long, rectangular table, behind the cabinet members. "Minister Zampi. Please order a comprehensive audit so we can understand the extent of the problem."

The mining minister mops his brow again, "Yes, Mr. President."

Jean Michel stops behind the mining minister and pats him on the shoulder. He then continues his slow walk around the table with his arms behind his back. The eyes of all the cabinet ministers follow Jean Michel. He stops and points at a man in an army uniform with medals across his chest.

"Major Akinyemi. I want you to work with Minister Zampi on finding who is responsible for stealing from our country. This is unacceptable and it is imperative that we retain the trust of the people. I encourage you to work with my special advisor, Ms. Mensa, on this matter. She has extensive security experience." Major Akinyemi nods, glancing in the direction of Anniesse, who is seated behind Jean Michel's chair. "I don't want to announce anything to the public yet, until we have more information and can give the people confidence that we have this in hand. It will also look good if the mining and security ministries appear to be working in concert on this." All the heads around the table nod in unison. Jean Michel has reached back to his chair. "I want to thank you all for making time for this meeting. I thought it was important for you all to be fully appraised of the situation." He raises his hand and gestures to the door. "Thank you."

The ministers all push back their chairs and leave the room. Anniesse stays in her chair, motionless and phlegmatic. When the room is empty, she gets up and stands beside Jean Michel.

"How is it that we were unaware of this surprise audit?" Jean Michel whispers.

"I don't know Jean Michel. I need to look into it."

"You do that."

"But you do realise that inquiries of that nature need to be very delicately made, so we don't expose ourselves. That means it may take some time."

Jean Michel waves his arm dismissively, "Yes, yes. Just get it done." He stands silently, thinking. "Any traces?"

'Nothing pointing to us."

"Storage?"

"The diamonds that have not yet been shipped will not be found."

"And the diamonds that have been lost? Since we cannot take anymore, it is imperative that we recover what has been lost."

"We have encountered some," Anniesse pauses, "problems."

"Problems?"

"The trail has gone cold."

"Well, warm it up!" Jean Michel spits. "Find me my diamonds, Anni. Do you hear me?"

"Yes, Jean Michel, but …"

"Anni!" Jean Michel's eyes are on fire. "Find my diamonds!" He says in a hoarse whisper, "Or die trying."